continued . . .

MYTH-TAKEN IDENTITY

ROBERT ASPRIN
and JODY LYNN NYE

ACE BOOKS, NEW YORK

THE BERKLEY PUBLISHING GROUP
Published by the Penguin Group
Penguin Group (USA) Inc.
375 Hudson Street, New York, New York 10014, USA
Penguin Group (Canada), 90 Eglinton Avenue, Suite 700, Toronto, Ontario M4P 2Y3, Canada
(a division of Pearson Penguin Canada Inc.)
Penguin Books Ltd., 80 Strand, London WC2R 0RL, England
Penguin Group Ireland, 25 St. Stephen's Green, Dublin 2, Ireland (a division of Penguin Books Ltd.)
Penguin Group (Australia), 250 Camberwell Road, Camberwell, Victoria 3124, Australia
(a division of Pearson Australia Group Pty. Ltd.)
Penguin Books India Pvt. Ltd., 11 Community Centre, Panchsheel Park, New Delhi—110 017, India
Penguin Group (NZ), Cnr. Airborne and Rosedale Roads, Albany, Auckland 1310, New Zealand
(a division of Pearson New Zealand Ltd.)
Penguin Books (South Africa) (Pty.) Ltd., 24 Sturdee Avenue, Rosebank, Johannesburg 2196,
South Africa

Penguin Books Ltd., Registered Offices: 80 Strand, London WC2R 0RL, England

This is a work of fiction. Names, characters, places, and incidents either are the product of the authors'
imagination or are used fictitiously, and any resemblance to actual persons, living or dead, business
establishments, events, or locales is entirely coincidental.

MYTH-TAKEN IDENTITY

An Ace Book / published by arrangement with Bill Fawcett & Associates

PRINTING HISTORY
Meisha Merlin hardcover edition / September 2004
Ace mass market edition / August 2005

Copyright © 2005 by Bill Fawcett & Associates.
Cover art by Walter Velez.
Cover design by Judith Murello.

ISBN: 0-441-01311-2

ACE
Ace Books are published by The Berkley Publishing Group,
a division of Penguin Group (USA) Inc.,
375 Hudson Street, New York, New York 10014.
ACE and the "A" design are trademarks belonging to Penguin Group (USA) Inc.

PRINTED IN THE UNITED STATES OF AMERICA

10 9 8 7 6 5 4 3 2 1

ONE

FizzZAP!!

A lightning bolt snaked through a crack in the door, barely missing my head. Little lower, and I would have been fried. Even the tough, green-scaled hide that every Pervect is born with wasn't enough to make me immune to fire.

This was starting to get serious! I thought they would give up when the two blue plug-uglies realized they couldn't simply break the door of our tent down, but now they were turning to magik. Who would have guessed the scrawny management type with them was a magician!

I smelled smoke and realized the lightning bolt had set fire to my favorite armchair. Trying to control my temper, I reviewed my options. I could wait them out and let them waste their firepower until they got bored, or I could open the door and tear the three of them into little quivering scraps.

At the moment, I was favoring the second choice. I had really liked that armchair.

Bill collectors!

I never thought one would come here, to M.Y.T.H., Inc.'s old headquarters in the Bazaar at Deva. Not one of my erstwhile companions was profligate with money; we're all too smart to stiff a creditor and had plenty of cash to pay their bills anyhow. Of all people, the least likely to attract unwanted attention over money was my ex-partner Skeeve. Yet the trio on the other side of the flap insisted he'd run up bills and stiffed the vendors.

"I say, Aahz," a deep voice beside me intoned.

"Chumley!" I said, spinning around. "You scared me out of a century's growth."

"So sorry! Doing a spot of interior decorating?" Chumley asked, nodding toward the burning recliner.

Purple-furred and possessed of a pair of moon-colored eyes of odd sizes, the Troll stood head, shoulders, and half a chest higher than I did.

"That smoke is bad for the paintings on the walls, what?"

"Don't tell me," I growled. "Tell the three bill collectors outside."

"Bill collectors?"

The Troll's shaggy brows drew down slightly. His brutish appearance was at odds with his natural flair for intellectual discourse, a typical misconception about the male denizens of the dimension of Trollia from which he hailed. Trolls deliberately concealed their intelligence, so as not to overwhelm beings in other dimensions who couldn't handle facing both mental and physical superiority at the same time. Chumley did good business as freelance hired muscle under the nom de guerre of Big Crunch.

"An error, surely?"

"Sure must be," I agreed. "They come from a place they call The Mall, on Flibber. They're looking for Skeeve. They say he skipped out on a big fat bill."

"Never!" Chumley said, flatly. "Skeeve's honesty and sense of fair play would never allow him to do such a thing. I've seen them demonstrated in many an instance when he had a choice to make between profit and the right thing, and he has inevitably chosen to do the right thing."

I scowled. Skeeve had let plenty of profit go by the way-side for some pretty outlandish reasons, not all of which I understood, though I had supported him.

"That's what I thought. Ever heard of this Mall?"

"Not I. Shopping is little sister's purview, what?"

The door behind me shook. They weren't going to get through that door with anything less than antiballistic mis-siles, and I hoped that the Merchants Association that ran the Bazaar would notice before they rolled up a launcher. Chumley threw his not-inconsiderable weight against the flap with mine, and it stopped quivering.

You may ask how a mere tent could withstand magikal attacks. To start with, most of the tents in the Bazaar were built to hold out against a certain amount of magik, but our place was special even here. It might look like a humble and narrow marquee on the outside, but behind the entrance was a spacious luxury villa occupying a large wad of extradimensional space. In other words, as a guy I used to know put it, it's bigger on the inside than it is on the out-side. My unwanted guests couldn't burn the place down or blow it up. For a spell to cross that dimensional barrier would take a lot more firepower than these guys could ever be capable of summoning up, but the interface that allowed us to walk out of the door that bridged the gap had to remain fairly permeable, hence my current problem. Except for back door into the host dimension, Blut, home of vampires and werewolves—a dimension, by the way, that had once tried to have me executed on trumped-up charges—the only way to walk out was obstructed.

"They're looking for 150,000 gold pieces," I said, with some irritation.

"A princely sum! You are certain that Skeeve couldn't have incurred the debt?"

"Pretty positive," I said carefully.

I hadn't been hanging around with him myself for some months. It was a painful subject, but Chumley knew that.

"Tananda's been with him for the last several weeks, on

Wuh.* She popped out of here a minute ago, headed for
Trollia. You just missed her."

"Oh, blast," Chumley said. The door flap responded
with an inward thump, and we shoved ourselves against it
again. "I came here looking for her, don't you know. Mums
sent me here to get her. The redecoration of the home
hearth has reached a stage where our dear mater wishes
another female's point of view on choices of color and texture. Still, there is a silver lining to the cloud: I shall be
glad to miss the resulting arguments."

"Go back when the shooting stops, huh?" I deduced.

"Quite right," the Troll agreed. "By the way, if it began
as a mere fact-finding enterprise on the part of our adver-
saries outside, how did this situation escalate to our present state of hostilities?" He nodded toward the door.

"I have no idea," I said, innocently. "They asked me
where Skeeve is, and I flat out refused to tell them. Then
they got upset. They threatened to ruin his reputation as a
deadbeat, and I offered what I thought were polite and
well-thought-out reasons why they shouldn't."

"I see."

Chumley must have run through the scenario in his
head. If he imagined a terse argument that got progres-
sively louder and ended up with the two toughs who
flanked the shrimp with the clipboard reaching into their
bulging tunics in a sort of weapon-drawing way, he would
have pretty much captured the sequence of events. We've
known each other for a long time, and he was more than
familiar with my temper.

"They are mistaken, of course?"

"Positive. Besides, this ain't his style. They read me a
list of things Skeeve's supposed to have bought, like Trag-
fur coats, a skeet-shooting outfit, a twelve-string guitar that
was supposed to have been owned by some famous bard,
and just about everything that'd be behind Door #3."

* See *MYTH Alliances*

I paused and shook my head.

"It's not what Skeeve would splash out on. A home for destitute cats, yes. Fifty percent of a casino, yes. A bucket of luxury goods adding up to a small kingdom's entire GNP? I don't think so. And besides, Skeeve never spends money he doesn't have. It's not like him. The signature they produced on some bills looks like his, but I am sure it's a fake. For one thing, it said 'Skeeve the Magnificent.' Even when the kid got a big head he usually saved the fancy titles to impress kingdom officials. I mean, he's surprised me a bunch of times in the last few months, but there's too many inconsistencies in this even for a Klahd."

"Then it behooves us, don't you think," Chumley said, "to find out who *has* run up this bill in his name?"

I glimpsed the D-hopper on the table where I'd set it down. It had been a gift from Skeeve, sent via Tanda, completely unexpected but totally within the character of the kid's sometimes foolishly generous nature.

"You bet it does!" I announced fiercely. "Nobody messes with my pa—ex-partner without having me to answer to. His reputation is worth more than any little bill, or any honking big bill, either. What are you doing this afternoon? I could use some backup."

"Nothing at all," Chumley said, with a grin. "I would be honored to aid in such an enterprise. But how do we leave here? The way is blocked, as you point out, and I have very limited skills in the department of enchantments. Mums sent me here. I expected to have Tanda transfer me back."

"No problem," I said airily, sauntering over and picking up the D-hopper. I smacked it into one scaly palm and brandished it at Chumley. "Poetic justice sent us a way out."

We barred the entrance to the tent with what remained of the living-room furniture, then *bamfed* out.

We flipped over to Klah first. Cross-spatial hopping is

how Chumley and I, who otherwise have little in common as species, are both occasionally called "demons," which is short for "dimensional traveler." Over the centuries the word has become corrupted in a host of dimensions, which meant that referring to ourselves by that handy designation occasionally resulted in us being met by angry mobs with pitchforks and torches. In any case our appearance would speak against us. Nowhere else on Klah, or so I assumed, would one encounter a well-muscled, green-scaled, yellow-eyed, debonair Pervect or a huge, shaggy, purple Troll.

We made sure to materialize nowhere near the remote forest inn where Skeeve had holed up to study magik on an uninterrupted basis (well, that was the theory, anyhow), but in the vicinity of the kingdom of Possiltum, where for a while Skeeve had held a pretty good job as Court Magician, with me as his "assistant" and financial agent. Chumley and I could provide all the muscle and brains we were going to need for any information-seeking mission, but we needed an expert on shopping centers.

"You *sure* we can't haul Tananda loose to help us out at The Mall?" I asked again, as the turrets of the royal palace hove into view at a distance through a spare haze of trees. "She's the most comprehensive power-shopper I know."

We started down the hill where we'd materialized, following a sheep trail.

"Not a chance," Chumley said with regret, kicking gorse out of his way with his big feet. "The fireballs Mums would throw if both of us turned our back on her project now I would simply not like to consider. What about Bunny? She has considerable skills in the retail-therapy sector."

"It'd be hard to extract her without alerting Skeeve something was up. I don't want to bug Skeeve over a minor misunderstanding."

Bunny was also a Klahd, but a sophisticated, beautiful, and streetwise one, the niece of a Mob boss known as the Fairy Godfather.

"Besides, it'd be good to make sure we have someone we can trust looking after him."

I felt in my pocket for a message ball. These handy-dandy little spells, which had been making their manufacturer rich in the Bazaar, could find whomever you addressed them to, even cross dimensions to a limited extent. I scrawled Bunny a quick note on the parchment, tweaked the spell into an outbound globe of golden light, and flung it into the air. It hovered for a moment, then zinged off in the direction of the inn.

"And you don't want to involve Skeeve personally because . . ." Chumley began.

I scowled. There were plenty of reasons, but I didn't want to talk about some of them.

"The last person you'd believe protesting his innocence is the guy you accused, right? That's just what you'd would expect him to say. It's like saying you're looking for the real arsonist, when everyone can see the lighter in your pocket. Why, I remember a number of years ago when I was pricing magikal security for a Gnomish funds transfer service, and one of the little guys whose cash register was always short kept going on about how he saw some mystery employee taking crates of gold out of the door just before the supervisor was coming through, and—"

Chumley interrupted me hastily. "So he would be a poor witness to his own defense, eh? That does leave Massha as our best prospect. Her grasp of bazaars and other vending emporia is unparalleled except by the aforementioned others."

Massha had originally signed on with us as Skeeve's apprentice, and had recently taken over his gig as Court Magician. She'd settled in nicely in Possiltum, making friends with Queen Hemlock and marrying the head of the army, General Hugh Badaxe, one hell of a guy, and a man of impressive physique to match Massha's own.

The large, round, chiffon-draped figure, definitely female, floated around the small room like a balloon. The Lady Magician of the court of Possiltum had a knack for dressing that would be gaudy even compared to a Mardi Gras float. Her bright orange hair was drawn up into a knot on top of her head, where it wouldn't war directly with the ruby-colored harem-girl pants and vest that left her wide midriff bare. Silk slippers in a screaming aqua only added a further jarring note. And around her neck, wrists, ankles, fingers, and waist hung dozens of gold or silver chains, bracelets, rings, baubles, bangles, and beads. If I knew our Massha, every single adornment packed some kind of magikal punch.

"So, what's the deal, Hot Shot?" Massha asked, sifting through her chests of impedimenta for the swag that packed the most punch.

Colorful scarves were draped all over the room. Necklaces and rings all sparkling with power even to my disenchanted eyes slithered through her fingers as she sought just the right items.

"You don't drop in very often, and the last thing I ever thought I'd hear fall from your scaly lips is 'do you want to go to The Mall with me?' I mean, I'm happy to help. I owe you for helping me out on Brakespear, and plenty of times before that."

"Never mind that," I said, preoccupied with the present predicament. (I knew I was teed off when I started thinking in alliterations. That poetic bumf was for Chumley or Nunzio. I like to think of myself as a straightforward kind of guy.) "How come you know all about The Mall?"

"I was wondering the same thing," Chumley added. The Troll was perched on the lid of a huge chest of drawers, where he was out of Massha's way as she bustled with intent. "Today's the first time I'd heard about it."

She stopped and gave us the kind of sardonic look you offer to someone who just asked how is it you know water is wet, then her face softened.

"Any woman could tell that it's been a long time since

either of you had a sweetie you wanted to buy something special for." Massha chuckled deeply.

"I've been rather busy," Chumley said uncomfortably. If his thick fur had been skin, it would have been deepening with embarrassment.

"What's your point?" I asked quickly, rather than give her another place to stick a needle. My personal life, or lack of one, was no one's business but mine.

"Well," Massha said, turning toward us with a handsome rosewood coffer, "if you had ever been there, you'd know that it is becoming *the* place to pick up hot items like these."

She grabbed a handful of swag out of the box and thrust it toward us.

I bent forward for a look. Even my jaded eye instantly detected there was something special about the jewelry. I picked up one piece and took a close look at the stones.

"Unusual cut," I murmured. "Unusual metals, too, if it comes to that."

Cabochon gems with incised slashes across their bases, which made pretty patterns when you looked down on their dome sides, were set in metals that flashed their own rainbow hues. I had never seen anything like them, but Massha was right about my not having any good reason at present to shop for jewelry.

"Hugh bought me these," she said, turning over bracelet after necklace after brooch. Then she brandished a handful of rings. "And I bought these for myself, each from a different magik seller. This one's a heat beam, this one can generate minor illusions . . . and this one's plain gorgeous. I had to have it. It'll just knock your eyes out."

We leaned close for a look, then everything went black.

"What the hell just happened?" I demanded.

"Sorry," Massha's voice replied.

In a moment light returned. She looked sheepish.

"I didn't mean to invoke the ring. It really does knock your eyes out, or rather, your vision. It's temporary. This is the kind of good stuff you can find at The Mall. It's vast, but they only seem to attract the high-end merchants. The Bazaar has a little of everything, but you're not going to find whoopee cushions or dragon-whistles in The Mall. What's your interest, since you have never gone shopping there?"

"It's Skeeve," I said, with a grimace.

"Is he in trouble?" Massha asked, cocking her head and pursing her big lips.

"I don't know," I replied.

I explained my visitors and their purported mission.

"My guess is someone is trying to pass himself off as Skeeve. That's smart *and* dumb, because no one is gonna question a wizard is he who he says he is, with the exception of that wizard's friends. I'm convinced that Skeeve was never on Flibber, or shopped at any Mall. It looks like my confirmation's here."

As if to echo my statement, a winking light appeared at the window. I opened the casement, and the fist-sized globe dropped into my hand. The glow was purple now instead of gold, indicating a reply was enclosed. As soon as I touched the globe it dissolved into a piece of parchment. The Deveel in the Bazaar who made them was growing rich—this month; next month some other manufacturer would undoubtedly figure out how to make them and undercut the first guy.

To my relief the writing on the paper was Bunny's. In the message she said no, Skeeve hadn't budged from Klah except for his outing to Wuh, he was fine, she would make sure to keep him at the inn for the duration, and where was this Mall? Women. Some things are just universal.

"That's it. Bunny says the kid's never been to Flibber. The debt's not his, and that's all I need to know."

"So you wish to deliver a warning to the counterfeit?" Chumley asked, aiming one moon-shaped eye at me.

To the uninitiated, a huge purple-furred Troll with odd-sized eyes might look amusing and relatively harmless, but no one ever makes one mad twice on purpose.

"I want to do more than that," I said, baring my teeth.

"There's the matter of over a hundred thousand gold pieces. Someone incurred those bills, and I want them cleared up with absolutely no doubt who is really responsible for paying, because it ain't Skeeve, and it ain't going to be me or either of you. And *someone* owes me a new easy chair."

"Agreed," Chumley said. "My goodness, a hundred thousand would put a largish hole in the family exchequer, what?"

"Whew!" Massha agreed. "With that kind of loot I could buy out the Gimmicks 'R' Us store, shelves and all. Just let me leave a note for Hugh."

With two sets of magikal means to transport us, there was an Alphonse-Gaston moment until we decided Massha ought to blink us there. I had a D-hopper now, but no one had the experience with gadgets like Massha. Using the directions we got from an infosearch spell Massha whipped up using an antique locket set with turquoise buttons, we popped in practically on the front doorstep of The Mall.

TWO

The *bamf* that was the displacement of air heralding our arrival also displaced several bodies. When we appeared, my arms were pinned to my sides by the sheer press of the huge crowd surrounding the gigantic white building ahead.

Pretty majestic, I thought, taking in as much as I could in one glance. The building had been constructed of white marble, stretching three stories to the gargoyles that ran around underneath the lip of the roof made of curved red tiles. A pediment underneath the peak on our side of the building displayed a frieze with a center figure that looked familiar to me. The place was a temple to Agora, a goddess of shopping centers who held sway in more than one dimension. As far as I knew she didn't have any influence in Deva; maybe she'd packed up in disgust. Her centers of worship tended to be orderly, and the only thing you could say about order at the Bazaar was that it had rules of engagement that if they pertained to fighting, you'd assume you were talking about street fighting, not war. I'd never had a tussle with Agora that I could recall. I wriggled to get loose from the crowd and tried to press closer toward the building.

"Oh, no, you don't get ahead that way!" a shrill female voice cried.

I felt myself grabbed from behind by a host of hands and tossed into the air. A snarl of protest from Chumley and a shriek of surprise from Massha told me that they had been seized, too. Massha had her gadgets, so she rose over the top of the crowd as the Troll and I were tossed like water buckets in a fire brigade until we landed with a thump on the ground behind the horde. Female faces glared at us as we scrambled to our feet.

"What's going on?" I said, trying to hold on to my dignity and temper.

"A sale!" a female Dragonet exclaimed, fluttering her light blue wings excitedly.

"Is that unusual?" Massha said.

"There's one every day in The Mall," the Dragonet's pale green partner asserted glumly.

"But not at Cartok's," his mate corrected him. "Seven percent off everything in the shop!"

Seven percent didn't sound like much of a discount to me, but most of the shoppers seemed to think it was a good deal.

"How come there's a crowd out here?" I asked.

"They don't open until ten," the blue Dragonet said. A clock in Agora's belly up on the pediment showed that the minute hand was still a short distance from striking the hour. "We saw you try to line-hop. They'll tear you apart if you try."

"We'll stay back here," I said, holding my hands up in surrender.

But one small male with a domed head, deep blue skin, and tall, narrow, double-pointed ears seemed heedless of the danger. I watched curiously as he shoved his way into the mass of shoppers and plunged doggedly forward. Got tossed back again and again, landing at Aahz's feet. Had to admire the little guy's perseverance in the face of an obstacle I wouldn't face myself. Tossed back, clothes torn, the beginning of a bright purple bruise under one eye.

"That's it," he swore as he landed almost at our feet. He picked himself up and dusted himself off. "One more time they throw me back, and I'm not opening The Mall."

"I'll help," Massha said.

She levitated downward like a big orange balloon and scooped the little man up in her arms. Lightning bolts and missiles of various types flew at her from the irate crowd as she flew him toward the front of the line, but she dodged them all. At the door she let the little man down, then sailed up out of the way as the twelve-foot-high doors flew open, and the horde of shoppers poured forward.

Massha sailed back to us and settled down, a satisfied look on her face.

"Not a bad thing to start the day with a good deed," she remarked.

"Let's go," I said impatiently, as people surged past us on every side. "C'mon, Chumley."

Massha yelped as a furry shape hurtled past her.

"He's got my purse!" she shouted.

"I'll get him," Chumley offered gallantly, and made as if to dash after the little brown creature. Massha grabbed the Troll's arm.

"Never mind," she said with a smile. Putting two fingers in her mouth, she blew a sharp whistle.

The bounding creature hauling the orange purse nearly as large as it was let out a cry of despair as the purse seemed to grow legs. It galloped forward, caught up with its captor, opened its mouth, and engulfed the creature in one bite, then snapped shut. Massha retrieved the struggling handbag.

"Now what'll I do with it?" she wondered.

"And what is it?" Chumley asked, as we bent over the purse to look. I opened the handbag a crack and stuck my hand into it. My skin's pretty tough, compared with Trolls and Jahks, being covered with a handsome layer of scales. The critter tried to bite my fingers, but I got it by the scruff and hauled it out.

"A rat!" was all I had time to say before it went for the tendons in my wrist.

It caught the pressure point under my thumb between its long, sharp front teeth and chomped down. I snarled in pain. My fingers went limp. Before I could grab the little monster with the other hand and squeeze the life out of it, it had clambered up over our shoulders and disappeared into the crowd.

"Son of a flea-bitten blankety-blank," I said through gritted teeth, clutching my hand.

"Rats are a big problem in The Mall," a female in a white, fur-trimmed coat informed us as she swept by.

"You okay, Hot Shot?" Massha asked, with concern.

"Dammit, yes," I snapped.

The skin wasn't broken, but I was going to strangle the critter if I ever caught up with it.

Her eyes gleamed. "Well, then, come on. The Mall is open!"

I maintain a method for going into a situation that I try not to vary. Step one: identify the problem. Step two: evaluate the situation at hand. Step three: figure out a solution. Step four: implement that decision. Step five, when possible: collect reward.

In this case there was no chance of a step five, but the first step had already been determined. Someone was ripping Skeeve off, hoping he would take the rap or defend himself in the face of unanswerable accusations. At the very least Skeeve would end up with a blot on his character. At the very worst, he would feel he had to cough up the dough The Mall was asking for, and maybe have to stand trial for fraud. I didn't know which end of the spectrum was worse.

Cash you could always recoup, though I hated to admit it. I never like to let go of a copper coin I don't have to. If you're thrifty, you don't have to go out and earn money over again. It works for *you*.

Reputation, on the other hand, was impossible to rebuild. At our level of *perceived* expertise (the kid was at the beginning of his studies as a magician, and I currently had no powers), what people believed about you was every bit as important as what you could actually accomplish, and made it possible for you to do less work than the other way around. If word got around that Skeeve was a welsher, no amount of bibbity-bobbity-boo he picked up over the next few years was going to help.

Step two involved surveying our environment. We followed Massha and the huge, eager crowd into The Mall.

On the other side of the threshold, we were hit by a solid wall of sound. I thought the Bazaar was noisy! This aural assault you had to fight against like an avalanche. My ears, which stick out in modified triangles from the side of my head, and one of my most fetching features, I like to think, are far more sensitive than those of a Troll, a Jahk, or a Klahd.

Massha and Chumley were cringing at the echoing barrage. I was, too, but I would rather have been skinned with a butter knife than show it. It was only my reputation as a tough and focused investigator that kept me from unlimbering my new D-hopper, bopping on out of there posthaste, and finding a nice, quiet hurricane to stick my head into.

"Should we withdraw?" Chumley shouted.

"Hold on, High Tops!"

Floating above us, Massha fumbled at her belt. Suddenly, the sound died to a manageable level. I could still hear the music and footsteps and endless chatter, but it no longer felt like there was a steel band around my head playing island melodies.

"Cone of silence," she said, pointing to a triangular golden charm hanging from a fluttering pennant of orange chiffon. "I bought it for a gag, but it's turned out to be pretty useful."

Shaking my head to clear it, I had to agree. Relief from the noise made it possible for me to think while I surveyed our surroundings.

If at first I wondered how anyone could drop a hundred thousand gold pieces here, I soon changed my mind. The Mall reminded me of the Bazaar, but cleaner, less fragrant, and cooler—much cooler. A chill breeze blew down my neck at intervals as we pushed our way into the hordes of shoppers, mostly female. The greatest majority of visitors looked eager and excited, but a few with dark circles under their eyes trudged in like zombies, pulled inexorably toward the bright lights of the stores.

I'd seen some of these pitiable beings in the Bazaar: they were shopaholics. A few of them looked to be in the last stages of the disease, their trembling, clawed hands clutching canvas or net bags, with no joy in the process, only hard-core need. Where were their friends? Friends don't let friends shop themselves to death.

Business was brisk in The Mall. Ahead of us lay a long avenue lined tightly with stores on either side, reaching up three gallery levels under a vaulted roof held up by thick, carved beams where birds and flying lizards roosted. Their cooing and cheeping added to the cacophony. I couldn't see the end of the passage. It seemed to roll on into infinity.

We found Cartok's with no trouble. A thread of perky, up-tempo music piped out of the ceiling, warring with the local bands, making a piercing counterpoint with the howls and cries of the shoppers, who were climbing over one another to get at the patchwork jackets and shawls that seemed to be the main items of attraction. Massha gave a longing glance, but turned her eyes forward as we moved past.

Clothing shops and scarf vendors weren't the only sellers there. Far from it. Jewelry booths tempted the eye with a rainbow of sparkling color. From this distance I couldn't tell what was real and what wasn't, but the effect was impressive. Sword shops, with a sweaty smith bending steel over the breath of·a chained dragon, caught light with a different kind of gleam. A host of Vikings stood around the smith, trying out axe blades on the balls of their thumbs and nodding with approval. Beside the smithy were a couple of bookstores offering tomes wrapped in exotic leathers with gem-studded bindings. A few booths with their doorways draped with gauze had all the earmarks of magik shops. This Mall was a high-end operation, just as Massha had said.

"We came in Doorway D," Massha announced, coming over to us with a thick scroll in her hands. "You can tell by the relief of the dragon over the entrance." She pointed back toward the doors we had just come through.

"There's a map?" I asked, reaching for it.

"It's an encyclopedia," Massha countered, thrusting it at me. I peered down at the illumination. A glowing blue disk indicated YOU ARE HERE. I kept unrolling it until I was wrapped in a coil of papyrus. I was impressed. The corridor off Doorway D was one of a dozen entrances. The shopping space contained within these walls was vast, with several floors in each wing. You had to squint at the flowery writing to read the names of the stores, but it wouldn't help to memorize them, since unlike an ordinary chart, this one was constantly updated by magik. The green square on Gallery Two that was the Bilko Shop vanished and repainted itself in a bigger location just up the hall from where we were standing. I glanced up in time to see the store appear in a fusillade of fluttering banners, parting the crowds of shoppers, who went on browsing and buying without missing a single pace.

"There's thousands of stores here!" I said.

Massha gave me a quizzical look. "This from the guy who practically lives in the Bazaar?"

"Yeah, well, that's different," I pointed out. "There's no roof over it."

The heavy foot traffic plunging in and out of their doorways also had pushcarts and peddlers trying to attract their attention. I watched a Deveel, looking out of place in the pristine surroundings, steering a huge spoke-wheeled gypsy van painted every color of the rainbow. As soon as he stopped his cart and rolled up the side curtains, he was surrounded by shoppers of every race I'd ever seen and more than a few I hadn't, all clamoring to look at the brilliantly colored toy wands. Half of the wands shot bright blue fireballs, and the rest played rainbows all over the walls. Plenty of the lookers were ready to buy, thrusting coins into his ready palm. I wasn't surprised by the greedy grin on his face. This was not only paradise for shoppers, but sellers. Not one of the buyers attempted to bargain, and I knew the Deveel had to be recouping at least fifty times his investment per item sold. I was surprised the place wasn't full of Deveels, but if I was the toy merchant, I'd hide news of this El Dorado from my fellow demons. My palms itched. I found myself wondering what kind of business I would set up here, to take advantage of the outpouring from constantly open wallets, purses, pokes, and coffers. But I digress. I wasn't there to collect a reward. I was there for an important purpose. I hauled myself back to step one, and Skeeve.

"Okay, people, let's focus," I said. "We're not here to shop. We're here to find someone."

"Right you are," Chumley agreed, dragging his attention away from the rainbow seller. Massha reluctantly came to hover close. "Do we approach the management and ask for their assistance?"

"Let's scope out the place, first," I said. "If they knew why we were here, they might want to lean on us for repayment of their imaginary debt, and I am not going to give them a dime. Let's ask around, see if anyone's seen the kid, or someone identifying himself as Skeeve."

We started up the right side of Avenue D, asking the shop owners or their assistants if they'd seen a Klahd calling himself Skeeve. That didn't prove fruitful. We jammed ourselves into stall after tent after shop, asked a few leading questions, and got nothing. Massha had with her a copy of the official court portrait of Skeeve from back when he was Court Magician of Possiltum. I thought it was a pretty good likeness, since it portrayed a tall, very young Klahd with strawlike blond hair and big, innocent blue eyes who wasn't exactly the high roller and big-time kingmaker that he sometimes thought he was, and sometimes even succeeded in being. This image showed him for what he was, a good-natured, friendly kid who could be taken advantage of. Crom knew I'd done it myself half a dozen times. For his own good, of course. No one we talked to could ID Skeeve, nor could anyone recall having sold him anything, expensive or otherwise. I couldn't see inquiring into every single booth in The Mall. The map didn't give a total number of retail establishments in the building, but I stood by my original assessment of four digits or better. We'd be there for years, and I wanted to kick this problem in the butt before the bars opened.

I was finding it hard to think. Thanks to Massha's spell the noise level had abated somewhat, but nothing she could do could improve the quality of The Mall's music system. A group of bards was situated about every fifty feet. They were universally lousy, and placed so that a walker wasn't completely out of earshot before the next group's sound intruded.

"There's the sporting-goods store that sold the skeet-shooting outfit," Chumley shouted over the sound of a krumhorn, an accordion, and a steel guitar mauling jazz. He aimed a large, hairy hand toward the opposite side of the corridor.

"I'll go." Massha rose above the crowd and floated toward the indicated establishment. Suddenly, I saw weapons rising to aim at her.

"Massha!" I roared.

Her eyes widened. She yawed to starboard, but too late. Six crossbow bolts ripped through the air. Four of them ventilated the fluttering cloth of her costume. Chumley and I leaped into the crowd and dragged her down. I popped my head up above the shoulders of the crowd of shoppers. The crossbowmen were reloading. I felt my blood pressure rise.

"Take care of her," I instructed the Troll.

Disregarding the glares and yells of protest from the crowd, I stormed across the passage, tossing shoppers out of my way as I went. The row of Klahds in the front of the sports store stared at me uncomprehendingly as I yanked the brand-new weapons out of their hands and crunched them into sawdust between my palms. Dropping the tangle of wood and wire, I advanced upon the cowering bowmen.

"No one, I mean, *no one* shoots at one of my friends without answering to me!" I bellowed.

The Klahds backed away, babbling. One of them fell to his knees. I went to seize him first, intending to use him as a bat to clobber the other five.

A blue figure scooted in between me and my rightful prey.

"I am so sorry, shopper!" the Djinn proprietor declared, bowing his apology.

The meaty, blue-skinned being flicked a wrist, and the Klahds vanished.

"It was a misunderstanding, truly. Please! They mistook her for a target. I was just a moment too late to stop them. You see?"

He pointed at the high-beamed ceiling, where a dozen round bladders, a couple painted the same color as Massha's gaudy outfit, were tethered among a clutch of nervous-looking pigeons.

"Let me make it up to you," he offered, as Chumley stormed down upon him, fire in his mismatched eyes.

Massha floated behind him, her bright red harem pants in tatters.

"I am the owner of this fine establishment. My name is Gustavo Djinnelli. I am pleased to make your acquaintance." He bowed deeply. Surreptitiously, I waved Chumley back.

"What are you offering?" I inquired.

"What do you need?" the Djinn countered, with an airy wave. "I have game equipment of all kinds. No heavy weaponry. The Mall's rules forbid it. Or perhaps one of my many cousins has something in one of his or her stores that you might like? We Djinnellis have shops all over The Mall."

He looked at Massha hopefully. "I would be happy to give you anything you would like to make up for the *dreadful* error."

"Well . . ." I glanced at Massha, judging how much I could shake this guy down for.

"I'm not hurt," she assured me quickly. "Just shook up, but look at my clothes!" She held up a fold of floaty silk, shredded into fringe.

"No problem," the Djinn cooed, moving around her with the magikally enhanced speed of his kind and looking her up and down. "My cousin Rimbaldi will have exactly what you want. He stocks wonderful clothes in all kinds. His establishment, The Volcano, is famous! Such generous beauty! He will love to dress you, you will see! He will have such scope to show style!" '

A wide, slow smile spread across Massha's face.

"Thanks, Hot Foot. I'd appreciate that. A girl my size has to keep track of clothiers who cater to it."

"I will send you there now!" the Djinn said, gathering his arms together under his chin.

"Just a minute," I said, opening the picture of Skeeve. "Have you seen this guy?"

Gustavo's brows drew down.

"This rotten thief?" he snarled. Clouds began to gather around his head, and lighting licked out of them. "I will never again trust Klahds! He collects up a load of my best equipment and pays me with a note for good nothing! I will never again fall for the fancy credit card."

I perked up my ears. "Credit card?"

"Yes," Gustavo exclaimed. "He pulls it out of the air— I should never trust magicians, either, but they run in the family, what can I do?—and presents it to me. The spell said his credit was top, simply top-rated. I took it. I wrap all the goods in a nice parcel. He vanishes. The moment next, poof! I get back no confirmation, because the card is not good. No credit is behind it. The bank will not honor it, and I am out fifteen hundred gold pieces."

Magicians. I could feel Massha's and Chumley's eyes on me.

"Coincidence," I said, trying to stay cool. "Anyone claiming to be Skeeve had better be some kind of magician. Some guy who looks a lot like him."

"*Exactly* like him," Gustavo countered. He felt in the big sash at his belt. "We keep watch for the dead bumps around here."

"Deadbeats?" Massha asked.

"Them, too. Here." The Djinn handed us a small crystal ball.

I peered in and saw a thin, pointy-chinned Deveel's face. It was replaced in a few seconds by the profile of a green Dragonet. The next one sure looked like Skeeve. I thrust the ball away from me. Massha took it. She and Chumley looked into it with interest.

"He cheats my brother, too," Gustavo added. "*And* eight of my cousins. They have sworn to take his heart out with their fingernails. My cousin Franseppe send me this image. I keep it, and if I find him again . . . ggggrrrrgh!"

He twisted air into a knot.

Massha gulped and handed back the crystal ball.

"Thanks for the graphic description, blue and bouncy. We'd better be going."

"Of course! I am so sorry, luscious madame! Your clothes! My cousin awaits!" He assumed the position again, preparing to magik us out of there. "Come back again! I still owe you a favor! Come again!"

"Perhaps when the air's not so full of arrows," Chumley muttered into my ear, as mist gathered us up.

As soon as the cloud lowered us to the floor again I consulted the map, turning it over impatiently until I found the little YOU ARE HERE disk. We were near Doorway P, beside a huge facility through whose doorway belched clouds of smoke.

"The Volcano," I stated shortly, pointing at the tent beside us.

"Are you sure you don't want to go back to Klah and ask Skeeve if he's been here?" Massha said gently. "Learning magik can do funny things to people. You know he's been studying all alone for a long time . . ."

"No way!" I snarled. "There's a lot of explanations for what that guy just told us."

"He wasn't lying," Chumley reminded me. "He did recognize the portrait."

"I know!" I said, shaking my head. "But I don't want to get Skeeve involved. Think about it," I reasoned, not wanting to let even a glimmer of what my two former employees were suggesting to worm its way into my brain, "magikal research does make people do funny things. The kid always tries to fly before he can walk. Look at the possibilities. Skeeve has lots of potential, and not as much control as he thinks he does. If he hatched himself a doppelganger by accident, we'd just have to come back here and dispatch it for him. He'd die or go nuts if he faced it himself. You know how doppelgangers work."

I looked at their faces and saw a hint of worry—not skepticism. They believed in Skeeve as much as I did. I was worried, too.

"Or if it's just the kid himself sleep-shopping, Bunny can't handle that alone, and Skeeve won't even be aware he's doing it. We'd need to do an intervention. That's what friends are for."

"Quite right!" Chumley exclaimed. "I say, Aahz, when you put it like that, I do see your point."

"Me, too, Green and Scaly," Massha agreed. "I don't want the boss to fall into a trap."

"Right," I said. "So let's not stand around here gabbing." I plunged into The Volcano.

"Gah!" I coughed. "Reminds me of Pitsburg!"

Once you made it through twenty feet of smog, the air

cleared, giving you a good view of the vast interior of the store. The floor was largely black, with aisles picked out in hot orange and red, like hot lava snaking through cooled magma like a gap in reality. When the color shifted suddenly I gave it closer scrutiny. Beneath a barrier of protective magik the floor was an active lava flow. I became uncomfortably aware that if the juice went out of the spell, everyone here was cooked, including me.

"Nice clothes!" Massha observed.

"Not bad," I admitted. I've got a natural flair for fashion, if I have to say so myself. The goods in The Volcano had cool, comfortable style. Most garments were cut on a relaxed bias from cloth of muted but interesting colors like brick red, mustard yellow, moss green, toast brown, and blue, blue, blue. Blue was definitely the default hue for The Volcano's merchandise. Racks and shelves were full of trousers shaded from glacier to midnight. I took one good gander around, then ignored them. Blue does nothing for my complexion.

I turned my attention to the facility itself. The walls, rough-hewn above as if really cut from the sides of a volcano, were skirted with long brown-and-green curtains from about eight feet down to the floor. Customers plunged in and out of them followed by Djinns with armloads of clothing. The line of curtains stretched back farther than the eye could see.

"Reminds me of our HQ," I pointed out. "Looks like M.Y.T.H., Inc. isn't the only firm to make use of extra-dimensional space."

On the map a wavy line showed at the rear of the store square that the key indicated meant "continued on next page."

I wondered how come I'd never found my way to The Mall before. It must have been known on Perv; plenty of my fellow Pervects were there trying on racks of clothes before the lines of magik mirrors. A male with frilled ears that I thought maybe I knew held up a green chambray shirt, and the enchantment made it look as though he had actually donned it. He turned around, judging the fit and color. I thought it was a winner. My opinion was shared by the two slender blue Djinnies who were assisting him. He grinned widely, making the nearer clerk jump back a pace, and reached for the next shirt on the rack.

My attention was caught by a very attractive Pervect lady standing in the curve of a three-way mirror. She had a huge pile of merchandise draped over her arm. She glanced up and met my eye, and gave me a dimpling smile that made her four-inch teeth gleam in the store's orange lava light. I felt my heart beat faster. She gave me a con- spiratorial wink as she shuffled through a pile of plastic cards in her hand. Suddenly, the fetching vision was gone. In her place stood a puny male Imp in a loud black-and-red shirt and lilac slacks. I shrugged and turned away. Not my business if she wanted to shapechange.

Out of the corner of my eye I noticed a flash of white. The little female in the white fur coat who had spoken to us outside The Mall was edging toward the door, her eyes darting nervously about.

Two Djinns flashed into being two steps from where I was standing. I jumped back.

"I tell you, she was here a moment ago," the younger one declared. "As bold as brass monkeys!"

"Find her," the older one growled. "I want her highly ornamented hide! Keep looking!"

I glanced again, but the white-clad female had made good her escape.

Another Djinn, probably yet another relative of Gustavo's, by his family resemblance, was demonstrating the wonders of a pair of blue pants to a goggle-eyed gang of Klahds, all standing around a dais in the middle of the store with their jaws dropping open.

"These blue djeanns are durable!" the Djinn boomed, tugging on the waistband. "Comfortable! Stylish! And," he added, pointing to the pair of gold fabric patches attached to the fanny of each pair, "these flaps of cloth at the sides and back provide you with modest storage space right inside the garment! Yes! These pants have their own magikal security system that only you control! Think of it! No more cutpurses making off with your belt pouch, because it's right here in one of these pockets!"

The Klahds gasped; a few more were moved to applause. One of the women burst into tears of joy.

"What's the fuss?" Chumley said. "Why are they so excited. In-garment storage system? What is so tremendously wonderful about that?"

"Ah." I waved a hand. "Klahds never discovered pockets. Skeeve never saw one until he started hanging out with me?"

"I say," Chumley exclaimed, intrigued. "I did not realize they were so . . . limited."

"Well, Skeeve's not." Massha leaped in to defend her former tutor.

"Unschooled ain't stupid," I chimed in.

A sudden puff of smoke left us coughing. A large, prosperous-looking Djinn with a chest-covering beard appeared before us.

"Welcome to The Volcano!" he said. "I am Rimbaldi! How may I serve you?"

"Gustavo sent us," I replied.

"My beloved cousin!" Rimbaldi exclaimed. "Then you are doubly welcome! I know why you have come! This lovely lady needs my assistance!"

Suddenly we were at the nexus of a retail whirlwind that would have made the Deveel merchants of the Bazaar sit up and take notice. Two gum-snapping Djinnies flashed into being beside Massha and began to hold up garment after garment to her ample chest. The magik mirror showed how she'd look at every angle. Massha preened under the relentless stream of praise Rimbaldi kept flowing in her direction.

"Ooh," Massha crooned, turning to get the full effect of a pair of rose-colored djeanns that matched her harem jacket. The legs hugged her roundness to the ankles, where they flared out to cover Massha's feet, almost the opposite cut to the floaty bits of silk they replaced.

"Would madame like to try these on?" one of the Djinnies asked. She held her hands up under her chin and blinked.

"Ooop!" Massha squeaked, as her ample lower half became encased in red denim. "A little snug, aren't they?"

"But that's all the style, madame," the Djinnies hastened to assure her. "And the fit is so becoming!"

"Me like," Chumley grunted. "Look good."

"They're fine," I emphasized, as Massha appeared to dither. "Take them, and let's get out of here." I turned to the proprietor. "How much?"

"Free of charge, of course!" Rimbaldi assured us expansively. "A debt owed by my cousin is a debt owed by all us Djinnellis! Is honor satisfied?"

Massha beamed. "It sure is, tall, blue, and handsome!"

Rimbaldi's huge beard parted in a grin. "You are most welcome!"

"Just one more thing," I said, holding up the parchment with Skeeve's portrait on it. "You ever see this guy around here?"

Rimbaldi's good humor evaporated like water on a griddle. "This deadbeat?" he roared. "Look here!"

He held out a hand, into which suddenly appeared a sheaf of papers.

"All these receipts, paid for by his so-impressive credit card! And every one remains unpaid! No, I have not seen him these many weeks, and lucky for him!"

I stalked out into the noisy corridor, pursued at a trot by my two companions.

"Aahz, I am certain that all this is a mistake," Chumley murmured, catching up with me.

Massha achieved my other side and tucked her hand into my arm. I shook both of them off.

"No one calls my partner a thief and gets away with it!"
The halls echoed with the sound of my voice. Silence

fell briefly, then the inevitable music, salesmen's chants, and footsteps filled up the void.

"Take it easy, Green Giant." Massha calmed me. "I'm sure it's a mistake. I agree with you. It's not in character. But it sure looks like everyone thinks it is him."

"Yeah," I replied glumly. "It does."

The lutenist of the nearest muzak group hit a sour note and a string broke with a discordant twang.

"I need a drink."

THREE

Plenty of little cafés and establishments that I would have called open-air taverns if they'd been out in the air instead of under the roof lay on either side of the main pedestrian walkways. I signed to the others to accompany me to one adjacent to the bards. I could ignore the music; it was terrible. I wanted to reach out and grab the instrument out of the lutenist's hands and show him he was holding it upside down, but considering his skill level it probably would have sounded the same either way up. I'd have done a public service by bashing him over the head with it. The lizard creature playing the caradoogle was pretty good. He huffed away, the red pouch under his chin inflating, then slowly deflating to fill the multiple air sacs on his instrument that released the requisite polyphonic whining.

A pickpocket sidled close, attracted by the pockets on the back of Massha's new trousers. He pretended to be studying the menu on a standard near the table where we were sitting. Chumley showed all his teeth in a growl, and the would-be thief sidled off at a much higher rate of speed. I signaled to the miniskirted blue Flibberite female holding a tray on one palm high above her head. She nodded a head full of blond braids and came over to us, brandishing an order pad.

"Whattaya want, darlinks?" she said, beaming at us, her cheeks a healthy sapphire.

"What've you got on tap?" I asked.

"Freakstone's Old Oddball, Bidness Asuzhul, Perving Cheer, Double Dragonette—"

"A gallon of Perving Cheer, and keep it coming," I said, giving her a friendly pinch on the bottom. The other two gave their orders. In a moment, a tankard larger than my head was smacked down in front of me. Kind of small, I thought, tossing it back, but the Flibberite was already pulling another one. Good service.

I set down the first tankard and chugged the second one. The key to drinking Pervish beer was to get it down your gullet before the fumes hit you. Then, after the fifth or sixth one, you were immune to the effects and could slow down to sipping, if you felt like it. The cheerful server also plunked down bowls of finger foods. The café must be used to my species: my snacks immediately tried to climb out of the container. I slammed my hand down on them to stun them, then grabbed a few to chew on. Massha, trying not to look at my snacks, took a healthy slug of her Double Dragonette, a green brew that released a haze of steam into the chilly air.

"Are you all right, big spender?" Massha inquired, as I downed my third beer.

"I don't like this," I said. "The guy we're after has all the advantages. He's obviously been masquerading as Skeeve for a pretty long time. He skunked a lot of merchants, and he hasn't gotten caught—pretty clever, because it means the blame falls squarely on Skeeve. We've got to come up with a plan of action! Look at this place!"

I swept out my arms, just in time to grab another cutpurse by the collar, a skinny, pink-skinned Imp. I held him up over my head until I could determine that he hadn't gotten ahold of *my* wallet. A dozen billfolds and pokes rained down from his pockets onto my head.

"Sorry, sir. Sorry," the Imp protested, crushing his hands together in supplication. "It was just a mistake. A mistake, I swear . . . aaaaaggghh!"

"Apology accepted," I replied, heaving him overhand into the nearby fountain, which stood about thirty feet away.

The authorities were on the guy almost before he landed. A couple of the blue-skinned Flibberites in comic-opera uniforms, complete with white marching-band-style hats, Florentine quilted-front tunics, and puffy trousers, looked my way. I glared back, daring them to call me out over the incident, but they gave me point-nailed thumbs-ups. I even got a few grins from my fellow shoppers. Brushing money bags off my shoulders, I turned back to my companions.

"The moral of that story is that people-watching always pays off."

"I see," Chumley acknowledged.

"That just leaves us with one problem," I said, downing my fourth, or maybe fifth, beer. "How are we going to find the person who's masquerading as Skeeve?"

"By following him," Chumley exclaimed, jumping to his feet. "There he goes now!"

I turned in the direction he was pointing. I saw a yellow-haired Klahd in a dark purple tunic come out of a jewelry store with a parcel in his hands and head up the corridor away from us.

"You! Klahd! C'mere!" Chumley shouted, in his Big Crunch voice, trying to sound friendly.

The person turned toward us, then away without a flicker of recognition. I felt my jaw hit the ground. The blue eyes, the narrow nose, the strong jaw, the mobile mouth with the ready grin and puny rectangular teeth—it was Skeeve to the life—but it wasn't. This Klahd looked astonishingly like my ex-partner, but I knew deep down inside it wasn't the real thing. An impostor!

I felt my ire rising like lava in a volcano. Someone, some magician, some shapeshifter was running around this dimension pretending to be Skeeve, and ripping him and a whole lot of merchants off. I sprang up.

"Get him!" I roared.

Massha floated away from the table and arrowed away after the Klahd. Chumley and I bounded out of the café, dodging past the bards and the security guards hauling the wet Imp out of the fountain.

The impostor's eyes widened, then he took off running. He might not be Skeeve, but he had the same kind of long legs and slim build. In the thick crowd, those were an advantage, unlike my more muscular frame and shorter limbs. I plowed ahead, tossing shoppers out of my way right and left.

"Allow me, Aahz!" Chumley called, and thrust in ahead of me. "Aaaarrrr-aaaggghhh!" he yelled, waving his mighty arms. "Get out of way!"

No being who heard a full-throated growl would obstruct our forward passage for long.

So much for a subtle approach. With a full-sized Troll trained in crowd management, we soon cut the distance to about ten yards.

It was a weird feeling, pursuing my ex-partner. You'd think that with all the experience I had exposing magikal fraud I could put the disassociated sensation to one side, but I couldn't. I kept getting the feeling that if we jumped this guy, it might really turn out to *be* Skeeve.

We entered a crossroads. Our quarry faked left, then right, then right again, loping into another avenue filled with stores, tents, and stalls. Massha, sailing along overhead thanks to her gadgets, stayed right with him. She fumbled with her jewelry, clearly trying to find one gadget in particular.

"Can you grab him?" I called to her.

"My tractor-pendant's on the fritz!" she shouted back, holding up a smoking topaz.

But she gamely dipped down, stretching out a ring-filled hand toward the running Klahd's shoulder. She made contact. With a snarl, he spun around and raised three finger-tips in her direction.

"Whoa!" Massha levitated suddenly.

A lightning bolt crackled just underneath her belly and impacted upon the center pole of a white pavilion tent in the middle of the corridor. The carved golden griffin at the apex fell like a downed pheasant.

"Massha!" I yelled.

"I'm okay!" she called back, and rose into view once more.

The creep really was a magician! With a grim set to her shoulders, Massha continued the aerial chase. I made a promise that if this jerk wasn't Skeeve, I was going to give him the walloping of his life, just before I tore his arms and legs off. If he *was* . . . well, I would think about it if that unlikely situation arose.

Arms forward, our suspect dove into a pale blue tent with iridescent circles embroidered on each flap. I took a deep breath as I plunged in after him.

No air filled this one; the interior was awash in eight feet of water, in which mermaids sold jeweled brassieres to the general public. My prey kicked off in a dog paddle. My physique was much more suited to dry land than sea, so it helped when Massha grabbed me by the collar and dragged me along over the surface. I spared a quick glance back for Chumley.

The Troll was doing a creditable crawl stroke and gaining rapidly on the two of us. I seemed to recall one night around the table in our tent in the Bazaar when Tananda had revealed her big brother had been a champion swimmer at school on Trollia. The big lug was too modest about his accomplishments. Such reticence never paid off, in my philosophy.

At the far end of the tent, our prey hit the ground running. I sloshed out after him, into a tiny boutique that sold ladies' unmentionables (even more unmentionable than the mermaids' wares). Now I had him!

The shimmering white tent was hardly bigger than a boudoir. Reaching the back wall, he turned at bay, his long arms and legs poised for some kind of single combat, which I was confident he'd lose. I slowed up, gathered the muscles in my legs, and sprang! He dodged to one side.

I landed on my face, my arms empty. The back of the pavilion was illusionary, not an uncommon practice when persons of modest virtue (or less than modest) wanted to disappear discreetly. The shrieks of females surprised in various states of dishabille pierced the sound-deadening spell protecting my ears.

"A man!"

"Sorry, ladies! Just a routine inspection," I said hastily, over the screaming.

Maybe that hadn't been the best choice of words. As I scrambled to my feet, I was pelted with shoes, purses, and shopping bags by half-naked women from fifty different dimensions.

Making a hasty retreat, I fled back into the small pavilion. The sturdily built gray-furred felinoid female, one of her own red satin foundation garments supporting four rows of two bosoms each, pointed sternly to the wall at the left. Sheepishly, I followed her direction, and picked up the wet footprints left by my quarry and Chumley, whose head I spotted above those of the surrounding crowd as soon as I got outside.

The blond head swiveled back at us. Those familiar features were twisted into an expression of alarm I never thought would be directed at me. It gave me the creeps, but I didn't let it slow me down. I bounded past another set of bards, then another, passing through modern jazz, back into plainsong, and forward into punk rock. He made another break, this time into a wide tent full of mirrors.

The first thing I saw was my own handsome countenance. The proprietors, a couple of Deveels who probably broke a few pieces of merchandise behind unwary shoppers when business was slow, gawked at me when I dodged the framed mirror at the door and started running toward

the image of Skeeve I could see close to the back. When I
got there I realized that it was another image. I spun
around, just in time to see a flap of the tent waving. I shot
out into the corridor again.

"Chumley!" I shouted, holding my hand high and pointing toward the fleeing impostor.

"After him!" Chumley called, then changed his voice.
"Er, get Klahd!"

In a scramble of long legs, our prey dashed out and
headed up a side passage that led us through tent flaps and
hanging banners, with Massha flying point above. We
weren't going to lose sight of him now.

"There he goes!" Massha shouted from overhead.

I glanced up. She pointed. Still running, I pulled out the
map. The little blue dot looked pale from having to follow
us all over the map, but it gamely pointed to the location
we occupied. I smiled grimly. This time the fake Skeeve
had boxed himself up. There was no way out of the dead
end ahead. I put on a burst of speed that propelled me past
Chumley.

We shoved through a metal door left flapping by the
passage of the man we were pursuing. The little dot on the
map in my hand kind of hung back, as if ashamed to go
into the leg of The Mall in which we found ourselves.

A wave of stench that reminded me fondly of Pervish
cooking wafted past my nostrils. Unlike the absolute pristine cleanliness of the building everywhere else, this area
was furnished with heaps of garbage, dumped in between
huge stacks of crates, piles of cages, and skids full of bags.
This must be where shipments came in and trash went out.

A loud beeping noise cut through the air, and a heap of
carved wooden boxes higher than my head appeared into
being underneath an ornate letter W etched on the wall.
Obviously, someone's expected delivery had just arrived.

Ahead of me the kid was flagging. He must have been
aware that the stone wall ahead meant the end of the chase.

"He could try and pop out, Massha," I called, though I
doubted it.

If he'd wanted to dimension-hop, he could have done that anytime while we were running after him. Before I'd lost my powers, I had *bamfed* out on the fly I couldn't tell you how many times. An experienced traveler would have done it without all the running around. I was beginning to draw a mental picture of what kind of being we were dealing with.

"I'm ready," she shouted back, holding up a chain with a green eye pendant hanging from it. "This'll tell me where he's gone. It's a new gizmo from Kobol."

Movement caught my eye in the dwindling light toward the end of the corridor. I spared one erg of attention for the clutch of huge brown rats that were crawling around in the rotting heaps of food that had come from one of the restaurants and hadn't yet been cleared away by magikal means.

Twenty steps now. Ten. Five. The three of us converged on the "Skeeve" as he neared the shadowy wall.

"Now!" I bellowed.

All three of us dove for him—and cracked our heads together before bashing into the stone barrier. He was gone. Chumley clutched his head with one mighty hand as he felt around in the garbage for our quarry. I sprang up.

"Where'd he go, Massha?" I asked.

The Court Wizard of Possiltum wrenched her hefty self out of the trash and applied her skill to interpreting the beeps and twitterings coming from the green glass eye. She shook her head.

"It says he's still here," she informed us with a puzzled expression.

"Invisible?"

"Not possible." Chumley shook his head. "I had my hands firmly around his neck for one moment, then he was out of my grasp."

"At least we know he *was* substantial," I said, kicking aside heaps of paper.

A large brown rat, unearthed from its burrow, glared at me with little beady eyes. I glared back, and the vermin retreated with a scared squeak.

"It's not some kind of illusion. He's a magician or shapeshifter of some kind. Keep looking. There must be some clue as to where he went."

I pushed over a stack of worn wooden skids and started to dig through a pile of burlap bags.

"Smile, boys," Massha said, from behind us. "The locals are here."

FOUR

"Hands-a up!" a gruff voice barked. "Turn around, very slowly."

I know when I'm outnumbered. Very slowly, I turned around, with my hands up, as instructed. Chumley did the same. Hovering in midair Massha had already raised her arms over everyone's heads.

Facing us up the soiled corridor was either the chorus from *Rose Marie*, or a large portion of the security force of The Mall. I stopped counting at a hundred, as more and more of big, strong, blue-skinned beings in Renaissance costume pointed a nasty array of weapons in our direction. I recognized the guy with the extra set of feathers on his hat at the head of the posse as one of the officers who had arrested the pickpocket I'd soaked in the fountain.

"Hey, buddy," I called, giving him a friendly grin.

He recoiled a pace, his face sewn up in the solemn grimace of officialdom. His hands tightened on the polearm that even I, in my disenchanted condition, could tell packed some kind of nasty magikal punch.

"Who is it? Who is it? Who are they?" a voice demanded.

The white hats shifted backward and forward as someone made his way up through the crowd toward us. The last two security guards parted about a foot, and from their midst came a little bent figure, his eyes concentrating on the floor about two yards ahead of his feet. The little guy straightened up enough to look me over, then turned his gaze to Chumley, thence to Massha.

"You I remember from this morning," he smiled, nodding at her. "Nice girl, doing an old man like me a favor. So, what's all the fooferang?" He gave an impatient wave. "Down with the hands, *capisce*?

Keeping a wary eye on the captain of the guard, I lowered my arms.

"Look, friend," I began, in my most businesslike manner, "my friends and I are sorry to upset your routine. I know you're all busy. So are we. So if you don't mind, can we get back to our own business?"

The old man turned to the captain for an explanation. "Parvattani?"

The guard snapped to attention, which made the feathers on his hat dance. I wouldn't have been caught dead in an outfit like that outside a Mardi Gras parade.

"We've been in-a pursuit of these three for over a mile, Mr. Moa. They've disrupted shopping for the past half hour or so. I have a sheaf-a of complaints from customers and store owners"—he snapped his fingers, and another rent-a-cop came forward with a handful of papers—"regarding breakages, disturbances of-a the peace, intimidation—"

"Come on!" the old man exclaimed, spreading out his hands to us. "You don't look like disturbers of the peace, especially this helpful lady. What's the story?"

I tried to sound just as friendly and reasonable as he did. "We were trying to catch up with an acquaintance of mine."

"And you followed him back here?" the old man asked,

skeptically. "I take it your 'acquaintance' didn't want to meet up with you, did he? So, where is he?"

"He was here just a moment ago . . ." Massha began.

"He owe you money?" the old guy interrupted, with a shrewd glance.

"Not exactly," I replied, peeved that he kept interrupting us.

"I recognize him, Mr. Moa," one of the other little Flibberites exclaimed, shoving forward. "This Pervert is an affiliate of the Great Skeeve!"

"That's Pervect!" I growled.

I recognized him, too. When I last saw him, immediately before I slammed a door on him, he'd thrown a bolt of lightning at me.

The little squirt ignored me. "We tried to get information from him regarding Skeeve's whereabouts, but he refused to cooperate."

He gave me a dirty look. I showed my teeth, and he backpedaled. He wasn't so tough without his two goons. I didn't see them in the crowd; they must have been off elsewhere pushing little old ladies off curbs into traffic.

"Now, hold the phone!" the third Flibberite sputtered, starting forward on bandy legs. He was built on more hearty lines than his two companions, and reminded me of an old cowhand. "You could've gotten the wrong house. It's happened before. You aren't so all-fired accurate as you think you are."

"I did not get the house wrong," the squirt groused.

The old guy raised an eyebrow at me. "You know this Great Skeeve?"

The whole of The Mall guard contingent leaned in a little closer.

"Look, is there somewhere we can talk in private?" I said, lowering my voice to a confidential level.

"My office," Moa snapped out.

I liked a guy who didn't have to think before making a decision. Since that had the added effect of causing the

weapons to stop pointing toward us, I liked him even more.
The little guy made a sharp gesture. The guards parted to
form an aisle. Captain Parvattani stepped out as if he was
passing a reviewing stand. Moa gestured to us to precede
him and his companions.

"Mr. Moa—"

A small figure darted into our midst, the female in the
white fur coat we'd last seen in The Volcano. Cute little
face, if you liked them peaky with black, pointed noses.

"Not you again!" Parvattani groaned, rolling his eyes.
He took her by the arm. "Get out of here!"

"Mr. Moa!" the female pleaded, trying to get past him
to the little old executive. "Please. I've got some information for you!"

"Now, now, darling," Moa chided, patting her cheek
with a paternal hand as he went by. "I'm busy. I'll listen to
your fantasies some other time."

"—That's why I'm sure it's not my friend."

With one emphatically raised finger, I finished up my
explanation, which had taken a long while to expound.

Moa's office was furnished the way I like to see executive suites. All the furniture, including the bookshelves
behind Moa's desk and the very well stocked bar on the
wall opposite the cut-glass windows, were fine-grained
mahogany-colored wood. The green, leather-upholstered
chairs, both behind and in front of a bronze marble desk
smooth enough to ice-skate on, were deeply and very com-
fortably padded. Mine kept trying to engulf me whenever
I sat down, so I had to perch on the end to keep from having to wiggle out of it in an undignified fashion every time
I wanted to get up to make a point.

Parvattani had insisted on standing near the door at
rigid attention, and now looked as if he wished he'd sat
down as Mr. Moa had invited him. The Flibberite was a

good listener, keeping his eyes on me the whole time and only pausing momentarily to take notes.

"Okay, that all?" he asked, as I sat down and at last gave myself up to the upholstery gods.

A pretty young thing in a modest dirndl skirt and bodice brought me a pint of whisky in a thin crystal glass. I tossed it back in one grateful gulp and set it down gently for a refill.

"Yeah, that's it."

Moa leaned toward me over his folded hands. "Mr. Aahz, I've heard everything you've got to tell me, and I wish it was a new story."

I sprang up, with some difficulty.

"It's not a story," I roared, making the crystal sing. "If you've heard one syllable through those twin peaks on either side of your head . . ."

Moa's little hands patted the air. "Sit, sit." He sighed wearily. "I don't mean it's a story like a fairy tale. I wish it was. Mr. Aahz—"

"Just Aahz," I interrupted, glad to get a chance to stop him for once.

"Aahz, then. Look, I'm going to tell you something I don't want known outside of this office. I'm a cosmopolitan kind of guy. I've traveled off Flibber. I've heard of M.Y.T.H., Inc., and I know something about its reputation. Can I count on your discretion?"

I glanced from Moa to Chumley and Massha.

"Why not?" Massha said for all of us. "Just because we're not active—at present—doesn't mean we aren't the same people you've heard about."

"Good." Moa nodded, settling back in his chair with a sigh.

He picked up his cup of tea and took a healthy sip.

"Chamomint is good for the stomach. You should try it. All right, you don't want to waste time. Neither do I. Here's the scoop. We've got a ring of identity thieves operating in The Mall."

I shook my head. "Could be several groups with the same M.O. They may just overlap the same territory."

Moa's gesture of negation was emphatic.

"No, I'm pretty sure there's just one ring."

Chumley's ears perked up. "Like the—" he began, sitting forward eagerly.

"*No,* not like that," Moa retorted peevishly. "You're as bad as that, that girl out there, what's-her-name. Forget about it. We know a lot about these thieves, and I'm sure they're just one band working together. They're a pain where I sit. You said your pal has a credit card. Most of the problems we have from this particular gang comes from credit cards. Once you've got them, it's easy to use them. No more hauling around big bags of money or letters of credit from Gnomish banks. No more weighing gold dust and disputing the grams, or wondering whether the scale's crooked." He sighed. "The biggest problem is that it is easy to use them. With money, when your pocket's empty, you're done spending. When you flip out a card, it feels the same when you're ten thousand gold pieces overdrawn as it does when you've got cash in the bank. The Gnomes say it's our problem. They get their cut no matter what."

"What's the scam?" I asked, frowning.

"Easy," Moa snorted. "Like with your friend. These characters cotton on to someone. Sometimes they get ahold of the card itself, don't ask me how. Maybe they've got a spell that lets them make a copy of the card owner's face and personality, and put themselves in the way to get it instead of the rightful owner. Here's what I do know. It's easier if the victim's got a credit card—it's as if he, or she," he added, with a little nod of his head toward Massha, "has put a little self into it. It's an extension of you."

"I get it," I growled impatiently.

"Okay, then. They must have some way of utilizing that little bit, because we've had face-to-face encounters just like the one that happened today with you and your friend's double. He's one of the easy ones to copy."

I nodded. I had known that damned card was trouble the

second the kid flashed it at me, but I wasn't about to air family troubles in front of strangers. Massha and Chumley exchanged knowing looks with me.

Moa continued. "But I know it's happened to plenty of people without cards. We've got regular thieves; every merchant knows some of their goods are going to walk away under their own power. You've got to accept that as a fact of life, or you should never open your doors to the public. It's not a good thing to consider, but it's reality. Am I wrong?"

"Nope," I agreed tersely.

"I'm not wrong. I know. Anyhow, we only hear about it after it starts to happen. A customer, or maybe even a stranger, starts to run up big bills, uncollectable bills. Sometimes there's a protest. If they can prove they were somewhere else when the fraud was committed, we let them off."

I narrowed an eye at the squirt in the chair against the wall.

"We have to try to recover our losses," the little Flibberite explained imperturbably.

"I'm sending you a bill for my living room," I informed him. "So what am I doing here?"

Moa spread out his hands. "I'm explaining you our problem. This ring of thieves consists of one or more magicians who can duplicate the appearance of a legitimate, innocent shopper. All I know is that we see the person come into a store, commit what amounts to daylight robbery, then disappear like a wraith." Chumley let out a wordless exclamation. Moa held up a warning finger. "Don't start again. I don't know why, but instead of hanging low and getting what they want, these thieves like to make with the flamboyant purchases, the big ones. They go away for weeks or months. Then they're back again. With the same faces. We've tried, Oximit knows, but we've never caught one of them yet. It's either a huge gang, or they have some way of maintaining several identities at once."

Enlightenment shone a beacon in my eyes.

"Option B," I said, firmly. "I'm pretty sure I saw one of your thieves today, in The Volcano."

"What did he look like?"

"She," I corrected him, and described my Pervect enchantress. "But she flipped through a stack of cards and turned into a he. It looked pretty effortless. Whatever magik is involved, it's pretty sophisticated."

"Mr.—I mean, Aahz, that's incredible news!" Moa exclaimed. "We've got spies and magik eyes everywhere in this Mall, and no one has ever seen what you have just described."

"It's a hell of a way to run a railroad," Skocklin, the bandy-legged Flibberite opined. "Cards! Consarn it! It just figures! Them cards is a burr under my saddle." I had already decided he must have been born in the land of outdated phrases. "But it sure sounds like you folks have earned your reputations for observation."

"Thanks," I said.

"And yet," the peaky Flibberite began, tapping his fingertips together in a manner that seemed to pave the way for bad news, "this could all be a story, concocted to keep from paying off the debts of your friend, the Great Skeeve."

"You can take that attitude and—" I bit off my words as the guards came away from the walls with their weapons pointing at me. "Didn't I just prove to you that it couldn't be the real Skeeve out there?"

"You didn't really *prove* anything," the squirt announced with satisfaction on his narrow little face. "All you told us was something we have already deduced and might have found out in time. There's nothing to determine that it's actually *true*. It's just one of many suppositions that we're exploring."

I had hated the jerk from the moment I had seen him. Bean counters were the same all over the dimensions. I wanted to take the little creep and squeeze his head until there was only one four-pointed ear on top of his neck. I knew a bureaucrat when I heard it.

"Who the hell do you think we were chasing for an hour? The will-o'-the-wisp?"

"I have no idea," the squirt smirked, and I really wanted to commit mayhem on him at that moment. "For all we know you're in league with the thieves."

"WHAT??? That's it—it's clobbering time."

I kicked out of my chair, only to find Parvattani and his spear in my face. Chumley picked him up by his collar. Five of Parvi's guards surrounded the Troll with their magik polearms. Massha geared up with some of her jewelry. The little guy flung up his hands, one pointed at her and one at me, readying a spell. I cracked my knuckles and prepared to dive in. I could probably take half a dozen of the guards before it got complicated. It was going to be a beautiful brawl. Then The Mall manager stepped in between us.

"Enough!" Moa held up his hands. "No fighting!" Everyone sagged a little, disappointed. He shook his head wearily. "You know, and I know, that we don't think any such thing. We've heard of M.Y.T.H., Inc. We know who you are."

With an eye on the obnoxious squirt in the corner I nonchalantly flipped my chair upright and sat down in it again. Massha kept her hand on the glowing jewels on her jangly belt.

"Then what the hell do you want?" I demanded.

"Well," Moa suggested apologetically, "we've just finished telling you that we've been unable to break up this ring of thieves. Maybe our approach is wrong."

"Duh," Chumley chided him, in his Big Crunch voice. "Not catch."

"Exactly," Moa remarked, with an emphatic upward swing of his forefinger. "Look, gentleman and madame, I'm a businessman. I'm not a detective. I sell goods. I don't solve mysteries." A thin eyebrow climbed up his shiny bald dome. "But you do."

I'd known the conversation would take this turning the moment Moa asked us back to his office.

"Sorry," I snapped. "Not interested."

Moa looked surprised. I knew he'd do that, too. "What?"

"You're about to ask us to investigate the thieves here in The Mall. Right?"

"Of course, right. We do want to hire you. You want the same thing we do. The sky's the limit on fees. Why not?"

I held up a hand and ticked off the fingers. "Several reasons. One: we *don't* want exactly the same things. I'm here to figure out who's impersonating my friend. Nothing else. Two: I don't like to get tied up in local issues in which I have no stake. Three:"—and here I fixed the squirt next to Moa with a full-throttle glare—"I might have considered differently, but your partner here decided to try and burn my office down."

Moa gave a chiding look at the peaky-faced Flibberite, then turned large and sorrowful eyes toward me.

"Please, Mr. Aahz, my associate here was doing his job. Won't you reconsider? We'll offer you . . . ten thousand gold pieces."

Now came the hard part: a cash offer. I'd already anticipated that, too. In my day I've been on both sides of this kind of negotiation. I thought about it, hard, but loyalty won out over greed. I folded my arms.

"No."

"Each."

My palms itched, but I held firm. "No."

Now Massha and Chumley looked surprised, too.

"Twenty," the Flibberite offered, growing panic in his eyes.

"Mr. Moa!" the financial squirt protested.

"Enough, already, Woofle," Moa replied, not taking his eyes off mine. "Thirty."

"No!" I roared. The picture of bags of shiny coins fluttering away on gossamer wings was almost too much for me to take, but I hung on. My efforts weren't lost on my associates.

"Aahz," Massha asked gently. "Are you feeling all right?"

"I'm fine," I snarled. "It's the principle. I want to get to the bottom of Skeeve's shoplifting double. I want to tear his head off and spit down his neck, then I am going back to Deva to finish the book I was reading when this whole mess started. If it didn't burn to ashes," I added, with a glare at Woofle.

He quailed. That was good. I felt like scaring hell out of *someone.*

"Maybe," Chumley grunted at Moa in his Big Crunch voice, "you nice, we help if possible." He turned his big, moon-shaped eyes at me. "Re-con-sid. Later."

Moa glanced at the Troll, as though surprised that he could actually talk. Trolls often hired out as muscle in other dimensions. Rarely did their employers get to know them as we did, which led to the widespread misconception that they had about five brain cells each. In reality, Chumley had about five *college degrees.* After me he was probably the smartest guy in M.Y.T.H., Inc. He certainly had the Flibberites' attention.

"Yes, Mr. Troll," Moa asserted eagerly, leaning forward with his hands outstretched. "How nice do I have to be?"

Chumley pursed his big lips as if trying to make words was difficult. "Place sleep. Food. Guard help. Yeah?"

"Yes," I picked up on my associate's suggestions, wondering what was wrong with me that I hadn't thought of that myself. "If you put us up, give us a . . . reasonable per diem for meals and drinks and so on, and give us an in with the local security, if, and it's a big *if,* we come across something during our personal investigation that helps you out, we might shoot it your way."

"You're free to reward us afterward if you want to," Massha interjected hastily.

"We'll be happy to," Moa promised, his enthusiasm

returned. "We'll deputize you. You'll be free to come and go wherever you want. Parvattani!"

"Yessir!" The captain of the guard snapped to attention.

"These three fine people need to operate as secret guards here in The Mall."

"Yessir!" Parvattani responded, with a salute that nearly knocked him unconscious. "Bisimo! Secret guard insignia for three!"

The guard nearest the door flung it open and tore out into the hallway.

In a very short time he was back with three more guards, each carrying a bundle of cloth.

"You're a little heftier than the average Flibberite," Bisimo offered apologetically.

He shook out the first bundle and held it up to my chest. It was a tunic. At least, if there'd been a volume control on the incredibly loud fabric so I could dial it down to dark blue serge from wild blackberry-and-orange-dyed spotted herringbone tweed, I might have identified it as a tunic. It was so tasteless even an Imp wouldn't have worn it. Huge epaulets in metallic aqua adorned each shoulder, and frogs in the same shade marched down the front, framing huge shiny brass buttons. The color scheme actually hurt my eyes.

"What's this?" I demanded, blinking.

"All our undercover agents wear these," Moa said, surprised. "It's meant to blend in with the local scenery."

"All of it at once?" I said, shaking my head. "No wonder you've had no luck sneaking up on your frauds! Any thief with half an eyeball could see these coming four dimensions away!" I shoved the cloth back at Bisimo. "No thanks, pal. I prefer my own style. Maybe, just maybe if I have time when we finish with what we came here to do, I'll help you set up a real undercover corps. And maybe," I added, trying not to look at the psychedelic ball of cloth in Bisimo's arms, "we can have a talk about camouflage. In the meantime, just stay out of our way. We'll try to keep it subtle. We don't want to tip off the perpetrators. We want their butts as much as you do."

"Well, you can't walk around without a guide," Moa countered. "One of the guards can accompany you."

"No," I retorted at once.

"It's a good idea," Moa offered persuasively. "He'll make sure you have no trouble with the locals, get you into secured areas, and all that. You did say you've never been here before. You should take one with you to show you the course."

I considered it for about one second.

"All right," I agreed.

I pointed at Captain Parvattani.

"We'll take him. That'll be Par for the course." I guffawed at my own joke and waited for applause, but in vain. Everyone looked at me blankly.

"But he's the captain of the guard," Moa protested.

"I know. That means he'll be brighter than the others, I hope," I said. "If he's at the head of your squad, it means he's the best you've got. Right? If he's worth what you're paying him, he'll have the whole layout of The Mall in his head, including the parts that aren't on the map."

Parvattani straightened his spine and tried to live up to the hype I was giving him. I always find it makes people give their all if you set an ideal for them to live up to. Still, Moa looked doubtful.

"Besides, he might learn something, hanging out with us," I added.

That was enough to convince Moa. That suited me. We wouldn't have to learn the terrain, and Par wouldn't try to take control of the situation.

"But you're not wearing that thing," I instructed the elated guard. "You stick out like a clown nose at a cotillion."

"But it's my uniform, sir!" my new guide protested.

"Don't 'sir' me." I sighed. He might stick out anyway, with that gung ho Boy Scout attitude. "I work for a living. Mufti, or we find our way around without your assistance.

How are we supposed to sneak up on your problem if they can see you coming? You handle situations like apprehending pickpockets and breaking up riots just fine; we saw you. But this is detective work. We're going to observe, not be observed."

Par blinked once, but nodded. He didn't need further explanation. Good. He was trainable. By the time we left he ought to be a better security officer than he was when we came. With a look to Moa for permission, Par disappeared out the door.

"So that's all settled," Moa said, with a sigh of relief. He signed to the nearest guard, who moved toward the sideboard. "Let's drink on it."

I grinned. "That's an offer I never refuse."

FIVE

"I've seen and heard enough," the voice in Strewth's ear squeaked. "Get your tail back here."

Hidden among the crystal decanters on the heavily carved wooden sideboard, the white-footed mall-rat backed slowly away from his listening point. Suddenly one of the Flibberites moved a hand toward Strewth. The rat panicked and scurried out of reach. The hand halted and settled onto one of the bottles. Strewth chittered.

"Missed me again, you big nincompoop!" he squeaked. "Nyah nyah nyah!"

Following the Master's standing orders, Strewth left a personal calling card on the shelf of the liquor cabinet, then slunk through the hole he and his fellows had chewed in the back and clambered down the concealed hole in the wall to an orange-curtained enclosure in the store adjacent to the office.

The hideout lay many corridors distant from his current location. It'd be good to use longer legs to get there. Strewth huddled under the bench in the dressing room and flipped quickly through the stack of cards he kept in a pouch on his back, chose one, and recited the incantation.

A second later, a big, burly Moolar with an impressive spread of pointed horns shoved back the drape and strode out into the shop with his hooflike thumbs hooked into his silver concha-laden belt.

"No, didn't see anything I wanted back there," he drawled.

A dozen mothers reacted to his appearance with alarm.

"Peeping Tom! Pervert! Monster!" they shrieked, battering him with their shopping bags. "What were you doing in there? Our precious children! Someone call the security guards!"

"No, don't," Strewth protested. "Coo! Er! Gosh! I didn't do anything to your children. Hey!"

The mothers paid no attention to his protests.

"Guards!" they shrieked. "Help! Monster!"

Strewth ran for the door. The mothers grabbed pieces of display and even the arms off mannequins to batter him. Strewth shielded his head as he dashed into the crowd, looking for a place to hide so he could change identity again.

"Strewth!" he exclaimed, as he shook off the last pursuer some eight or nine storefronts away.

As he ducked underneath a velvet rope in front of the Magik Lantern Emporium, a mother Imp shook a pink fist at him. Her other hand clutched a sniveling Impling rubbing his eyes with one fist. The moment she was out of sight, Strewth scooted behind a tent flap and changed the Moolar face for an Imp in a yellow-checked suit.

"I didn't know it was a children's clothing shop! Last time I was in here it was a haberdasher's!"

"Fool! Get back here!" Rattila's laughter rang in his ears all the way to the hideout.

.   .   .   .

At the concealed entrance Strewth disembodied and wriggled through the rathole into the Master's presence.

"All right, so it was stupid," the white-footed mall-rat said, straightening up to his full one foot eleven inches in height.

Rattila crouched over him from his throne of garbage, gazing down at him with glowing red eyes. He was twice the size of a mall-rat, his black fur gleaming in the faint light, his curved claws yellow. He pointed to the badge on his chest that read LEADER.

Strewth cowered down into the steaming muck. It was always hot in the Rat Hole, which raised the level of stink occupying it to a virtually visible state. It was a nasty, dirty, wet hole, full of the ends of worms and an oozy smell, as if a hundred layers of compost had been distilled down into its very essence, a huge contrast to the oppressive cleanliness in The Mall above. It always reminded him of home, Rattila was fond of saying to his followers.

"You made a mistake," the lord of the rats hissed. "You were not supposed to be observed. That was not a quality withdrawal from your listening post."

"Yeah. No. Sorry," Strewth said, groveling in the dirt. Did Rattila have to use such big words? "But the administrators didn't see me. Or their guests."

"How good was that? A whole storeful of women saw you. They could have followed you. We don't want anyone accidentally finding their way here," Rattila asked, leaning forward threateningly, "now, do we?"

Strewth groaned. It was going to be another lecture.

"No, Ratty. We don't."

"Don't call me that!" Rattila recoiled, rolling his eyes toward the stalactites hanging from the ceiling. "Will you never learn the correct way to address me?"

"Sorry, Ra—I mean Rattila. Mighty Rattila. Lord Rattila." The mall-rat sighed and launched into the litany. "King of Trash, Marquis of Merchandise, Collector of Unguarded Property, Magikal Potentate Extraordinary,

Rightful Holder of the Throne of Refuse, and, er, Ruler of All Rats and Lesser Beings."

The red eyes slitted with pleasure, and Strewth breathed with relief. Sometimes coming back to the hideout gave him more of a thrill of terror than his daily rounds of shoplifting. Rattila's fur crackled with power, something that had always struck Strewth as not quite normal. But then, nothing down below had been normal for years.

The Rat Hole would have surprised the shoppers who passed through The Mall every day. It extended off in every direction except up, several levels that covered near-ly the whole footprint of the vast building. It had only one entrance, concealed virtually under the Flibberites' very noses, but that never stopped them carrying tons of loot down into their domain.

The hard, cold fact was that once somebody was carry-ing a piece of merchandise in the corridor, everybody else assumed that it had been purchased. The trickiest bit, the one that gave Strewth the emotional high he loved, was conveying the object of his desire from a store shelf or hanger all the way to the door of the shop it came from. That nourished him more than food or drink, none of which they ever paid for, either. But responsibility was a new thing, imposed upon them when Rattila had arrived. In exchange for doing tasks, they were having more fun than they had ever had.

One of the most important duties was keeping an ear on the administration. Moa and the other executives had a magik-repelling stronghold on the floor above the chil-dren's store. Rattila had tried several times to plant a bug in the offices to hear what was being said, whether the greenies had figured out who he was or how his operation worked, but the bugs always died. The insects sent a dele-gation to complain, and though they still professed loyalty, refused to allow any more of their contingent to go up to the executive suite.

Instead, Rattila was forced to send a rat spy up to watch and listen in person, under the desk or on the sideboard or behind one of the picture frames. He also established listening posts in the security stations, in the buying office, and even in the janitorial department. He hadn't kept hold over The Mall for so long without having infiltrated most of the departments. Nothing went unobserved for long.

"What else do you have to say about the visitors?" Rattila demanded.

"Nothing but what you saw and heard," Strewth said. "Thanks to that Pervert, they know about the cards."

"But they do not really know what they mean!" Rattila laughed heartily.

Strewth hated when he did that. He thought he was so superior, coming from another dimension. If he was so great, how come he hadn't been born a Flibberite?

"Because I am Ratislavan, of course, and that's superior to any other dimension!"

Strewth gulped. "How'd you—"

"I hear a faint echo of your thoughts, mall-rat!"

"All the time?" Strewth squeaked.

He flung his hand-paws up to his ears to keep his thoughts from leaking out.

"That doesn't work." Rattila laughed. "You think my hold on your senses just flickers out like a candle when the job's over? Don't you like having your eyes and ears conscripted for my use? What is a good minion for, eh?"

Strewth's shoulders hunched guiltily.

"Sorry, Ratty."

"Don't call me that!"

Rattila rose on his haunches, his thick black fur bristling between his shoulder blades. The rest of his henchrats giggled shrilly to one another. Everyone liked it when someone else got called on the carpet. Rattila grinned at his subjects, his teeth yellow in the glow from the magikal toys strewn around his throne. Every vermin in The Mall worked for him, but the mall-rats were something special. It was as though the species had been tailor-made for his purpose.

Mall-rats lived to hang around in shopping areas and

pick up things that other people had dropped or turned
their backs on for a moment. Not just merchandise, but
outdated expressions, cast-off clothing and fashions. All of
it came in useful to Rattila's quest and the means of dis-
guising how he accomplished it.

All around him, the wealth of objects glowed with the
aura of the beings who had owned them last, the ones who
had made them, and the ones who reaped the raw materi-
als. From that horde of shop clerks and factory workers
and farmers he squeezed out the basic spark of their lives.
True, most of the power that he gleaned was boring,
earnest, and straightforward, but it provided him with more
energy to pursue higher-quality targets. For his quest was a
holy calling: to transform him into the most powerful wizard in existence.

He had seen it as a blazing burst of light, the night that
he first beheld the Master Card. Touching it, he had had a
vision what life could be like for him. From that moment,
the purpose of his life was fixed.

But he needed living energy, lots of it. His own dimension, Ratislava, was a poor source, having few wizards, living or historical. He had since learned that power did not
come from beings themselves, but rather from lines of
force that crisscrossed the landscape. He needed to tap into
people with the potential for magikal talent, until he had
gathered enough to instill it in himself. But The Mall on
Flibber—what was it the house agents always said were the
three most important characteristics of the perfect piece of
real estate? Location, location, location. Through the doors
of this gigantic building, every day of the year, came thousands of beings from nearly every dimension, to buy goods
from everywhere. The trait that made it possible for each
of them to hop to an out-of-the-way land for the mere purpose of shopping? Magikal talent. They had it, in gobs,
bunches, and tons. Rattila didn't merely want a piece of
that, he wanted it all.

How easy it had been, to establish his headquarters there,
in the last place the green ones would look. The basements

had been roughed out in the natural caverns of the mountainside and never used once the builders of The Mall figured out that their shoppers didn't like to go underground. Rattila took the vacancy as another sign that fate meant to make his dreams of power and conquest come true.

He had found a ready-made workforce waiting for him, a people just desperate to be led forward into a glorious future. The mall-rats had been living such a pathetic existence when Rattila had arrived, second-class citizens in a world of several competing intelligent species. Most of them he let run wild under his direction. Nine of them showed special promise. He took those as his protégés.

While he knew that they weren't cut out for world domination, he had shown them how they could use their natural talents and inclinations to prosper, and enjoy an interesting and varied existence that let them wear a new face every day, several times a day, if they liked. All they had to do was whatever he said. They could use their free time and newfound wealth as they pleased. They served him enthusiastically. How much of a pity was it that they would never know or appreciate the power he was gaining through their actions? None at all. They did what they were told, and that was all he really cared about. For him, they were the means to an end. They would benefit, but he would rule over them, and every being in the overworld. He was patient. His goal was within his reach. He listened once again to the words bumping around inside Strewth's head.

"So, we have visitors." Rattila said. "The Pervert might be fun to play with. He's so emphatic no one will question what he does. If we can turn him, he'll be very useful. The Troll . . . they never have any money, but who cares? He can carry a lot of booty for us. And that Jahk—now, she has possibilities."

"Not to mention all that bling-bling," Yahrayt added, showing his pointed front teeth. Rattila's red eyes shone.

"Ye-ees," Rattila breathed greedily. He waved a hand, and visions of the Jahk Massha's wealth rotated in the air before their eyes.

Rings! Necklaces! Earrings! Anklets! Bracelets! Bejeweled, engraved, damascened, twisted, wrought, linked, and braided, and all of them brimming with magikal potential. What was the use of having power if you never used it for something you enjoyed?

"All that lovely jewelry for you, and all the power for me."

Oive, Mayno, and Garn went so far as to try and touch the illusion. Rattila swept it away with one wave of his paw.

"Awww!" they protested.

"You want to see it again?" Rattila snarled. He pointed at the ceiling. "Go get the real thing! Bring it here. Everything there belongs to us! Bring it to me. All of it!"

The others looked around. Wassup blinked stupidly.

"We don't have enough already? This place is full."

The others groaned. Wassup had a way of taking all the wind out of their sails.

"And you call yourself a mall-rat, eh?" Mayno asked, twirling his long black whiskers in disdain. "Nevair do we have *enough*. The pursuit is all."

"You're just no good at analytical thinking," Garn sneered, polishing her long claws on her fur.

"Ana-what?" Wassup blinked. "Like, I'm totally confused."

Oive groaned. "So, what else is new?"

"What do we want?" Rattila demanded.

"More! More! More!" the rats chanted.

"All right!" he said, grinning. "Who's got something for me?"

Oive pushed forward, a bag clutched between her slim pink paws. "Pretty, pretty," she cooed.

Rattila could sense the magik from the short distance.

"Give it here." From the red-beaded handbag he drew a new, bright orange credit card. "Barely used," he complained.

"Can't help that," Oive piped nervously. "I mean, like, I could wait until it got used more, but then I wouldn't have gotten it. Like, do you get that?"

"Good thought," Rattila praised her.

The mall-rat was overjoyed as he tossed the empty purse back to her. By the Big Cheese itself, they were easily pleased.

"Let's see how much of its owner's essence it's managed to absorb anyhow."

Rattila put the card to his forehead. By the power of the Master Card underneath his Throne of Refuse, he had the power to be the Card Reader. Visions began to crowd his vision, full of linoleum and chintz.

"Kazootina. An Imp, husband, dealer in used wagons, three children, favorite color sky-blue-pink." Typical of an Imp, couldn't even like a real color. "Belongs to a bowling league. Cheats a little. Good. Loose morality will make it easy to intrude on her reality. Yes. She'll be a good addition to our stable."

"I want her!" Garn shouted.

"No, me!" Oive shrilled. "I found her."

"You'll all get her," Rattila said, opening one eye. "You idiots know that!"

Wassup looked hurt. "You don't have to call us names."

"Settle down," Strewth ordered, turning a large beady eye on his associates until they quieted.

Rattila watched him with alarm. If he had to worry about any of his subordinates, Strewth was the one. He seemed brighter than the others, and observed more closely. Perhaps, if the day came when Rattila had achieved his purpose and no longer required The Mall, he would leave his domain to Strewth. But if he interfered with Rattila's scheme at all—slllcch! The street-cleaners upstairs would find yet another pathetic little body, which the puffy-pantsed guards would be at a total loss to explain.

Strewth nodded to Rattila and crouched down in a submissive manner, which Rattila completely distrusted. But he could wait no longer. He plunged a claw down into the Throne of Refuse, past the mouldering fish bones, past the wadded-up aluminum foil, past the square of gray-white chocolate with spoiled raisins, to the glowing heart of his power.

The solid gold rectangle clung to his pads as he drew it forth. He could feel its store of power almost burning his flesh. He could see the gauge in his mind—the card was 75 percent full. So near to world domination, and yet so far. The card yearned to break free and rule all existence. All it took was the right magician to wield it, and Rattila knew he was the one.

"One day, my pretty, one day," he whispered.

The card burst with golden light, increasing the paltry glow that illuminated the Rat Hole a hundredfold. He touched the newfound credit card to it, and snarled at his subjects.

"Now, chant!" he ordered.

Their eyes fixed on the Master Card, the mall-rats broke into a singsong.

"One Card to rule The Mall, One Card to Charge It, One Card to cruise The Mall, and in the darkness Lodge It."

"Again!"

"One card to rule The Mall, One Card to Charge It, One Card to cruise The Mall, and in the darkness Lodge It!"

"I can't heee-aaar yeww!"

The mall-rats repeated the litany, over and over, until Rattila could feel the new treasure warming and flowing. The Master Card seemed to reach out tentacles to surround it, sucking its essence into the golden light. For a moment the orange card was an empty husk. Then, he let a little power trickle back, *his* power. Kazootina belonged to him now! The housewife from Imper had just joined Rattila's Raiders.

The orange card multiplied in his paws until there were nine of them, all completely indistinguishable from the first one. He dealt them out to the eager paws of his mall-rats.

"Now, go," he ordered them. "Buy! Follow the strangers. I want to know everything they do, everywhere they go. And make sure you use the Skeeve card a lot. Go everywhere with it. I want his all his power before his friends up there get any wiser to us than they are."

SIX

Parvattani, now in an embroidered blue tunic and breeches and a pair of black tights, came running up to us as we left the executive offices. He scrambled to a halt, all out of breath, and threw me a vigorous salute.

"Ready to go, sir! I mean, Mr. Aahz. I mean, Aahz—" He swallowed.

"Take it easy, kid," I said, raising an eyebrow.

Boy, he was young! I couldn't remember ever having that much nervous energy.

"And stop doing that! We'll never be able to observe anybody secretly if you keep saluting."

"Yes sir!" Parvattani acknowledged, hammering his forehead with another straight-handed blow. "Whatever you say, sir!"

"Cut it out!" I snarled. "We have to figure out where to get started."

A voice piped up from behind us.

"I know where to start."

We all spun around. Trotting in our wake was the little blond female with the black gumdrop-shaped nose in the white fur coat whom I had seen sneaking out of The Volcano and who had confronted Moa on our way out of the alley.

"Go getta lost," Parvattani snapped.

She met my eyes, ignoring the fulminating guard.

"I hope you have more sense than this toy soldier here. I know what you're looking for."

Par took my arm and turned me back in the direction we were heading.

"Pay no attention to her, sir—Aahz. We'll go and-a interview the shopkeepers who actually waited on the person masquerading as your friend. Perhaps one of them heard-a him—or her, we can't disregard that possibility, since we are dealing with shapeshifters—speaking with a confederate-a—or make any reference to who is behind the theft of identity."

The voice interrupted, more insistently.

"I know who is behind it, too."

Par's face became more set, but he kept marching forward.

"Now that we have a particular face we're looking for, we can inquire as to how many fraudulent purchases he or she made and see if we can distinguish a pattern. We should concentrate our efforts on the shops where the false 'Skeeve' repeated the most often."

"That won't help," the little female scoffed.

I shook off Parvattani's arm to confront her.

"What do you know that we don't?"

The little female's jaw dropped.

"You're actually willing to listen?"

"Try me. If you're trying to sell me a load of clams, I can ignore it after I hear it."

The guard looked surprised, then insulted.

"Sir, pay no attention to her. She's mad. She keeps insisting that there is a vast secret conspiracy intending to undermine The Mall."

"No, I don't," the female said. "I keep telling you the truth, and you pretend I don't know what I'm talking about."

"You two argue like you've been married twenty years," I said, drily. "Before we go any farther is there something going on that I ought to know about?"

"Eyugh!" Par and the female chimed in chorus, exchanging looks of mutual dislike, but they shut up.

"Good. What's your name?" I asked the nonbride.

"Eskina." she replied, looking sullen.

"This is Massha and Chumley. I'm Aahz." She nodded to us gravely. "Let's go somewhere you can talk and I can listen. Preferably with a beer in my hand. That suit you?" I asked my companions.

"Beer good."

"Fine by me, High Roller," Massha added.

Parvattani bowed to us and began striding up the long corridor, threading his way in between crowds of people like an old pro. Massha floated beside the diminutive Eskina.

"Where'd you get the fur coat?" Massha asked, with a fashion-hunter's gleam in her eye.

Eskina glared. "I grew it," she snapped. "I'm a raterrier from Ratislava, a sworn officer in the Pole-Cat Investigation Department and the Ferret-Prevention Department."

"Oh," Massha said in a small voice. "Sorry. I'm from Jahk. I've never been to Ratislava. Your coat is very pretty."

"Sorry," Eskina said, with a toss of her fair head. "I am perhaps a little touchy. It is so long since I have been treated with any respect."

She treated Parvattani to another fierce look.

After one more glance of distrust toward the little female, Parvattani took over as tour guide. Eskina didn't utter another syllable the entire way to the hotel bar to which Par led us, the mere fact leading me to believe she was something unusual. Most females would have yakked their heads off, trying to make their case.

. . . .

The corner of the Mystikal Bar at the hotel seemed quiet
enough. The intimate lighting seemed to make people
automatically lower their voices. No one sat within two
tables' radius. I settled into the corner seat of the burgundy
velvet-covered, deeply upholstered banquette.

"It's a far cry from the Yellow Crescent Inn," I said, "but
it'll have to do."

"Oh, Aahz," Massha chided me. "It's a classy place.
Wait a minute, let me make sure we're alone." She took the
cone of silence off her wrist and waved a hand over it until
the purple glow extended outward to surround the entire
table. "That ought to do it."

Chumley came back from the bar with a tray of drinks
and lowered his big furry posterior into an armchair.

"Okay, talk," he uttered tersely in my direction.

We had known each other a long time. The two-word
sentence meant that he had spoken to the bartender and
intimated that we didn't want to be disturbed by anyone. If
we wanted more drinks, we'd come and get them.

I turned to our visitor, who was sipping carefully at a
Mango Lassie.

"So, you say you're an investigator. What are you doing
here?"

Ignoring the disapproving Parvattani, she reached into
the thick fur on the front of her torso and slid a small
object across the table to me.

"My badge. I am field agent for Ratislavan Intelligence.
I know who you are. If you are sensible, we can help each
other."

"How?"

Eskina leaned forward conspiratorially.

"I have been on the tail of a small-time wanna-be wizard named Rattila. He stole an experimental philosophical
device from the Ratislavan Research Workshops."

It was a new name to me, but Massha nodded.

"I've got a few things from them." she said. "Very nice
work, and dependable, too. Very upscale presentation.
They work mostly in precious metals."

"True," Eskina agreed. "This is a solid gold artifact I seek. It is very distinctive, but, alas, very small. I have asked these fools to help me"—she threw a scornful hand toward Par—"but they sneer."

"She is making it all up," Parvattani insisted.

"And you would know, how? You never listen to me!"

I was growing tired of their bickering.

"Ain't love grand?" I inquired of Massha and Chumley.

"All right!" Eskina said, embarrassed. "Here is what I know. Perhaps after I tell you, we can work together."

"How do you know what we're here for?" I asked, suspiciously. "For all you know we're looking for shoes for this lady."

Eskina waved a hand.

"I have been following you all day. I heard what you told Mr. Moa and what you asked the shopkeepers. Unless you are fibbing to everyone, then our purposes lie together."

"Go on," I offered, intrigued.

She was an observant character, if nothing else. I wish half the people I ran into had that going for them.

"This device, it is a magikal amplifier of great power. Ratislava is proud of its accomplishments in both magik and science. Our alchemists were working on it to enhance spells and other great workings in places where there are few lines of force, such as our own dimension. We know we are capable of more, but our native talent in manipulating magik is limited. We hope to accomplish greater things. We know we are capable. Only the means escapes us. The grand chief wizard, who, if you will forgive me, is not much in the enchantment department but is a great talker, believes that this will be the big breakthrough that will enable Ratislava to evolve a few real magicians. At present only prototypes of the device exist. It doesn't work for everyone; the basic potential must be there. This was the most powerful. Our leaders had great hopes for it. And then it disappeared."

"Do you know who took it?" I asked.

"Who could it be but Rattila?" Eskina countered, spreading her tiny pawlike hands out before us.

"One of your potential wizards?" Massha inquired, cocking a professional eye.

Eskina spat.

"Cats, no! He worked as a cleaner in the building. A menial. He is not very intelligent, I am afraid, but very ambitious. When he and the device disappeared at the same time, we investigated. No trace of him could be found, so it was assumed he employed the latent power in the device to flee the dimension. His mother was surprised. She said he was always such a quiet loner."

"Uh-huh," I acknowledged. "Those are the ones you have to watch."

"Yes." Eskina sighed. "Now we wish that we had. But how many eyes can we keep on the janitorial staff? Must we never hire quiet loners? Eh? For a job where one pushes a broom or uses a cleansing spell to clear the air of ectoplasmic matter late at night when no one is there, must we employ a jocular and outgoing individual? I would think that would create much more trouble than taking chances upon employees who do well alone."

"Don't look at me," I said. "I only deal with rampant individualist self-starters. The others get complacent and lazy and never solve a problem on their own."

Eskina nodded. "I see we understand one another."

"This has nothing to do with our thieves," Parvattani grumbled.

"Far from it," Eskina corrected, but speaking directly to me. "My assignment is to get the device and return it to the alchemists' lab. Misused, it will transform the one who invokes it in such a way that he is no longer a natural being but a creature of energy."

"So? It sounds like the problem will solve itself."

"Eventually! It is a very long process. In the meantime, the problem is that it gleans its energy from a chosen source. It is designed to tap into force lines. That is no trouble; those are nonsentient and eternally replenished."

I held up a hand. "I see where this is going. You think this Rattila is drawing his power from living beings."

"I feel certain of this," Eskina insisted. She poked a sharp finger into Parvattani's fancy tunic. "You have seen the husks yourself, the sad ones who shuffle around. They have no minds, no will of their own. They go forward with no memory of who they are or what they are doing there. They are the remains of normal shoppers who have been drained by the talent device."

"That's bad," Massha declared, horrified.

"How? How does the object gather power from those people?" I demanded.

I remembered the people she was talking about. I winced, picturing Skeeve meandering around like a mechanical windup toy.

"Through the Law of Contagion, direct contact, or contact with something that once touched the target. It is more difficult with force lines, which is why this is still a prototype. Making a physical connection with a force line is still in the theoretical stages. But living beings, though their potential is much less, are very easy to reach out and touch. It takes draining many to accomplish what would be quite swift and harmless if the device could be used in the manner it was intended."

"What's this got to do with the shapechangers who impersonate honest shoppers?" Par asked, pugnaciously.

"Everything! That must be an intermediate stage, manifested by the device. Taking action in the form of a targeted being strengthens a connection. Hence the purchases—affirmation of his tastes, his wealth. The longer that another person pretends to an identity, the more readily it is stripped away from the person to whom it belonged in the first place. Because this device is only an experimental one, we do not know precisely how Rattila manages to transfer the energy from one person to another. This is where your friend is in the most danger: Rattila seeks especially those who have magikal talent."

Parvattani seemed to be wrestling with a thought. It finally made its way out of his mouth.

"Tell her," he spat out.

"What?"

"I can't reveal information that came to me in an official capacity. You must. Tell her what you saw at The Volcano."

I did. Eskina's round brown eyes grew rounder as I gave her all the details I could remember about the shapechanger with the deck of cards by the clothes rack.

"But this must be related! The device, too, is in the shape of a card. The eventual and irreversible mindlessness will happen to Skeeve unless Aahz can stop it. Rattila wants to collect enough power to transform himself into the greatest magician in the universe, using a device obtained from a wizard he ripped off many years ago."

"I refuse to let Skeeve get shopped to death," I said, darkly.

My companions agreed heartily.

"What do we do first?" Massha asked.

"Cut him off," I said. "If the key to draining someone is by impersonating him, then the impersonator can't be allowed to make any more purchases in Skeeve's name."

"I'll put out an all-points bulletin at once," Par said, reaching into his pocket. His hand came up empty, and his cheeks turned a bright shade of green. "My globe's in my uniform. I'll have to go back to my quarters for it."

"Make it snappy," Massha urged him.

"But what about you? I am supposed to show you around."

"I can guide them," Eskina suggested.

When Parvattani made a face, she made one back.

"What do you think? I have been here for a long time looking for Rattila. I know this place as well as you do— better, maybe! Come on," she urged us. "He can find us later."

SEVEN

"I'm overwhelmed," Massha admitted, as we left the Mystikal Bar. "This place is too huge! I mean, normally I would be overjoyed to have more stores at my fingertips than I could ever shop in a lifetime, but I'm at a loss. How do we cover them all?"

I had no idea, but as the leader of this expedition, I had to show leadership, and the first key of good leadership is delegation of responsibilities.

"You're the friendly almost-native guide around here," I said to Eskina, who was trotting along a pace ahead of me like a tiny Sherpa. "Where would you start looking for someone?"

"We are going there," the Ratislavan investigator informed me, with an airy wave. "The center of The Mall is the center of the community."

"Community?" Chumley asked.

"But of course! When you work day by day next to someone else, you get to know them, no? It is a neighborhood. Even if you do not sleep there, it is as though you live there. People you see every day, customers who come in all the time, the complainers, the bargain hunters—"

I slapped my forehead. "It's the Bazaar except indoors," I exclaimed, feeling like a dope. "Who's in charge here? A Merchants' Association?"

"The administration," Eskina replied. "The shopkeepers do not have an association, but that is a good idea. I will begin to talk it up with my friends. They have some concerns that the administration does not always address."

I grimaced. If I'd just provided the seeds of subversion, I wasn't going to let it get traced back to me if I could help it. "No, I mean who's *really* in charge. The administration's in charge of the physical plant, assigning spaces, collecting rent. Who's the mayor of this burb? Who's the go-to guy, or the one you really don't want to piss off?"

"Ah!" Eskina nodded. "This is more sense. The Barista, of course. I will take you to the coffee shop."

I began to get a better idea of how The Mall was laid out as we walked. Big stores formed anchor points at intersections, with strings of small, smaller, and downright tiny establishments linking them. According to the map most of them were as modest as they appeared. Not many had taken the transdimensional route as The Volcano had.

The parallels between The Mall and the Bazaar became more obvious the farther we went. I noticed a delicate little Gnome female weighing out gems for a pair of burly horned-and-hooved travelers at the booth of the currency exchange she ran. Behind them, out of their line of vision but fully in sight of the Gnome were a couple of Trolls from the bar next door, each holding a club in case the travelers got rowdy. The transaction came to an end, the customers thanked her and departed, and the Trolls melted unobtrusively back into their establishment. Eskina was right: neighbors, looking out for one another.

A sign pinned to the wall read "Rub My Belly, two silver pieces." Underneath it, on the floor, a large dog lay on his back, wiggling seductively. He lifted his nose and sniffed, then whined.

"Eskina!"

The Ratislavan hurried over to fondle the dog's belly.

"How are you, Radu?" she asked.

"Very well. No sniff of the scent you seek."

"Ah, well." The female sighed. "Thank you for being vigilant."

"How about you?" Radu looked up at us with big brown eyes. "Reduced rates for friends of my friends?"

Massha smiled. "Why not?" She stooped to tickle the dog's hairy stomach. "Reminds me of my Hugh." Radu writhed all over with pleasure. "That reminds me of Hugh, too."

I groaned. "Too much information, Massha." I strode on.

"Hey, friend," a whinnying voice hailed me. I glanced in that direction. A huge, dappled gray horse stood at the door of a well-lit shop with a swinging sign emblazoned SHIRE OAT MEALS hanging horizontally on a pole over his head. Inside I could see a host of customers of several species, including Klahds, standing at a high bar, dining with spoons or eating right out of the dish. He tossed his head, making his long white mane dance. "Come in and try a bowl! Best oatmeal you'll ever taste! Today's special is whole grain cereal, with a bright red pippin on the side."

"No, thanks," I called back. "I like my food a little more active."

"Perverts," whispered his coworker, a smaller black steed.

It was meant to be an aside, but my species has very keen hearing. I don't take that kind of abuse from anybody.

"Do you want to be the main course?" I bellowed.

"Neigh!" she whickered in alarm, backing into the diner with a clatter of hooves.

The gray rider blew out his lips at me. "There's no need to be offensive," he chided.

"Maybe you'll remember next time: it's Per-*vect!*"

"Aahz!" Massha poked me in the head with a finger. She was floating above our heads. "Say, Eskina, is it always this warm in here?"

"Not really," Eskina replied. "Normally the climate is very well controlled. The volcano underneath the mall generates geothermal energy to run the technology that many of the shops are selling. And it keeps us very warm in the winter. But this is summer, and it is much too hot. The building engineer is falling behind in his job. Ah, here he comes! Jack!" She jumped up and down, waving to a fair-haired male in a pointed red cap with a bobble on the end.

I saw him skimming toward us as the crowd parted to let him by. He stood about my height, clad in a red jacket and breeches. Effortlessly, he nipped in and out of clusters of shoppers, gliding smoothly on one foot, then the other.

He didn't have skates on. I realized, as I saw vapor condensing around his body in the hot air, that he had to be a weather wizard or something equally powerful. As he got closer I saw a trail of ice form where his feet touched the floor. With his heels together and feet pointing outward in a straight line from toe to toe, he skimmed around us in ever-decreasing circles until he came to a halt directly in front of the Ratislavan.

"Eskina!" he exclaimed, sweeping her up in his arms. He had the features of a well-fed elf, with light blue eyes and strawberry blond hair framing an agreeably round face, pink on the apples of the cheeks and the tip of his sharp nose, but pale everywhere else. His ears, unlike the locals', had only one point each.

"Put me down," Eskina chided him, tapping him on the chest. "You will freeze me."

"Sorry." He grinned. "I don't know my own BTUs, sometimes."

"Let me present new friends," she offered, introducing us each by name. "You have probably heard of Jack Frost?" she asked me.

I received a solid handshake and drew back a hand chilled to the bone.

"The Jack Frost?" I asked. "The elemental?"

"Yup!" that dignitary replied cheerfully. "Nice to meet you! Are you shopping for something special today?"

"No, they are not," Eskina corrected him, before I could speak. "They are going to help me find Rattila."

"Wait a minute, I didn't say that," I argued.

The pale blue eyes met mine sincerely. "That's really good of you. Eskina's kept her nose to the ground, but she's only one person. This is an awfully big place. It's too easy for an interdimensional criminal to hide out here. I'm only a contractor, so Mall administration doesn't listen to me, but things are really heating up around here, and I do not mean the temperature. Speaking of which," he added, raising his nose as though sniffing the air, "it is too warm. Stand back a bit, folks."

Jack inhaled deeply, then blew. His breath shot outward in a white cone, and the whiteness radiated outward to the walls. I prefer a cool room to a hot one, but this was one abrupt change. If there'd been a bag of peas hanging in front of him it would have been flash-frozen. My teeth chattered hard enough to hurt my jaw. Massha pulled her flimsy garments more snugly around her. So did the hundreds of shoppers in the hall. Some of them shot dirty looks at the elemental. Only Chumley and Eskina, clad in their own lush fur, were unaffected.

"Sorry, folks," Jack apologized, after taking a second breath. "It'll even out in a moment. Got to keep on top of things, or it'd be the end of The Mall as we know it!"

"Wait a moment," I exclaimed, as a thought struck me. "You say this place is on top of a live volcano? The steam rising above the mountain outside isn't an effect?"

"Nope! The Volcano, the clothing store, is named for it. You've seen the floor? My work," he announced modestly. "Living art, I call it. Free-flowing lava. Really pretty. You should go and take a look."

"Maybe later," I suggested, promising myself never to set foot in that store again. I remembered the orange-and-black floor, but I thought it was a piece of magik intended to impress the shoppers. A live volcano! These people were definitely crazy.

"So you'll be around for a while?" Jack asked, sticking

up a finger to test the atmosphere. The temperature had
dropped to a pleasant level. Elemental magik was some of
the most powerful around.

"Not one minute more than we have to," Massha
answered, cheerfully. "We want to help our friend, then
I've got to get back to my job."

"They are staying," Eskina insisted. "They have a friend
who is being thieved from. Only if they help me catch
Rattila will they solve their friend's problem."

"We'll see about that," I glowered.

"Hey, hey, then, welcome to the neighborhood," Jack
Frost boomed. "Gotta go." He offered each of us a hand
again, then shot off down the corridor.

"You had to tell him everything?" I asked, moodily.

"Everyone knows everything about each other," Eskina
acknowledged. "I have had to become acquainted with so
many because the administration is so bad in not helping
me. I will introduce you to all my good friends. They are
all very nice, giving me food and places to sleep. Some are
not so kind, like the proprietor of The Volcano and his
cousins. That is why you see me sneaking in and out of
there, but I must patrol where my nose leads me." She
tapped that small feature. "Come with me! I will take you
to the Barista."

Looking around. Now that I was tuned in to it, paid
more attention to the blank-eyed shufflers, worrying that
Skeeve could become one of them. A haggard female with
long, graying black hair and a narrow face caught me
regarding her with pity, and snapped, "What are you looking at, scale face?"

So not all of them had been mind-stripped. I stopped
thinking that they were all alike and wondered how many
of them were just moody.

"Sir!" a perky young female in a green uniform and cap
accosted me, thrusting a pen and a clipboard in my face.
"Would you care to apply for a Mall card? Unlimited credit, only thirty-five percent interest per annum. Just fill your

name in here, put your birth date here, and your shoe size here, and sign!" She pushed the pen into my hand.

I shoved the clipboard aside and stuck the pen in her hat. "Bug off."

"What about you, madame?" she asked, flying up to meet Massha. "For today only, all purchases will be eight percent off with your new card!"

"Eight?" Massha inquired, showing some interest.

"Just put your name here. And your favorite color. And your favorite season."

She reached for the pen.

"Massha!" I bellowed.

"Oops, no, thanks," my companion informed the Mall clerk.

The young woman showed no disappointment. She beamed brightly as she dropped back into the crowd. "Have a nice day," she wished us.

"Sorry, Aahz," Massha apologized. "But, eight percent!"

I frowned. "You could get twenty off in the Bazaar without having to fill out a form. Fifty off if you really bargain."

"It sounds silly when you put it in perspective." Massha blushed. "I just got caught up in the moment."

"Hi, Esky!" A horn player stopped blatting into his instrument and greeted our guide. The other members of the band surrounded her.

"I talk to them all," Eskina confided. "They are paid a minimal amount. Their original bargain was to include tips, but the management said no, so they don't practice."

"You mean they play like that on purpose?" Massha asked, horrified.

"It is their protest," Eskina shrugged. "Very few people ever notice."

"Eskina!" two female Tigrets cried, running up to her as we rounded the next corner. They were slender catlike females with striped skins and wide green eyes. Each of them was carrying eight or nine shopping bags.

"They are here every day," Eskina explained, as soon as

the Tigrets had ducked into the next shop. "They are very wealthy."

"Sweetie!" A very large Bugbear at the door of a bed shop waved at her. "Got new stock. One I think you ought to try out!"

We all stared at her. Her cheeks pinked up. "He is very effusive, but there is nothing between us. He lets me sleep in the storeroom. I cannot afford to stay in the hotel."

I raised an eyebrow. Along the way we came across more friendly musicians, more charitable shop owners, and more of Eskina's friends. I wanted to ask them to keep a lookout for Skeeve, but Eskina kept telling me to save it for the Barista.

"Mmm, smell that!" Massha exclaimed in delight.

"Goo-oood!" Chumley agreed.

My sensitive nose had been picking up the aroma for several blocks. A burst of fragrant steam surrounded us from holes in the floor. I felt an inexorable force pulling me, and everyone around me, inward, toward the small, round, redwood-sided booth at the center of The Mall.

Hot white lights blazed in our faces. I threw up my hands, momentarily blinded. When my vision cleared, I realized that we were approaching moving spotlights, salamander-occupied mirrored cylinders being cranked in spiral patterns by a quartet of Imps in tight, frogged tunics and pillbox hats.

"What is that?" I asked, squinting into the glare.

"That is the Coffee House," Eskina informed us reverently. The others were impressed into awed silence, but I had a feeling I was walking into a familiar place.

As we approached, I noticed a sign high above the shack that said THE COFFEE IS THE LIFE. Bubbles of golden light welled up to the ceiling from the roof and cascaded down on the surroundings. Most of the crowd lurching forward held out their hands. Bubbles landed on their outstretched palms and burst into decorative china and pottery cups and mugs from which steam rose. Massha tentatively put out her hand.

"Espresso!" she crowed, taking a sip from the tiny cup that appeared there.

The bubble that burst on Chumley's broad palm became a huge bowl filled with beige foam. His face split in a broad grin. "Latte."

"Hold out your hands," Eskina instructed me, demonstrating. The bubble that touched her tiny fingers melted into a plain china mug sloshing with dark brown liquid. "You shall receive that which you need most."

"Nah," I replied, peering forward in between the beams of light. I kept my fists balled tight at my sides. "Don't think so."

"Don't refuse the Barista's bounty," Eskina cautioned me, alarmed. "If you do, she might refuse to serve you. People would turn themselves inside out to avoid displeasing the Barista! How can you get started in the morning without the coffee?"

But I was on the scent.

"Only one person I've ever known brews coffee that smells that good," I muttered, striding toward the booth.

And I was right. When we neared the little building, a door in the side burst open, and a large blue-white blur zipped out of it and straight into my arms.

"Aahz, you old deveel!" crowed Sibone. The Cafiend's long, sinuous body wound her way around me, the end of her tail flicking side to side with delight. "My goodness, you're looking handsome."

"Suspicion confirmed." I grinned as I introduced her to my friends.

"You know the Barista?" Eskina asked, astonished and, at last, impressed.

"We're old friends," I announced, my arm around Sibone's waist, or where her waist would be if she wasn't a twelve-foot serpent with arms and living hair. "Chumley, Massha, this is Sibone. She's from Caf." Her hands, as flexible as her body, curled about my ears, tickling places that obviously she hadn't forgotten in all these years. I enjoyed the sensation, then snapped back to the realization that I had a mission. "Hey, we've got an audience," I protested.

"And when did that ever stop you?" Sibone purred. Her hair crawled around the back of my neck and caressed it. But she turned to my companions and threw her arms around them. "Come and let me give you love. Any friend of Aahz is a friend of mine."

"What are you doing here?" Sibone and I asked one another in unison.

"You first." I laughed.

"Oh"—Sibone sighed, fanning her pale cheeks with a twist of paper held in a coil of her tail—"too much pressure." She took a refreshing drink from one of the many cups standing on tiny shelves adorning the walls of the Coffee House, and curled up in her basketlike chair like a big white pearl in a ring. I kicked back with my feet crossed on a chaise longue with gold tassel fringe. Massha lounged easily in a contraption like a padded hammock. Chumley perched uneasily on an ottoman too small for his big Trollish posterior. Eskina huddled against a wall between the ever-filling coffee cups and stared at the Barista in deep awe.

Unlike its simple exterior, the interior of the small booth proved to be much bigger on the inside than it was on the outside. A surreptitious glance at the map in my pocket showed no detail about the kiosk at the center of The Mall, but Sibone had clearly gone extradimensional for comfort. The room was an easy thirty feet in diameter. The air was filled with the rich, slightly oily aroma of fresh coffee, which brewed in dozens of gigantic urns that stood in arcs flanking the window and in the crystal decanter that stood on a pedestal in the center of the round, mahogany-tiled room. We could see blank-faced, hopeful customers staggering toward the building, their hands held out in supplication. One of Sibone's bubbles would usually do the trick, one sip of elixir restoring character and energy to the customers' faces. Another coin or two clanked magikally into the overflowing golden crock under the counter. Sibone supervised the process for a moment, then turned back to us.

"Everyone in Caf is frenetic, no problem there. It's always crazy, but a few years ago someone in the government decided that anything that feels as good as coffee must be regulated to the bitter dregs. We need coffee to live, so this was very unfair legislation. I was running a multiregion-distribution business of gourmet goods—only the best, of course."

"Of course," I agreed.

"I oversaw picking and processing personally. It was wonderful. I had a slate of faithful customers, and all of them began to get questionnaires from government regulators. Now, you're like me, you don't like snoops. I started asking questions back. They didn't like the fact that some of my blends are made with beans that come from other dimensions. But you know that Caf explorers seeded those plantations thousands of years ago. Those trees are *ours*. If you like, I was only importing sunlight and water. But the pests did not see it that way. They started to demand that I justify my extradimensional purchases. And then when they asked for full lists of all my customers, and all of *their* customers, I realized that *someone* was getting too hyper."

I nodded. A being like her whose blood is mostly caffeine would know how bad that was. She uncurled her long hands in a gesture of helplessness.

"So I have returned to my roots. I have one outlet, here, which I run myself. It is supplied by one farm, which I own myself. I give the gift of life to all those who come to me. I am appreciated."

"Why here?" I asked. "Why not somewhere like Perv, where you'd be a star?"

Sibone patted my leg with one of her tentacle-like hands. "Perv is too focused on the pursuit of the moment. I wanted to go somewhere I was really needed. Here there

was a center with nothing to fill it, where people were looking for direction. I provide them with the strength to do
what they choose. In the end it is only people that matter."

"Now, that sounds like the old metaphysical Sibone I
used to know," I exclaimed. I reached for a hefty brown
mug hanging on the wall. Pervects like their coffee like
they like their beer, at optimum temperature and in suffi-
cient quantity to drown their tonsils.

"But what about you? I had last heard you were acting
as a balance in a lawless place."

I narrowed an eye. That wasn't the way the Merchants'
Association would like to have the Bazaar described, but it
pretty much explained M.Y.T.H., Inc.'s job.

"Temporarily retired," I stated shortly, hoping that
would do. However much I trusted Sibone to understand all
that had happened to me recently, I wasn't going to go into
any of it in front of Eskina. "I'm here to help out a friend.
Someone in The Mall's been masquerading as him, ripping
him and a bunch of merchants off, but Eskina here thinks
there's a more sinister purpose."

Eskina launched into her story, aided by the picture of
Skeeve I was carrying. About five cups of coffee later she
sputtered to an end. Sibone patted her on the back.

"So your good friend is being drained by this evil creature Eskina is seeking," Sibone summed up neatly.

"So she says," I replied. I still wasn't completely convinced. "It explains the mechanism as well as anything
else. I'm willing to have help chasing down the SOB."

"Help? You?" Sibone asked, astonished. "Why don't
you just reach out and grab him, trounce his sorry behind,
and spit on the remains?"

I scowled. "It's not so easy. I've lost my powers."

Sibone put out a sympathetic hand. "I'm very sorry. Oh,
but then I have to warn you: Cire is running around here."

"Cire!" I exclaimed. A fellow wizard and a friend, but
he had a sense of humor you might call playful if you
weren't the brunt of it.

"Yes. He just came off a very lucrative contract, has

money to burn. He thought he would blow it at The Mall and spend his afternoons drinking my coffee."

I leered at her. "Well, that's half a good reason to hang out here."

Sibone tapped me playfully. "You! Well, let me see if I can help you." She shook her head at me, then stared off into space over our heads. Cafiends never closed their eyes. Close as I'd been to Sibone, I still wasn't sure if it was because they had no eyelids or from living on a steady diet of coffee. "I see all, in the course of the day: the lonely ones who come here, the unready, the sleepy, the unaware, and those who just need a good jolt of joe. I do not believe I have ever seen this face." She tapped Skeeve's portrait.

"We'll have to get ahold of the other people who've reported having their credit cards ripped off," I suggested. "Parvattani can do that for us. Where do you suppose he is?"

"Oh, that one?" Sibone asked, an annoyed look on her face. "He has been waiting outside the booth for half an hour."

EIGHT

The Mall guard captain had a fixed look of distaste on his face when Chumley brought him inside.

"Sorry, pal," I offered sheepishly. "I forgot you didn't know where we were."

"Oh, I knew where you had gone," Parvattani corrected me, holding up a small orb like a miniature crystal ball. "We have eyes all over this facility. I could not enter this building."

"And why should you just be able to sashay in and out?" Sibone demanded. "This is not a police state, however you believe it should be?"

"Now, see here, madame, we are the security of this Mall, and as such ought to have access in the event . . ."

Uh-oh. Two of my allies shared some past history, and it sounded like it wasn't resolved yet. I flung up my hands.

"Hold it!" I shouted, over the growing argument. "We're all working together!"

"You are right," Sibone admitted. "Forgive my lack of manners, Captain. Would you like some coffee?"

"Not while on duty," Par emitted shortly. I could tell he was still smarting for having to stand outside like a sentry.

Massha came to the rescue. She floated up from her cushy hammock and alighted beside Par, cuddling close and insinuating her arm into his.

"Hey, big guy, don't be upset! We couldn't let the grass grow under our feet. We were just following up a lead or two. You understand that. Your boss hired us for our expertise. We're just using it."

"Yes, of course, but I wanted to observe—" Parvattani shot a yearning look at me, and I realized what we were dealing with was a bad case of hero worship. I ignored the twinge of nostalgia that awoke in me.

"Well, you can observe now," Massha promised, with a tight hug that nearly pulled the guard captain off his feet. "And we're counting on your help. You were going to cut off the fake Skeeve's credit line. How did you do that?"

Par responded instantly to a call to show off his competence. He held up the little globe.

"With this," he explained. "All of my guards have one. If you cannot find me, you can stop any one of them and have them contact me. With it I can speak to one or all of the security force. It is also hooked into the eyes all over The Mall. If the eye of a statue or a painting look-a like it follows you, it's probably one of ours. I can also talk to the shop owners who are on-a the system. Not everyone can afford a globe."

"Ah, but everybody knows somebody who's got one," Eskina put in.

"Yes," Parvattani snapped tersely, not liking his thunder stolen. "So word will get around. I have issued a bulletin not to permit 'Skeeve' to make a purchase anyplace, not-a even a newspaper or a doughnut. They are also requested to summon the guard if he comes into their shops. I cannot ask them to apprehend him; that is our job, not theirs. Now we will be notified directly if anyone sees the Skeeve."

"Good enough." I sighed. "Pretty soon the thief will have to abandon the disguise."

.   .   .

"So, if you'll just wait a minute," the Djinnie salesclerk suggested, with a perky smile at the tall, thin Klahd, "I'll run in the back and see why your receipt hasn't materialized yet."

Wassup knew he wasn't the brightest candle on the mantelpiece, but he knew the signs of a clerk about to call a security guard.

"I'll just wait out in the hall," he offered, edging swiftly backward, away from the counter. He shot a final, regretful glance at the crystal chandelier. Too bad. It would have been really pretty hanging in the Rat Hole.

"Oh, no, sir, it'll just be a moment!" The Djinnie fluttered after him, trying vainly to catch his hand, the one holding the Skeeve credit card. Once Wassup was over the threshold she had to abandon the chase. Those were the rules, written and unwritten. He hadn't taken the merchandise with him, and he was outside the store, so he was no longer the clerk's problem. He strode away as fast as his long shanks would carry him. Being a Klahd was like trying to balance a bag of groceries on stilts. Mall-rats were much more aerodynamic in shape, being low to the ground, but he had to admit this body had a pretty decent turn of speed.

"What's wrong?" a low voice hailed him.

Wassup's ears perked up. "Hey, Oive," he chirped. Mall-rats recognized one another no matter what faces they were wearing. His fellow thief had on a teenage Dragonet body, a power shopper she particularly liked impersonating. Her arms were full of bags. "Man, I am bummed. That was the fifth place in a row where they tried to bust me for being this guy."

"Bummer," Oive agreed. "Hey, want some of this stuff?"

"What have you got?" Wassup asked.

"I dunno. I just look at the price tags. Let's see: high-heeled boots, a power saw, an enameled altar set, and a commemorative plate for the Diamond Jubilee of King Horace of Mindlesburonia."

"Where's that?" Wassup asked.

"Never heard of it. But it's pretty."

"Good stuff, man," Wassup praised her. Oive preened.

"And it only took me an hour! Hey, there's Garn."

"Word up," Wassup hailed him, or rather her, since Garn was in the shape of a young and attractive Flibberite Mall employee.

"Hail to thee," Garn replied.

"Where'd you get the cool phrase?" Oive demanded, admiringly.

"Like, there was this guy, you know, actually reading out loud to an audience?" Garn related, his eyes wide with disbelief. "I mean, words off a page! They sounded neat, like music without a tune."

"How come you went into a *bookstore,* man?" Wassup asked, curiously.

Garn shrugged. "They were playing The Mall's sales music. Had to go, man. Had to be there."

"Cool," Oive and Wassup breathed in unison.

"I liked it. Otherwise, the day's been dry, dry, dry. I was following the visitors, like the Big Cheese told me? You know? I was trying to get facts about them so Ratso could make a card out of them? I'd like to be the green guy. He's as strong as a horse, man. But no-ooo-oo. They wouldn't give me names, or anything."

"Tough nuts," Oive offered, sympathetically.

"They're totally nuts, man," Wassup complained. "Hey, you hear? Like, they cut off my Skeeve account!"

"What?" Garn exclaimed, outraged.

"I know." Wassup sighed. "The Big Cheese isn't going to like it. But I better tell him before he picks it out of my mind. He's going to have to come up with something else."

The Deveel spa owner picked up a hank of Massha's hair and examined it critically.

"Darling, you're overprocessing this poor stuff just hideously," he proclaimed. "You need a hot oil treatment." He aimed a casual hand toward the sinks, where an Imp was boiling a barrelful over a salamander-controlled flame. "You, too, tall, dark, and hairy," the Deveel informed Chumley, walking around him. He tilted an avid glance up and down the Troll's huge body, to Chumley's embarrassment. "You're just letting yourself go to pieces. I hate to see a big, good-looking Troll like you neglecting that pelt. Come in in the morning when I give this little girl her treatment, and I'll condition the both of you. Friend-of-the-family rates."

"Thanks," Chumley grunted out.

"Sorry I couldn't help you find this fellow," the Deveel added, tapping the portrait of Skeeve with a long, pointed fingernail. "I certainly never did his hair, because if I did, he wouldn't be wearing his hair like *that*. Cute, though."

"What's wrong with my friend's hair?" I demanded. Chumley put an arm around my shoulders and hauled me out into the corridor.

Eskina tittered. "Broscoe is very scathing about anyone's talent but his. I thought it was very funny when he wanted to give Aahz a facial right there."

"Like he'd understand about Pervects and being stylishly scaly," I grumbled.

"If we have a moment, I might let him do my hair," Massha mused. "To be honest, Queen Hemlock's too cheap to attract really first-class stylists to the capital."

"I will, too," Chumley confided. "Can't get back to my barber for ages. May as well take advantage of the local talent."

Eskina's eyes flew wide open. "Did you just say all that?"

"Please, keep your voice down," Chumley whispered. "As long as we are to be allies, we must lay all our cards upon the table."

"One thing I would have thought you'd have figured out," I added, "is that not everything is always as it seems."

Eskina regarded us all with respect. "I see," she said.

Eskina was a pretty quick learner. I began to feel a lot of respect for the intrepid little investigator. She'd put up with a lot of hardship in pursuit of her case. I could tell from Par's nonstop gibes as she led us from one establishment to another that Mall security had not given her any kind of a hand, but she'd pretty much made her own way, making friends with most of the longtime owners. Besides the Deveel barber who let her use his spa every morning, the Djinni cousins furnished her with clothing samples, cast-off books, shoes, and other merchandise they claimed that otherwise they "couldn't sell." The Shire horses who'd given me a hard time let her cadge free meals once in a while. So did most of the other restauranteurs. Out of admiration for her devotion to her mission, which incidentally would help keep them in business, they kept her housed, fed, and groomed. I was impressed; I'd before never seen a Deveel part with anything for which he wasn't well paid. Either he was soft, which I doubted, or she made him and the others feel safer than Mall security did. Par didn't like that aspect a whole bunch. He had to stand back and let the Ratislavan look like a hero or diminish his own status in their eyes by making a fuss about it.

"Let us go on," Eskina proclaimed, leaping up as soon as she had finished a snack furnished by the owner of the Jolly Dragon pub on the corner across from Troll Music, a huge bardic emporium which sold little magikal boxes that played dozens, even hundreds of songs when opened. I hadn't finished the rest of my fifth beer, but I was glad to get away from the racket pouring out the door across from us. The way the cacophony blended or, rather, failed to blend with the bands within earshot made me lose my appetite. Not that a ham, a dozen-egg omelette, and a broiled half pineapple was more than a light snack.

"You don't sit down long," I observed, as we strode out again. The innkeeper had promised to keep a discreet eye out for the fake Skeeve. "This must be an exciting new case for you."

"No," she contradicted me. "I have been on this assignment five years. We of the Ratislavan Intelligence are nothing if not . . . dogged." She grinned, showing her sharp little incisors. "I pursue Rattila, and I will continue until I have arrested him and brought him back to face Ratislavan justice. Many leads have come and gone, but I am sure mine is right, and I shall be vindicated. That is what gives me energy."

"Mmmph," Parvattani grunted, skeptically. But no matter what he thought, most of the denizens of The Mall were on his rival's side.

"Any friend of Eskina's a friend of mine," was a litany we heard over and over again. And we heard plenty of stories about how the shapechangers had ripped them off. If they'd been in the Bazaar, the Merchants' Association would have caught up with the thieves and traced them back to their master in nothing flat, with none of this five-year delay because of a mental turf war.

"There are procedures," Parvattani argued, as we left another stall.

"Tell me," I confronted Par, "if you'd figured out yourself there was a foreign master criminal running a crime syndicate in your Mall, you'd go after him *mach schnell*, wouldn't you?"

"Maybe," Par admitted. "But then I would be approaching it with evidence. She has never produced anything that I can call evidence. Show me, and I'll believe!"

"Bah." Eskina waved a dismissive hand. "This is the closest he has ever come to showing me professional courtesy, by listening, and it is all because of you."

They marched ahead of us. Par strode rapidly, covering a lot of distance with each pace, but Eskina stayed abreast of him, trotting on her little legs. I grinned. The rivalry between them disguised the fact that they had a lot in common. I thought they even admired each other a little, but they would rather have had the floor open up, swallow them, and burp before they'd admit it. But they went on trying to impress us with their knowledge, all the time pretending they didn't care if they impressed the other.

"That is Banlofts," Eskina explained, nodding toward a two-headed Gorgon trying on a pair of hats at a stall. "They're a personal shopper on Gor. Very popular in The Mall. Very good taste, too."

"Always pays cash," Parvattani added. "No problem with theft, either, since they can shop and keep an eye on their purse at the same time."

"Their business flourishes because they always compare their impressions before they buy."

"So two heads are better than one," I chortled. "But in the case of a tie you have to let the right prevail, huh?" Chumley and Massha shot me pained looks. "What?"

"Arrest her," Eskina whispered suddenly, pointing to a long, skinny Wisil sauntering toward us. She was dressed in a fancy blue satin dress and a picture hat and carrying a big handbag studded with jeweled beads.

"Why?" Par demanded.

"She has stolen that purse! It is from Kovatis's shop."

"How do you know she didn't buy it?" I asked.

"Because Kovatis only works to order," Eskina hissed urgently. "And I was in the store with the Klahd lady who ordered it."

"Do you see, Master Aahz?" Par asked, furiously. "This is the kind of nonsense she has been treating us to for years!"

I might have agreed with him, but something about the Wisil's too-careful walk pushed my alarm buttons, too. "Get her," I instructed Chumley.

"Right ho," he agreed. He stuck out a large hand, raised the Wisil by her shiny satin scruff, hauled her over until she was eye to eye with him, and boomed out, "Give purse back."

"Oh! Oh!" the Wisil screeched, twisting this way and that to escape. "Don't hurt me! I—I just wanted to take it for a test walk to see if I wanted to buy it! Here, here!" Hastily, she shoved the jeweled bag into my hands.

Parvattani hadn't hesitated once he'd realized he was wrong. A quick word into his long-distance orb brought a pair of uniformed guards running. They took the Wisil and the bag into custody.

We started walking again. Palpable in the air between Eskina and Par was the phrase "I told you so." Again, I had to give the little raterrier credit: she didn't say it, but boy, could Par hear it. After another block or two, he cleared his throat.

"Good call," he murmured.

Eskina's head turned slightly toward him, then away to scan the shops on her left. I could see that she was smiling.

"Aren't they adorable?" Massha sighed. "If I didn't know better, I'd swear the two of them were a little sweet on each other. I love a budding romance. It reminds me of me and Hugh."

"For pity's sake, don't say anything like that where they can hear you," Chumley warned her. "That would surely nip it in the bud, so to speak."

"I'm with him," I added, although in a million years I would never have seen a comparison between the wall-pounding lust fest that she and Hugh had indulged in before they got married and a couple of shy kids who happened to be rivals in the same profession. "Let them discover it."

"Oh, well." Massha shrugged, but she agreed. "It'll be hard not to say anything. They make a cute couple."

"Give 'em time," I advised. "If they don't figure it out before we leave, you can play matchmaker then."

Since I had a chance to watch the goings-on in The Mall, I realized that the gestalt was very much like that in the Bazaar. It wasn't long before I could tell a denizen from an occasional customer. The people who frequented The Mall, both employees and visitors, were a lot classier in demeanor and dress, but the merchants had the same summing eye to decide whether the warm bodies walking in had money or not.

Just like in the Bazaar magik served as a deterrent here. I watched a party of rowdy young werewolves push their way into a store selling personal music boxes. In no time they materialized out in the corridor in front of us, shaking their heads, not sure how that had happened. I grinned as they marched back in again. And got beamed out. They tried again. On the third trip out, Eskina strode up to them and took them each by an ear.

"Now, they told you to go away, yes?" she asked. The teenage werewolves grimaced but remained silent. She tightened her grip. "Yes?"

"Yes," they grunted at last.

"Then come back when you wish to buy something. You can listen to music free in the dance halls and clubs, no?" She let go of her grip. The boys shook free, then retreated a few paces. With my keen hearing I overheard them agreeing with her suggestion, but they would rather be shaved bald than tell her so. "They ought to pay you to patrol this place," I suggested. Parvattani looked offended.

"I have my mission," she replied simply.

So did we. I kept my eyes open, and Massha read her magik detector as we watched the crowd. I really hoped the fake Skeeve would show his face again. The longer this investigation took, the more I really wanted to get my hands on him.

A loud buzzing sound erupted from Par's pocket. He brought out the orb.

"We have a situation," he informed me. "I think we have your Klahd."

NINE

"Get the hell out of my way!" I yelled.

Shoppers of all species dove shrieking for the walls to avoid the wall of flesh of a Pervect, Troll, and Jahk bearing down on them.

For obvious reasons teleportation within The Mall was outlawed, and magikal interference existed to keep it from happening. I cursed Mall policy as we ran and floated toward the far end near Doorway L. With the globe to his ear, Parvattani kept us posted with a running commentary.

"A yellow-polled Klahd, yes. Above average height, yes. He's-a doing what? With what?"

"What?" I bellowed.

Parvattani was clearly embarrassed to reply to my question.

"He's taking off his clothes."

"DA-da-da-da-DA-da! DA-da-da-da-DA-dum," the music blared. "Da-DUM-DUM-da-DAH! Da-dadada-DA-dum!"

The crowd never seemed thicker as we pounded into the raked amphitheater area just behind the troop of guards responding to Par's call. Thousands of shoppers hooted, clapped, and laughed at the figure down at the bottom of the wide bowl. It was the phony, all right. A manic grin on his face, he balanced unsteadily on the brink of the third tier of a huge ornamental marble fountain in the center. He hopped up and down on one foot, trying to pull off his left boot. His right was already off, leaving him clad in one magenta sock. The boot came free with an audible pop, to the delight of the audience. "Skeeve" whirled the suede shoe over his head and let it fly, all the time swinging his hips in time to the band behind him.

Massha gasped. "The boss would be red as a beet."

The impostor slipped and fell with a splash into the water. The crowd went wild. He climbed out and bowed, as if he had meant to do that. I felt as though I could shoot steam out of my ears. This guy was dead. He climbed out, grinning, and started to undo the lacings of his tunic.

"Get him!" I roared.

Chumley plowed downward into the crowd with me in his wake. Massha scooped up Eskina and carried her overhead. Blocked by Chumley's furry back, I lost sight of the faker, but by the roar of the audience, he had just untied his belt and thrown it into the front row.

"Do you feel that?" Massha asked.

"Yes," Chumley replied, surprised. "A . . . pull."

"What kind of pull?" I demanded. "I don't feel a thing."

"It's magikal," Massha explained.

"That is the draw of power," Eskina insisted.

I looked up, then scowled as I realized, for the millionth time, that I couldn't see the lines of force in this dimension—or any other dimension. What a pain in the butt it was not to have my powers!

"He's drawing power from force lines?" I asked.

"No, from the people around us," Massha explained.

"Some of them get their energy from the force lines, and it's flowing down to him."

"We have to stop him," I insisted. "Now!"

"Clear the area," Parvattani ordered, flashing the badge he was carrying. The green-skinned captain barked out orders to surround and disperse the mob.

Easier said than done. The phony had their full attention. Young women, and some young men, hopped up and down to look over the heads of the people in front of them. Little old ladies clambered up on the backs of Deveels and Ginorms to get a better view. As the crowd shifted, I got the occasional glimpse of a skinny arm or a bare foot down below.

"Da-DUM-DUM-da-DAH! Da-dadada-DA-dum!"

A howl of laughter arose from the watchers. Massha zipped upward as a tunic came flying overhead past her. I pushed apart the two Imps blocking my way, and caught sight of the impersonator still a hundred feet away. Now bare-chested, he started to fumble with his trouser fastenings. I stumbled down three more levels.

"Stop that Klahd," I bellowed.

"Catch, big guy!" Massha shouted. We glanced up. Massha dropped Eskina into my arms and started fumbling with the pouch of jewelry at her belt. A big plum-colored gem popped out into her hand.

Suddenly, the room went dark. The band music died away. The audience wailed with disappointment. I set Eskina down in the dark and started moving down toward the center of the arena. I kept my orientation by focusing on the sound of the fountain tinkling, pushing aside all the bodies I encountered, seeking out the right one. I didn't have to see the Skeeve-clone. Klahds had a pretty distinctive smell, and the fake copied it down to the last olf. If only he didn't change form before I got to him.

The next moment I caught a scent. It was him!

"He's down there!" I shouted. "Chumley, Massha!" I sped up, climbing over bodies where I had to. The aroma got stronger. I must have been within ten, maybe twenty feet. I threw out my hands, flailing for the impostor.

"I have him, captain!" a voice shouted. I felt arms go around me.

"Let go, you idiot!" I roared. I threw my weight forward, then spun, grabbing a pair of uniformed shoulders and shoving them away. I kept going toward the laughing sound of the water, but the invisible guard tried to tackle me again, leaping on me from behind. "I said, let go!" Tugging him over my shoulder with one hand, I heaved him up over my head and threw him into the crowd. If there was no mosh pit for him to land in, that was his problem.

I reached the cold marble lip of the fountain just as the lights went on again. Chumley, Massha, and I had all reached it at the same time. Except for the twinkling waters, the tiered marble basins were empty. No, not quite. A heap of clothes, including a blue, sequined G-string, lay draped over the edge.

"Awwww!" the crowd bleated. But without an attraction to keep it there, the audience finally drifted away. I kept my eyes open.

"He's around here somewhere," I yelled, waving the handful of garments, "and he's naked as a jaybird!"

Parvattani arrived at my side, already transmitting this information into the globe held to his ear. The other hand waved wildly in emphasis. "Be on the lookout for a naked Klahd. Above-average height, and-a . . . never-a mind! He's naked! That ought-a to be distinctive enough!"

"What the hell is wrong with your guards, Par?" I demanded. "I would have gotten him if one of your men hadn't jumped on my back! They're supposed to help, but I'd do better with a rubber crutch!"

"Whattayou mean?" the captain asked, his ears twitching defensively. He took a step back, but came right up to me again, his fists clenched.

"I mean," I explained, reining in my temper, "that just as I was about to take down that phony, that bad Xerox copy, that *fake,* one of your guys wrapped me up and tried to apprehend me! Even in the dark, how could anyone mistake my Pervect physique for a Klahd?"

Par's fury turned to surprise.

"My guards should-a been able to tell you apart in any condition. They are-a highly trained to recognize-a the residents of six hundred-a dimensions!" He lifted the globe. "All security forces-a in area L, report to the open stage. Right-a now!"

Within minutes the tiered steps were full of uniformed Flibberites. A few shot puzzled glances at their captain in mufti, but sucked in their bellies and squared their shoulders as Parvattani marched up and down their ranks.

"All right-a," he barked. "We just hadda situation. All you have to do is arrest one Klahd. He's not armed, he's not even-a dressed! And one-a of you mistakes this-a Pervert—"

"That's Per-*vect!*" I corrected him, peevishly. Par didn't miss a beat.

"—Pervect for the perpetrator-a! Now, whatsamatta with you? Who did it?"

The denials were instant and unanimous. "Not me." "Nope." "Not a chance." "I know what Klahds are." "Me, touch a Pervert?" "Nope."

"Come on," the captain bellowed, his voice ringing in the rafters. "Who is it? No punishment if you come-a clean now."

But no one admitted grabbing me.

"Mr. Aahz, maybe you recognize the fool who interrupted you?"

I eyed them all. None of the guards present fitted the silhouette of the guy I'd flung away. "None of them."

Parvattani goggled. "None of them?"

"No," I insisted. I turned away, disgusted with my own impotence. "None of them. Another shapeshifter had to be waiting in the crowd. In the dark none of your men could have identified him as a fraud."

"This is my fault," Massha moaned, floating down beside me. "Sorry, Aahz. My blackout ring went a little haywire. It was only supposed to plunge Skeeve in darkness, not the whole wing. I think the overload that was in the air affected my gizmos."

"It's okay," I reassured her. "I was tracking the shapeshifter by smell." I sighed. "I need a drink."

It didn't help my mood that the buzz about the stripteasing Klahd was already making the rounds at every bar in The Mall. I nearly coldcocked an Imp who was giving an animated description of the event to a group of his laughing friends, but it wouldn't have done any good. And it wouldn't have made me feel any better.

"It doesn't make any sense," I complained over my beer. "No one's giving the false Skeeve money or anything valuable. How can that draw energy from an audience."

"They're *paying* attention," Chumley suggested, after a moment's thought. "Have you never told anyone your time is valuable?"

"Time is money," Eskina interjected. "And money is power, and power is—"

"—What Rattila's trying to get," I finished, slamming a fist into my palm. "Well, we can't let it happen again. We have to head off any more performances like that. Par, can you have your guards patrol all the open spaces? If the impostor starts dancing or singing or reciting Hamlet's soliloquy, cut him off before he can gather an audience."

"Aahz, they tried," Par replied, his hands spread helplessly. "He had begun his act by the time anyone noticed. And then, you saw. Too many people were already there."

"We need to fight magik with magik," Massha insisted. "The flow cut off when the house went dark."

"But how can we do that?" Parvattani asked. "None of us are magicians."

Massha beamed broadly. "Nothing to it, honey. I know just what you folks need. Let's go shopping."

"Your boss can pick up the tab," I added.

Par looked dubious as Massha led him out of the bar. I tailed along, grinning. He was about to see a real expert in action.

"Beautiful, beautiful!" Rattila applauded Garn when he got back to the Rat Hole. "What a marvelous improvisation! I enjoyed the astonished expressions on all of those faces, and the eagerness they evinced watching you. Why have we never used mass entertainment before? It was fantastic!"

"I felt stupid," Garn admitted, handing over his Skeeve card. "I mean, all those dudes looking at me? I felt like, I was shaving all my fur off in public."

Rattila clutched the small blue square to his chest. Even without the Master Card in his hand to complete the transaction the delicious energy tickled his nerve endings. "Intoxicating!" he declared. "You may not have been comfortable, but you showed a natural talent for attracting attention."

"I do?" Garn asked, blankly.

"You do." Rattila looked at the rest of the mall-rats. "I am sure each of you conceals a hidden talent like Garn's. From now on you will all do that kind of performance art with the Skeeve card, at least once a day."

"C'mon, Ratty," Strewth whined. "We're mall-rats. We shop. We don't act. We don't sing. We don't dance. I mean, it doesn't come naturally. We haven't got any talent. I mean, what's our motivation?"

The lights in the Rat Hole went out, leaving Rattila's blazing red eyes as the only source of light. Strewth and the others cowered deep into the slimy muck.

"I suggest you look deep inside yourselves for the proper motivation," Rattila intoned. "In fact, I insist. Get me a handle on the visitors! And don't call me Ratty!"

"Let's see," the female Jahk beamed, floating ahead of the pack of guards up the hall like the banner before a troop of toy soldiers on parade. "Shall we try Meldrum's Magikland, or Binnie's Spell Box?"

"Magik shopping," Wassup whispered to Yahrayt. "She must have half the guards on duty with her."

"Awesome," Yahrayt breathed. "It'll be all clear for the others to shop."

"Totally!"

Disguised as an elderly male Imp and a Klahdish child of six holding his hand, the two mall-rats fell into line behind the others.

"Goin' on a lion hunt," Wassup sang happily. A Mall guard glanced back over his shoulder. "Goin' on a lion hunt!"

"Shaddup!" Yahrayt hissed. "Mayno should never have brought that Imp's card to Rattila. He's not right in the head!"

"You don't love me?" Wassup asked, forlornly.

Yahrayt had had enough. He tugged Wassup by the ear into the flap of a nearby tent. "Change cards! Now! *Anybody.*"

Wassup pulled out his deck and selected one at random. The cloth around them bulged as he expanded suddenly from an undersized Imp to a full-sized Gargoyle.

"Cool," he gritted. "Yer right. I feel smarterer now."

"C'mon," Yahrayt snorted, grabbing his arm and hustling him after the file of guards, now disappearing into the crowd. "Follow that Jahk!"

"Wendell's Emporium?" Massha inquired, thumbing through the index at the back of the atlas as she hovered over the heads of the rapt guards. I was bored already with the enterprise, but it would have shown a lack of faith in my associate to split.

"So," I asked the nearest Flibberite, a skinny youth whose

huge tunic was more or less wearing him, not the other way around. "How'd you decide to join The Mall security force?"

"My father was in it, sir!" snapped out the recruit. "And my father's father. And my—"

"Never mind," I interrupted him.

"Yes, let's try here," Massha suggested, levitating down to eye level.

"Hey, lady," a heavy voice grated. "Would youse mind answerin' a few survey questions?"

Massha spared a brief glance for the huge Gargoyle who shouldered through the horde of shoppers toward her bearing a clipboard. "Not right now, thanks."

"Hokay. Den would youse take dis survey, and drop it off anyplace when youse done wit' it?" The heavy fist proffered a sheet of closely printed parchment.

"Sure," Massha agreed absently, rolling up the paper and sticking it into her cleavage.

"How about youse, sir?" the Gargoyle requested, turning to me. "You gotta minute?"

"Hem!" Eskina cleared her throat.

I rolled my eyes. I didn't need the warning. I hadn't been hatched at The Mall door. "Sure, buddy? What do you want to know?"

"You gotta favorite color?" the Gargoyle asked, poised with quill in fist.

"Why do you want to know that?"

"Well . . . we always ask dat kinda question."

"And what do most people usually say."

"Blue," the Gargoyle answered promptly.

"Well, I ain't gonna buck the average," I insisted, in a friendly tone. "Blue's good. What else do you want to know?"

"What kinda tings you buy when you go shoppin'?"

"Whaddaya got?"

"Man, I knew you were gonna ask me dat!" The Gargoyle sucked the top of the pen thoughtfully. "Dere's clothes, shoes, toys, magik wands, posters, a real good candy store, candles, and incense—"

"Hem!" This time the warning came, not from Eskina, but from a little kid with pumpkin-colored hair and a missing front tooth.

"Tanks for yer cooperation," the Gargoyle offered hoarsely. "Hey, Troll, you spend a lotta money on discretionary spending?"

Chumley let his lower lip droop. "Huh?" he asked.

The Gargoyle grunted. "Never mind. Tanks, all of youse." He stumped away, clutching his clipboard, the tot following in his footsteps. I grinned.

"You're gonna have to do better than that, Rattila."

Massha and Par finished their conference and headed for the door of Wendell's. As she passed, I reached up and plucked the survey out of her décolletage.

"Hey," she protested.

"You're not gonna need that," I informed her as I shredded the parchment and let the fragments sift to the floor.

Massha didn't need to have the whole picture painted for her. She grinned at me.

"Thanks, Green and Brainy. I'd better be more careful. If I hadn't been so busy, I might have filled it in."

TEN

"That was useless!" Rattila's voice echoed angrily in Wassup's and Yahrayt's minds. "The Pervert turned every single one of your questions back at you, you idiot!"

"Hey, don't be mad, man," Wassup protested. "Dis—I mean, this Gargoyle's a mechanic, not a census taker!"

"Try another tack!"

"Tack?" Wassup's lips moved as he tried to figure out what Rattila meant.

Yahrayt came to the rescue. "I'll figure out a way to get close to 'em, Big Cheese. Over and out."

". . . And these amulets will tip you off when you're near a specific magik source," Massha continued her spate, piling silk-wrapped packets into Parvattani's arms. "Once we get ahold of one of these shapeshifters we can tune it to pick up that spell. The amulets are cheap, so they break easily—the gems are only glass—but the good thing is they're easy to replace, too. They're not like the Ring of Oconomowoc.

That'd be your best tracker, but there's only one in existence, and it's in a dragon's hoard about seventeen dimensions from here."

Par's eyes had long ago glazed over from her cheerful lecture, but he passed along his burden to the next guard in line.

"And these," Massha added, gleefully seizing a handful of gleaming pebbles and letting them drop through her fingers, "are terrific for keeping you from getting lost."

"We don't need those, madame," Par ventured timidly.

"Well, sure you do . . . I guess you don't," Massha corrected herself, with a sheepish grin. "Sorry. This is your stomping ground. I'll take a few, though. I·guess that's all here."

Par stepped up to the counter, where a Deveel merchant was rubbing his hands together in joyful anticipation.

"I have a letter of credit from Mr. Moa," Par began, reaching into his tunic for the document.

"Wonderful, wonderful!" the Deveel crooned. "I'll just take that—"

"Hold it right there," I pronounced majestically, before he could put it on the counter.

"What do you want, Pervert?" the Deveel snarled. "This Flibberite and I were about to do business."

"That's right," I agreed. "And I'm his business agent. Now, about these amulets. Six gold pieces each is out of the question . . ."

"I still can't believe you got us a fifty percent discount!" Parvattani kept saying.

I whistled as I walked. "That was a pretty nice piece of negotiation," I acknowledged. "Nobody who hangs with me *ever* pays retail."

Massha and Chumley rolled their eyes. I had to admit that maybe I had kept repeating myself, too, but it *had* been a damned fine deal. Because of all the years I'd spent on

Deva, all the arrangements I'd come to with other Deveels, I knew when to cut the offer and crank up the volume. About halfway through the negotiations we were yelling at one another at the top of our lungs just as if we had been in a dusty tent in the middle of the Bazaar. The low, civilized, conversational tone people generally used here in The Mall was left far behind. I found it kind of refreshing. The Deveel seemed surprised at first, but like any merchant of his species the bartering he learned at his mommy's knee came right back to him. The highest percentage I paid for any item was the first one we dealt on. After that I started a lot lower and fought a lot harder. It had been such a frustrating few days there in The Mall chasing shadows it was really nice to win at something for a change. I strutted all the way to the next store on Massha's list.

"—No, I don't want to enter a drawing," Massha exclaimed, batting at a fairy clad in diaphanous pink who fluttered beside her pushing ticket slips into her hands.

"Go 'way," Chumley ordered, swatting at the winged pest. The fairy flew hastily out of reach.

We got pestered a lot in between stops. Moa had assured me that all solicitors carried a license, a blue crystal that they had to display on demand. Most of these didn't have 'em. Rattila kept sending minions after us, some pretty, some obnoxious, some ugly and menacing, all of them nosy. I wondered how he managed to sneak all of these people in and out of the building every day. Then I realized that they looked like everybody else. For all I knew he had six shapechangers who could turn into a hundred or so customers apiece working for him.

"All the more reason," Eskina insisted, when I broached the subject, "that we be well prepared and well armed." She cocked a pocket crossbow and tucked it into her thick fur coat. It disappeared without a trace.

"What else have you got in there?" I asked, with a wicked grin.

She winked. "I must know you much better before I tell you that."

110 **Robert Asprin and Jody Lynn Nye**

"That one," Yahrayt whispered, pointing, as he hovered over the head of Lawsy, who was disguised as a Mall guide. The Flibberite female whose image she wore had been a find Rattila gloated over. Dinii was a deep-seated shopaholic who never kept track of the purchases on her employee credit card. She paid the minimum on whatever balance her statement showed. At this point she was years behind on her payments, but the card was the only one that the administration didn't have a watch on. She came in very handy when one of the mall-rats needed to be in a restricted area during business hours. Dinii's identification was all up-to-date. They had to be careful not to use Dinii up; she had to keep her job in The Mall, or the cloned pass card that was their key to going where she could go would be changed.

"She's friendly?" Lawsy asked, studying the big female who hovered just above the heads of the crowd.

"She talks the most," Yahrayt corrected Lawsy. "Like, the Big Cheese told us to look out for opportunity. I think she's it. The big purple guy talks in one-note words. The other one is nasty. Go where the going's easiest."

Lawsy straightened her neat uniform. "I get it. Later, man."

"Later, dude."

"—Well, you don't want to skewer this thief," Massha argued, as Parvattani pawed through racks of polearms looking for the most serviceable.

"I do," I put in.

Massha ignored me. "You want to snare him, at a distance."

"Before he can get away," Par nodded.

The weapons shop salesclerk, a bronze-skinned individual, nodded until his chin clanged. "May I suggest these?" He rapped his chest with a shiny fist. "You can try them out on me."

"How was that?" Massha asked in a low voice, as we left the weapons shop.

I twisted my mouth. "You did fine. You know, you're not an apprentice any longer. You really need to stop doubting yourself. What would—er, what would Skeeve say?"

Massha instantly snapped out of her funk. "You're right, Aahz." She sighed.

"Take a break," I advised. "Your part's done. Now I'm going to give Par and his men a pep talk on strategy. You can give them all the toys they can carry, but you're not going to turn them into operators overnight. I'm just gonna give them a few rules to follow."

"Wilco, Green and Scaly," Massha agreed, her good mood restored. "Guess I've spent so much time worrying about Skeeve I'm winding myself up in knots."

"Take a look at the big picture," I suggested. I'm not a big one for the Dutch-uncle routine, but she needed to cool down, or she was going to break down. "I want to tear that impostor's head off, but you don't see me wasting energy fidgeting. Relax."

Massha was pretty savvy, or she would never have risen to jobs as local chief magician in two different dimensions. She nodded and headed for the nearest jewelry store. Everyone relaxes in their own way.

"You'd make a good mall-rat!" the pert, uniformed clerk beamed approvingly. Massha removed her nose from the glass display case outside Sparklies 'R' Us. "Aren't those pretty?"

Massha glanced back at the glistening baubles on display. "They're all pretty."

"You like blue? I like blue, too. I noticed that you're interested in the bangles. Would you like to try one on?" When Massha hesitated, the girl grabbed her arm and started to tow her inside the shop. "Come on! You don't know if you'll love it until it's on your arm."

"Well—" Massha allowed herself to be persuaded. "I do deserve a chance to try on something nice. I've just spent the entire morning shopping for . . . utilitarian items."

The young Flibberite female looked blank.

"Guy stuff," Massha clarified.

"Oh! Well, come and sit down. This is my favorite store in The Mall. Even when the sale music isn't playing it's almost hypnotic to come in here, isn't it? So, what would you like to try on first?"

The displays of rings, necklaces, earrings, and other adornments were arranged by color. Massha glanced from red stones to clear to green to purple to black, and inevitably back to blue. "How about those?"

The girl opened the back of the case and came over with a trayful of rings. She pointed to them one at a time. "Invisibility, growth-shrink, talking to plants, poison detector, gold assayer, and that one will make you look five years younger."

"Only five?"

The girl looked a little embarrassed. "It's not very expensive, madame. You get what you pay for." She cocked her head. "You don't need a youth ring, really. Why would you even want to consider it?"

Massha grinned. "Well, my husband and I weren't kids when we met. I kind of wish he could have seen me in my prime." She poked fingers into the rolls of flesh at her sides. "A little less of this, and a few less wrinkles!"

The girl shook a finger at her. "I'm sure he doesn't see any of that when he looks at you."

Massha laughed. "You're sweet. All right, how about that one?" She looked approvingly at the plant-speech ring with its forest green gems arranged like petals around a carved purple center stone. The girl touched the golden shank. It grew to accommodate Massha's finger.

"Let me just get a begonia so you can try it out."

Massha looked around with approval at the rest of the shop. The cases against the wall gleamed with light generated by the jewelry itself. From the center of the ceiling swags of silk and velvet swirled down to the floor, which was lined with a plush silk carpet that matched the comfy padded chair she sat upon. An elderly Djinni gentleman across the room peered over half glasses perched on the end of his nose as he helped a large Impish matron try on enormous bejeweled necklaces.

A potted plant plunked down on the glass case.

"Why not try out basic conversation with this one?" the girl asked.

"Er, how are you?" Massha inquired of the tall stalks adorned with tiny, fragrant blossoms.

"Qui? Quelle disastre sous ensemble!"

"I'm sorry," the girl apologized. "That's French lavender, but it's the only plant I could find in a hurry."

"Never mind." Massha hastily pulled off the ring and replaced it in the rack. She didn't need a ring that let her hear vegetables making rude comments about her choice of clothing. The invisibility ring might be useful. She waited for the girl to size it, then invoked the spell. A glimpse in the mirror revealed an outline and a pair of disembodied eyes floating in its midst. "I don't think this one is working very well."

"Oops!" the clerk exclaimed, diving forward to make an adjustment. Massha turned her head this way and that, admiring the complete absence of herself she could see. "Nice workmanship."

"Only the finest alchemists and artifact manufacturers are represented here," the girl assured her. "Have you shopped here before?"

"Well, not in this store," Massha explained, taking off the ring. A few other customers browsed into the shop.

Massha kept an eye on them in the mirror. Which of them might be a shapechanging thief? The girl presented her with a tray of bracelets, chattering all the time as she helped her try on one glittering piece after another. Massha replied absently, enjoying the feel of quality magik items.

"That's beautiful," the girl noted. Massha admired the woven net of gold on her wrist. "And absolute proof against cold. I'm sorry it's so warm in here."

"I don't really need anything like that," Massha explained. "Girls my size are usually pretty warm."

"Well, then, *this* one"—the clerk proffered another wristlet—"is proof against heat. You'll notice that the weave is reversed."

"Really?" Massha asked, avidly. She turned it to admire from every angle. "I really do like that. It could come in handy in this place. How can all of you stand the heat?" Then she looked at the price tag. "No. Too much."

"Oh, well! It's fun to look, isn't it?" Lawsy burbled cheerfully. As soon as Massha's gaze shifted, she dropped the bracelet into the cuff of her boot. She had to be careful which way she moved, to avoid being spotted by the owner. All the walls had mirrors, but at present she was still hidden from his view by Massha's bulk. "How about this beautiful piece? Or this? Or how about this?" She shuffled out an array of bracelets and bangles. The Jahk tried them all on.

She kept returning to one arm ring studded with square, deep blue stones. According to the tag, the bangle was a powerful artifact, useful for increasing the potential of another item placed in contact with it. Lawsy grinned to herself and removed the tag. That could be a lot of fun if the Jahk bought it. Rattila would approve of her initiative.

"This is a very pretty piece," she stressed. "Do you have a lot of blue clothing?"

"Not really," Massha admitted. "I tend to go for warm colors. They go with my personality." She let out a big, hearty laugh. Lawsy concentrated on memorizing every single nuance. "But I like this."

"Do you prefer jewelry for its looks, or its ability?"

"Oh, ability," Massha confided. "No one ought to know better than me how unimportant looks are to what's inside. Don't get me wrong; I love pretty things, but a plain old hunk of silver won't fetch my coffee for me."

"You are so right," the disguised mall-rat agreed, with a friendly smile. "So, would you like this wrapped, or will you wear it?

"I'll wear it," Massha decided. "How much?"

"Only thirty-five!" Lawsy exclaimed. "Very reasonable for such a beautiful piece, don't you think?"

Massha nodded. "Not bad. Yes, I think I will take it."

She pulled open her purse and began to count out coins.

"What's going on here?"

Lawsy looked up in alarm. Hovering above them, his face deep blue with fury, was the store owner. She hadn't been paying attention. The other customer was on her way out of the shop. She gave the fizzing Djinn a helpless grin.

He wasn't mollified.

"What are you doing back there?" he demanded.

Lawsy rose at once and moved out from behind the counter.

"I was just helping this fine lady try things on," she chirped. "I could see you were too busy. We were having a nice chat! It's my job, to make the customer feel at home."

Massha, alarmed, gawked at the mall-rat.

"She doesn't work for you?"

"No, charming lady," the Djinn replied, in a milder tone. "She's a survey taker here in the mall. See the badge? Thank you for your help," he added, though he didn't sound grateful, "but next time, don't do that."

"Of course," Lawsy exclaimed. She reached over and patted Massha on the hand. "I'll just be going, now that we have what we want."

"Thanks." Massha smiled at her. She waited as the jeweler snapped his fingers and summoned up a receipt.

"Shall I wrap it, charming lady?" the Djinn asked, then

did a double take. "I know you! My cousin Rimbaldi in
The Volcano tells me what a joy you are to dress!"

The Jahk's cheeks pinked up. "No bag, thanks. I'll wear
it." She tucked it onto her arm with the rest of her swag.
Lawsy backed hastily out of the store and ran as fast as she
could for the Rat Hole.

"Beautiful, beautiful," Rattila slavered, fondling the
bracelet again and again. "And she spoke to you. I heard it
all. How nice that she was willing to open herself up so
readily to your inquiries. Good job."

Lawsy quivered with happiness. She didn't get much
praise from the Big Cheese.

Rattila tasted the bracelet, his teeth rasping against the
soft metal. "Married, likes blue jewelry, sensitive about her
body, knows about magik devices—I can make use of her
expertise." He thrust his claw into the heap of garbage and
came up with the Master Card. He touched the bracelet to
it, and both of them glowed brightly. The gleam was
echoed in Rattila's red eyes.

"Yes, yes!" he gloated. "I feel her power joining mine!"
He closed his eyes and envisioned the credit balance in the
Master Card. It was not quite full yet, but it soon would be.
As the mall-rats chanted, he produced thin cards, flimsier
and less potent than the usual collectors. "These are tem-
poraries," he explained carefully to his followers. "Do not
stop trying to get her to fill out an application so we can
devour her completely. Now, spend, spend, spend! Do not
cross the visitors' paths. I want all of it to come as a surprise to Master Aahz when Mistress Massha falls into my
power."

ELEVEN

"Don't you love it?" Massha asked, showing off her wrist to me and Chumley.

"Nice," I offered shortly. I wasn't much for fancy baubles. I always think natural beauty shines through better. But, then, Massha wasn't a Pervect and didn't have that advantage.

"Very pretty," Eskina approved.

"What's it do, what?" Chumley asked.

"I . . ." Massha paused. "Do you know, I forgot to ask! It made my hand look so nice that was all I could think about."

A black cloak swirled around our feet and slipped into our midst. I resented the intrusion, and cocked an elbow into the ribs of the tall figure.

"Ow!" Eskina shrieked. "He hit me!"

"Sorry, kid, it was me," I apologized.

I realized my mistake then: the newcomer was a Spectre, the semi-insubstantial denizens of Spect, a mysteriously beautiful dimension I'd dropped in on once. Frustrating place in a way, because although the women could touch me, I couldn't return the favor, and they had been tall, sensual, and exotic.

So was this big lug, or so he thought. He picked up Massha's hand and began to nibble his way up from the tips of her fingers.

"Hey, watch the jewelry," she warned him. "I just polished—ooh—mmm."

A big, silly, trancelike grin broke out on her face. Then, she snapped out of it.

"Hey, buddy, we haven't even been introduced."

"I am the architect of your wildest dreams, baby," the Spectre whispered. "I like a woman with . . . substance." He eyed her up and down, the jet-black eyes in his hollow eye sockets evidently liking what they saw.

"So, what do you say, baby?" he asked, snuggling so close to Massha's back that his black robes brushed her rose-colored jeans. "We can get a room, and put a big DO NOT DISTURB sign on the door."

Massha spun abruptly, making him stumble. "Goodness me!" she giggled. "You wouldn't say things like that if my husband were here."

The Spectre grinned sepulchrally, his hooded eyes blazing with white light. "Oh? And what would your husband do if he were here?"

Massha winked coyly. "He'd stand right there and watch me mop up the floor with you. Now if you can't take a lady's hints, I'll say it straight out: *bug off*."

"I like feisty women!" The Spectre, laughing hollowly, tried to put his arms around her one more time.

Chumley started to move in from one side, Parvattani from the other. I put a hand on each of their chests to hold them back.

"Hang on. Let her enjoy herself a little, first."

The lesson in manners was brief but memorable. The big guy counted on being insubstantial to stave off physical jolts, but Massha pulled one of her gizmos out and dangled it in his face. I'd seen the glowing green charm before. Massha had told me it was specific for dealing with phantoms: glass covered in gold. The Spectre was not impressed. He stood with his big chin out. Massha hauled back and dealt him one hell of a roundhouse punch delivered all the way from the middle of her back. You could tell by the glazed expression on his face just before he folded up and sank that he thought her fist should have gone right through his jaw.

Massha stood over the body, shaking her hand up and down to restore the circulation.

"I really gotta remember what my mother always said about not hitting bone with bone."

"Very pretty, Massha." Chumley applauded her. "My little sister couldn't have cooled off a man faster."

"Thanks, Tall and Shaggy." Massha smiled, stepping over her would-be suitor. "I have a lot of respect for Tananda's talent, so coming from you—"

She paused, a blank look on her face. I wondered if the Spectre had grabbed her leg. I glanced down, but he was out for the count.

"You okay?" I asked.

"I'm fine," Massha assured all of us. "I just felt far away for a moment."

"Oive," Mayno breathed, as he prepared to rappel down the face of Unmentionables, the gigantic underwear store in Corridor G.

"What?" Oive asked, from the rafters above him.

In the guise of a black-furred Troll, she stood with her heels braced against a joist, ready to pull Mayno up in case of trouble.

"I wasn't call-aing you," he replied. "I was just . . . looking down."

"Don't," Oive reminded him. "If you do, you'll lose your grip and go splat on the floor. I mean, your guts could be spread out all over the entire corridor!"

Mayno gulped.

"I can't do zis!" he shrilled. "Zees is not fit activity for mall-rats. What is Rattila doing to us?"

"He thinks it gives him more of a buzz than stolen merchandise. Isn't that the weirdest thing you ever heard?" Oive's large eyes widened. "Maybe one of the personalities we brought him is making him crazy."

Mayno hastily lifted a finger to his lips. "Don't say that! He'll hear you!" He tugged on the ropes. "Can't we do this anoth-air way?"

"Find a happy place, dude," Oive advised. "Come on, pretend you're just lowering yourself into a giant cookie jar. You've got infinite pockets. Put all the cookies in the pockets . . ."

Mayno closed his eyes, and a blissful smile appeared on the Klahdish face he was wearing. "*C'est marveilleuse.* Okay, I go."

The Spectre turned out to be the first member of the newly founded Secret Admirers of Massha Fan Club. I'd wanted to split up the group into pairs, with Massha accompanying Par on his rounds, Chumley with Eskina, and me getting reacquainted—I mean patrolling—with Sibone, but I didn't like to leave her back uncovered, so to speak. Males of every species were coming out of the Mall's overly ornate woodwork to whistle, leer at, or bow to Massha.

Rimbaldi, the proprietor of The Volcano, appeared on his threshold, bowing and kissing his fingertips to her. Massha giggled like a schoolgirl. I raised my eyebrows at her.

"Well, it isn't every day someone appreciates my figure," she said. "I was so lucky to find Hugh."

"He's the lucky one," I stated. "Don't shortchange yourself."

Parvattani began to jump around as if he had a live fish in his shorts. He pulled the globe from his pocket.

"This way," he announced, pointing toward the hall to our left. His eyes danced with excitement. "It's a code S!"

"S?" I asked.

"Skeeve. We gotta another sighting of your friend. I mean the perpetrator that's not your friend. He's hanging from a rope on an underwear shop."

"Good," I announced, smacking my hands together. "This time the guy's gonna get it in the shorts!"

"He fly zroo ze ayair wiz ze gray-dest of eeeze—!"

"Why is he singing like that?" Massha asked, as we homed in on Unmentionables.

"Because it isn't Skeeve," I gritted, "and I'm going to kill him."

The gangly figure of the pseudo-Klahd swung from a rope around his middle, lying flat out as if he were flying. A large crowd had gathered to point and giggle at the Klahd dangling from the store's façade. A couple of tourists with cameras were taking pictures.

"This ought to be easy," I asserted. "His eyes are closed."

Parvattani brought his globe of authority up to his mouth and started to bark out an order. "All guards—!"

"Don't do it!" Eskina warned him. "If he hears you, he will vanish again."

Par frowned, but lowered his voice to a whisper. "All guards within G sector, converge on Unmentionables. Repeat, Unmentionables. Assist in clearing the area. Apprehend suspect Skeeve."

I wasn't going to wait for the cavalry. I was about to solve my own problem.

"Massha, you have anything to cut with?"

"Sure, big spender," she replied, floating over my head. "One cut line, coming up! Or, down."

I signaled to Chumley and Eskina to fan out to the other side of the pink-painted doorway. The name Unmentionables was spelled out in fireflies that were supposed to blink in patterns, but they seemed stressed out because of the presence of an intruder swinging in front of them. UM, they spelled out, some letters lit and others dark. MENTAL, and two words that flashed in sequence, UNS and TABLE.

"Who is the idiot?" a scantily clad Deveel woman demanded, gazing up at the impostor with her hands on her hips. She caught sight of Par. "Captain! I demand you get that moron down from my storefront at once!"

"We're attempting-a to do that, madame," Par averred, saluting smartly.

Massha flew toward the swaying body like a zeppelin homing in on a target. She pushed her sleeves up purposefully and brandished a hooked amulet like a miniature scythe. I ran to position myself underneath the impostor. Massha let the spell loose. A bolt of purple fire shot out from the charm.

The fake flew upward. I looked up and saw a shadowy form on the rafters hauling on the rope like a stevedore. So they were working in teams! I flung myself at the wall and started to climb up the blinking letters.

"#@%#@*!" they read.

The fake opened his eyes and shrieked. The purple fire snaked around the rope a foot above the knot holding him up and burned right through it. He reached the beam and scrambled onto it just in time. He and his big, dark, hairy accomplice ran away along the beams under the roof. I reached the top of the storefront. It was ten or twelve feet from there to the beams. I couldn't let the phony get away again!

I pushed off with all my strength, but it wasn't enough. I grabbed air just out of reach of my target. The crowd screamed as I fell. My breath was knocked out of my body as something caught me. I tried to twist to see.

"Stop struggling, big guy," Massha grunted. "My flight belt will burn out!"

"Thanks," I gasped.

"Don't thank me," she insisted, as she brought me the

rest of the way up to the white-painted beam. "Go get the phony creep!"

I didn't need the encouragement. I pulled myself upright and started running after the two thieves.

They knew their turf as well as I know every vein in my beautiful yellow eyes. They dashed toward a wall that I thought would be a dead end. At the last minute they clambered up and started running at right angles along another joist invisible against the white ceiling. I chinned up to the next level and continued my pursuit

Below me I could see the white hats of the guards jogging along, shouting warnings. Chumley made way for them, parting the crowd forcibly where necessary. Eskina, a foot shorter than the average shopper, had disappeared in the sea of heads.

Massha flanked me, readying a ring with a huge tan stone. The Skeeve kept glancing back at us, and as Massha raised her weapon, he spun on the narrow beam and pointed his joined hands at us.

"Duck!" I yelled.

Massha's eyes widened. She dove to one side as a tongue of green fire blasted by us. One of the dragonlings whom I had disturbed sleeping on the first beam let out a squawk of protest as it got a hot-seat. The beam itself was singed black for a significant diameter. I gulped. If one of us had been in the way of that spell, we would have been toast. Massha recovered quickly, firing off the ring.

A mass of writhing tan and gray flew toward the fugitives. As it neared them, it unwound into a coil of rope. The running figures flattened themselves on the beam. The rope should have followed their movements, but it expanded into a greater and greater mass and plummeted into the crowd. A cry went up as several shoppers were bound into a huge tangle with Chumley and some of the guards. An outraged, "Oh, I say!" escaped the Troll, who began to break the ropes one at a time between his mighty hands.

"Sorry, Chumley," Massha called, her face scarlet.

It was up to me. I tried to ignore the fact that the boards I was running on were a hair narrower than my feet. I tried to ignore the sixty-foot drop if I should trip. All I could see was getting my hands on the Skeeve-impersonator and beating the heck out of him before turning what was left over to the authorities.

Another turning appeared ahead. This time I was aware of their trick, so I studied the beams that lay ahead of me. This time there were two sets of cross braces, one higher and one lower. Psychologically speaking, the thieves had gone up the first time. I thought it was a better-than-even chance they'd go down. I almost grinned as they reached the end of the beam, and the big thief crouched to jump to the lower level. He stuck out a hand to help the shorter thief, the Skeeve-clone, who slowed down so he could make the transit more safely. I put on a burst of speed, gathered myself, and leaped out into space.

My hands touched smooth warm flesh. I had him! The Skeeve yelled. We found ourselves hanging on either side of the beam with our legs dangling six stories in the air. His accomplice, who turned out to be a Troll with purple-black fur, wobbled its way back toward us. He would reach us in a moment. I wasn't in a position to fight.

The Skeeve saw my expression as I considered the dilemma.

"Monsieur, do not drop me. I am afraid of heights. Please. Please do not drop me."

The Troll was two steps away. I had no choice. I let go of the Skeeve's hand.

"You dropped me!" he screeched, as we fell.

The crowd saw us dropping toward them and fled the area, screaming. A purple blur dashed into the newly cleared floor, and put out its arms. I collapsed into a nest of thick hair and lay there gasping.

"Thanks, Chumley," I croaked.

"Think nothing of it, old man," the Troll assured me gallantly.

I got my breath back and waved my arm. "Let me down." He set me on the floor. "Where is the SOB?"

"Right here," Chumley gestured, pointing to a body on the floor. It didn't look like Skeeve. It was small, hairy, and terrified.

"What is it?" I asked distastefully.

Chumley picked his foot up off its neck. The skinny creature, which would be up to my hip if I let it stand up, lay panting on the floor. It had a short, light brown pelt everywhere on its body except its tail, which was naked, and its head, where the fur was longer, blonder, and teased into a pompadour. Strapped to its skinny back was a pack like a book bag. Parvattani's men quickly wound the beast up in a coil of lightning, which I'd taught them to use only that morning, and confiscated the tote.

"It's-a a mall-rat," Par explained, a sneer on his otherwise pleasant face.

"A species indigenous to confined shopping spaces on Flibber," Eskina explained. "They are very greedy and like to steal. It makes sense that Rattila would employ one so close in type to his own species. But they are not very intelligent. It would be difficult to teach them to do what the other shapechangers are doing. Perhaps he is the only one of his kind in Rattila's employ."

"And who are you calling stupeed?" the mall-rat complained.

"Not you," Eskina acknowledged. "You can't be too stupid, anyhow."

"Thanks for nothing, madame," the rat grumbled, hunkering down in a heap between us.

Parvattani stood on its tail. The guards went through the backpack. Inside was nothing but a pile of cards.

"Those are just like the ones I saw the Pervect gal using," I insisted.

"What are these?" Par demanded, waving one under our captive's nose.

"I have no idea," the mall-rat said, a blank look on his face. "Rath-air pretty, eh?"

"Where did you get them? How do they work?"

"*J'ne parle Flibber, monsieur.*"

"He is stupid." Eskina sighed.

"No, he's not," I contradicted her. I shoved my face into the rat's. "He's smart enough to know that I'm going to start ripping his limbs off one at a time if he doesn't start cooperating!"

"Hey, cool down, cool down, Green-skinned Dude!" the rat protested, scrambling to put some distance between his face and mine. He looked plaintively from Par to Chumley to me. "They are my cards, monsieur. Give them back, *s'il vous plait?* I will get in real trouble without zem."

"You have-a been causing a lot of trouble with them," Parvattani asserted, triumphantly. "Mr. Aahz, will you do the honors?"

"Wait a minute," I cautioned him, holding up a hand. "Let's make sure we're dealing with the real·thing. Massha, is this the guy that we followed the other day?"

Massha hoisted her magik-detector amulet out from among the cluster of jewels hanging on her massive chest and waved it over our captive. "Yup."

"So," I deduced, "one of these cards is the one that lets him turn into Skeeve."

Massha shrugged. "That'd be my guess, but magik items are tricky. Unless he shows us how he did it, it's just a surmise."

"Which one is it? The tall Klahd with blond hair?"

I turned to the mall-rat, who stuck his long nose into the air. "Not a chance, monsieur. I do not do requests."

"Left arm first, or right?" I asked, casually. The mall-rat's eyes widened into twin blue pools of alarm.

"*Hein,* I did not say I wouldn't help out at all!"

"Good." I spread out the pack of cards in his face. "How do they work?"

The rat looked blank again. "You just—how you say?— I mean, I just hold it. You say the words. And then it works."

"That's real descriptive," I gritted, menacingly.

"Sounds pretty straightforward, Aahz," Massha soothed me. "You just invoke the card the way you'd invoke an amulet. What do you think, Eskina?"

The Ratislavan investigator nodded avidly. "It was meant to be easy to use."

"Aahz?" The rat's face brightened. "Yeah, I know you. I mean, the card does."

"Shut up!" I roared. I hated it that this piece of vermin might know anything about my ex-partner's inner thoughts. "Can anyone use these things, Massha, or are they keyed to him?"

Massha frowned. "I wish the Boss was here."

"Well, he's not," I snapped, probably sharper than I should have. "You're the real gadget mechanic, not him. This is your field of expertise. Think!" Massha looked a little surprised, but she got with the program.

"My guess is no," she offered, a little uncertainly. "If what Eskina said is true, that they work by the Law of Contagion, then they're generic."

"Do you have to be a magician to invoke it?"

"Doubt it," Massha stated.

"Good." I turned to the mall-rat. If furry creatures could sweat, he would have been soaking. "What are the words?"

"Oh, monsieur, I cannot say!"

"Sure you can," I insisted. "Say it, or you're going to have to eat oatmeal for the rest of your life."

The mall-rat's eyes widened with horror. "Oh, monsieur, you would not!"

I showed him all my teeth. "Try me."

The mall-rat muttered something low.

"Louder," I insisted.

"One Card to rule The Mall, One Card to Charge It, One Card to cruise The Mall, and in the darkness Lodge It."

I stared at him. "That's stupid."

The mall-rat shrugged. "The magician is not necessairily the poet."

"You can say that again." I picked up the first card, a

square of orange, and nodded to Massha. "Tell me what happens."

"Aahz, no!"

I invoked it.

TWELVE

It had been a few years since Garkin's moronic practical joke had robbed me of my powers. I could usually put the situation out of my mind; after all, it was temporary. In a few hundred years my powers would return normally. Or I could do some detective work and hunt down which of a hundred vendors in the Bazaar had sold Garkin the joke powder he used in the summoning spell. When I did think about it, it bugged me. So I didn't. Not that introspection wasn't a facet of my deep-thinking personality, but when you have an itch you can't scratch, it only makes it worse to dwell on it. If magik had been my only resource, I might have folded up and died, but I was a Pervect, I was intelligent, and I'd been around. Trying out an unknown magik item might sound ridiculously dangerous, but if a transformation card had been tried out extensively on a lab . . . I mean, mall-rat, chances were that it would be safe for a higher order of species to use. Like me.

"Well?" I asked.

Everyone looked taller, and the quality of the light was more blue. My voice sounded very high and a little hoarse.

I patted my chest, and my hand flew off it in surprise as I touched a couple of obstructions I wasn't expecting. I looked down. I was female, very skinny, with smooth blue skin. A tight band hoisted the small bosoms up for maximum eye catching. The arms were kind of nice, too, with slim wrists and long fingers, eight on a hand. Not a species I recognized. Then a memory whispered in my mind. Tantalusian. My host's name was Vishini, an animal trainer with a fondness for shoes. Except for her home dimension there weren't many places like The Mall that sold high-fashion styles in extra wide, to accommodate eight toes per foot.

"Effective," I nodded approvingly. "Totally painless."

Thinking of Garkin, I realized that a card like this would be a really good practical joke. What if you planted one of these where a buddy couldn't resist picking it up? I chuckled.

The others were still staring. I glared back.

"Knock it off, guys. It's still me in here."

"Um, well," Parvattani gulped, his cheeks a brilliant teal in embarrassment.

"Not Skeeve," Chumley rumbled.

"Yeah." I sighed. "Well, we can't leave this hanging around." I picked up the orange square and tried to snap it between my fingers. Her fingers. In any case, they weren't strong enough. "Hey, Chumley, do you mind?"

"Not at all."

"Hey, monsieur," the mall-rat protested, struggling with his guards. "Don't do it!"

"Shut up," I barked. "Break it," I ordered.

The Troll took the card from me and bent it in half. It broke with a clap of thunder.

The next thing I knew I was flat on my back, staring up into the anxious faces of Parvattani's guards.

"Back off," I snarled.

My body was my own again, my handsome scales restored to their bright green, my clawlike fingernails intact, the fingers reduced to the right number. The guards jumped back. I staggered to my feet and tested my head to make sure it was still fastened on.

"That kicks like a mule. Gimme the next one."

"Isn't that a bad idea, Aahz?" Massha asked, worry written all over her big face. Her voice seemed to echo in my head.

"Not if I disinvoke before we break them," I insisted. I gestured toward the rat, who was crooning a worried song to himself. "He didn't go into a fit when I fell over, did he?"

"Nossir!" exclaimed the two guards flanking the prisoner.

I turned back to Massha and Chumley. "See?"

The mall-rat stared at me in astonishment. "You must be of the ultimate toughness, monsieur. That snapback killed Farout."

"Who's Farout?"

The rat, sensing he had said too much, clamped his jaws shut.

"Never mind." I waved a dismissive hand and reached for the next one.

"Me try?" Chumley suggested.

"No way," I stated firmly. "If I become something large and hostile, you'll have to be the one to sit on me. Let's get this out of the way and identify the Skeeve card. We can be back at the Bazaar in an hour. We'll just wing through them until we get the right one."

Par cleared his throat. "Aahz, we must keep a list of the—er, people-a you become. They are all-a victims inna this, too."

I raised an eyebrow. Massha nodded.

"Just because we're getting what we want doesn't mean we can't spend a little more time and help The Mall," she pointed out. "Think how their friends and family feel about the violation of their identities."

"Aww." But Massha was right. "I'll do it," I agreed.

We repaired to Moa's office. We brought the administrator up to date, though he'd been following the chase by crystal ball. He was fascinated by the whole process, by the cards, and my experience with the first one.

"No wonder we've never been able to detect the thieves in all this time," he exclaimed, thumbing through the stack again and again. "Remarkable, remarkable." He glanced at Eskina. "Young lady, maybe I owe you an apology."

Eskina tossed her head. "And maybe I accept."

"We've got to go through the rest of these," I explained. "Thought it'd be nice to do it in more comfortable surroundings, where it's more private."

"Of course, Aahz, of course," Moa insisted hospitably, spreading out his hands. "It's nice to find such consideration in the world."

"Er, speaking of consideration" I began, then interrupted myself. "Never mind! I just need some space, all right?"

"Whatever you say," Moa assured me. "Would you like to use my office?"

I glanced around at the furnishings, especially the handsome upholstery and the range of breakables on the walls and tabletops.

"Better not," I stated. "If I can't control the cards, I might end up redecorating in here."

We ended up in an empty storeroom down the hall from the offices. Two of Parvattani's guards stood sentry outside the door. Four of them hung out at each wall. Massha, Chumley, and, to my extreme annoyance, Woofle stood at a safe distance, but close enough to jump on me if I needed it. All of them were watching me nervously.

I invoked the next card.

I have experimented with magik a lot. Not during my younger days, when I was way too serious, but later on, sometimes out of necessity, other times out of boredom, but I had never come across anything like the Ratislavan system. Like most magicians I was accustomed to taking my power out of the lines of force present in nearly every dimension to a greater or lesser extent. Nature renewed that flow. It was impersonal, neither good nor evil, and a magician could make use of it according to his, her, or its own talents, gifts, and inclination. This was different. I could feel power coming through me from the card in my hand, a weak trickle, and with it came a personality.

If you have never been possessed, don't. Let me give you my spur-of-the-moment reaction to using the card: it was weird. I knew who I was, Aahzmandius, Pervect, and all the millions of little details that make me me, but at the same time I knew I was also Dreo, a wood-carver from Creet. I thought of myself—my borrowed self—as a nice enough guy, but I didn't like to be around a lot of other people. I could almost sense through the walls the thousands of other shoppers. It made me jumpy. This was directly opposed to me, Aahz, who likes being in the midst of the bustle of a busy place. The two personalities rubbed one another raw. It was worse than telepathy; there was no place to hide from the other guy. I found myself feeling sorry for hydras.

"What's his-a name, Aahz?" Par asked, clipboard at the ready.

"Dreo. Cretin. I mean, Creetan," I corrected, at the fierce urging of the "visitor" in my head.

I pushed the card away. Soon, but not soon enough, I was alone in my head again.

"This could be marketable," Woofle was saying, as I snapped out of it.

"No," I bellowed.

He gave me an annoyed look. I liked the finance guy less than ever.

"Never. I can't even begin to tell you what a bad idea that would be. You'd be asking for assassination attempts, or worse, lawsuits, if you tried to sell this process over the counter. You like it so much, you try it."

"All right," Woofle snarled, accepting the challenge.

He took a card from Massha. Once he had chanted the spell, his scrawny body was replaced by a tall, black-shelled insectoid fashionista from Troodle.

"Now, look at the possibilities inherent in this . . ." Woofle began, gesturing at his/her figure. Then his mandibles clicked uncomfortably, and his multiple-lensed eyes started to roll. He clutched his head. "Stop that! Shut up! No, I am not a boring dresser! Be quiet! Aagh!"

Hastily he undid the spell and threw the card on the ground. His round Flibberite face contorted with fear and disgust.

"Get rid of them! All of them!"

"We're trying to, Woofle. Calm yourself," Moa advised.

"Name, sir?" Parvattani asked, politely. "We need it to compare with store receipts to verify fraudulent purchases."

"Do you think I want to remember?" Woofle shrieked.

I groaned. Wimp. "I'll do it." I picked the card up off the floor, and was in and out of the Troodleian in nothing flat. "Ch'tk'll."

"Thank you, sir."

"See what I mean?" I tried not to gloat, but I didn't like Woofle. "You only were in for a moment. If you stayed a different being too long, you might lose your own identity."

"Then how come a rat like that can keep using them over and over?" Woofle demanded.

"We have, how you say, not much mind to call ou-air own," the mall-rat acknowledged modestly.

"If you've got a healthy ego, this system could destroy it," I told Eskina.

The investigator waved a hand. "There will be bugs worked out."

"This isn't a bug, it's an infestation," I insisted. But I went on doping out the identities embedded in each magikal card.

The third from the last card in the pack was Skeeve. I didn't need the shocked looks on the faces of my friends to know I'd hit it. I could hear his inner voice talking to itself, probably at the last minute that his card had been stolen or copied.

Wow, that girl is really something. She's a vampire! Aahz wouldn't like that. He was really upset when he found out Blut was behind our tent. Sometimes he worries too much. They don't seem so bad . . . I think Casandra really likes me. I hope she's impressed. I feel like a phony, but everyone's treating me like a big shot . . .

I shoved the card away from me. I'd heard and felt more besides that inner monologue, a whole lot of things I really didn't want to know about my ex-partner's inner workings. I felt as if I was barging into his mind, like mental breaking and entering.

"Destroy it," I croaked. "Now!"

"Right you are, Aahz," Chumley asserted. He snapped the blue plastic rectangle in two, then four, then eight pieces.

"What about these?" Massha asked, holding up the last cards.

"Gimme a minute," I snarled. I recovered my usual composure and processed the final two, an Imp and a Gnome.

"Thank you, thank you, Aahz!" Moa beamed. "You have done us a great service. We realize you didn't have to assist us further, but we are grateful."

"Don't mention it," I grunted. "What are you gonna do with Fuzzy, here?"

I aimed a thumb at the mall-rat chained with lightnings.

"We will lock him up. Based on all the identifications you just made we can probably connect him with a lot of shoplifting incidents."

"That's it, then." I dusted my hands together with satisfaction. I turned to Massha and Chumley. "We can go home."

"But there are more members of this gang out there!" Woofle protested. "You're not going to help us solve the rest of the problem?"

I shook my head. "Nope. I set out our terms at the beginning. But we've weakened them a lot. We've just knocked out Rattila's access to a bundle of his victims. And you can get a lot of information out of this vermin. If you can't, I bet Eskina has some ideas."

The Ratislavan investigator showed her sharp little teeth.

"Certainly I do." She grinned. "Do you want me to start now?"

She advanced upon the mall-rat, who cowered back to the extent his bonds allowed.

"Please, monsieur, get her off me! She's rabid!"

"You be cooperative with this guy," I indicated Moa, "and he'll see that she doesn't shred you. Too much."

"I comply, monsieur, I comply!"

"Okay," I concluded, pulling the D-hopper out of my pocket. "We're out of here. Moa, it's been nice meeting ya. If you're ever in the Bazaar, look me up."

"Wonderful!" Moa shook our hands. "You all certainly deserve your reputations. I am very impressed. But don't go now! At least stay tonight. We'll have a celebration. A party in your honor. We'll have a feast, dancing, kegs of ale—"

"Don't mind if I do," I accepted, with a grin. Massha and Chumley agreed.

The Ratislavan marched back and forth, kicking boxes of new shoes out of his way with angry feet. His hairless tail lashed. The mall-rats, most especially the eight remaining "specials," cringed together in a fearful knot.

"One of our number has been arrested," Rattila shouted, for about the hundredth time.

"We tried to get away," Oive wailed. "That Pervert is too tricky!"

"You were stupid!" Rattila bellowed.

He pointed a finger at her, and lightning sprang from its tip. Oive looked at the burned patch on the ground at her feet and fainted dead away. Strewth and the other mall-rats edged backward.

"Hmm, that's new," Rattila mused, staring at his finger. "This! This is what real power is all about! They must not stop us now! I will drain all of their talent!"

"How?" Strewth asked. "They figured out about the cards, Big Cheese. They keep breaking 'em; we don't have any way to buy more stuff for you."

"Steal their essence! Use up the magicians we have until they're empty shells. They don't realize what they have done," the Ratislavan tyrant raged, "but this means *war!*"

"Dude," whispered Wassup to Strewth, "I think we, like, created a monster."

THIRTEEN

I pried open one eye, and some sick joker stuck a twelve-foot, flaming spear in it. I fell back, groaning. The spike in my eye eventually died down to a faint glow. I realized it was a mote of sunlight peeking through a gap in the curtains of my hotel room. I also knew that I had absolutely no memory of how I had gotten back there last night. I hoped it had been last night, but I had no way of knowing that, either. That had been one hell of a party. In celebrating our success, Moa had gone all out. The details started coming back to me: the best food, plenty of good liquor, entertainment, and a game of dragon poker that kept going until the wee hours.

I heard wounded dragons roaring in pain in the next room. I thought I'd better get out there and defend Massha and Chumley.

Thanks to the headache it took one or two tries before I extricated myself from the silk bedcover. I was still fully dressed, which suggested self-locomotion last night, but I would have taken either side of that bet.

Once I reached the sitting room in our luxury suite, I

identified the roaring dragons: Chumley and Massha. They were holding a snoring competition to see who could break the most windows by dint of pure decibels. I judged the contest a tie and went to wake them up.

Eskina, asleep in the walk-in closet, was curled into a little ball. If the noise didn't wake her, I didn't see why I should. After all, she didn't have to check out and go home. Moa might have her moved to a smaller room when we were gone, but she was entitled to decent treatment, having given us the tip that eventually led us to capture Skeeve's impersonator. With luck, the kid would never hear about the situation or its aftermath. He sure wasn't ever going to hear it from me.

The Djinn who delivered room service blinked in and out of the sitting room, pausing briefly only to hold out his hand for a tip. Massha was the first to emerge from her room.

"Do I smell coffee?" she asked.

I was already wrapped around a cup that was almost big enough. I shoved an equal-sized beaker toward her. The serving spell filled it to the brim. Massha grabbed it and gulped down half of the steaming liquid.

"That was some party," she stated. "My head feels like the conga line's still dancing through it."

"I have a hangover the likes of which I have not felt for sixty years," I admitted. "Maybe not since some friends and I closed down the bar next to the distillery on Tulla." I paused to remember past glory and compared it favorably with the present. "These Flibberites sure know how to party."

"Amen to that," Massha agreed.

Chumley staggered out. "Coffee," he grunted, sounding like Big Crunch, his nom de guerre. A cup or two later the veins in his odd-sized moon-shaped eyes receded, and he was able to resume his normal intellectual discourse.

"We ought to thank Moa before we head out," I suggested, finally able to face the pink omelettes and green ham in the covered serving dishes.

"Good idea." Massha nodded. "I want to pick up a little present for Hugh. I saw some beautiful swords in the weapons shop. There was a gorgeously balanced silver-hilted hand-and-a-half that he could use for sword practice."

"I'm going to take half a day and browse the book-stores," Chumley added.

Another rap came at the door. This one sounded a hundred times quieter than the first one. Moa stuck his head in.

"Hey," I called, feeling expansive as my hangover began to recede. "C'mon in."

The Mall administrator looked a little tentative, nothing like the plucky little guy who had braved thousands of angry shoppers the first morning we saw him, or the same guy who had danced on the table with a Gorgon's head pinata about five hours ago.

"You had a good time last night?" he inquired.

"That was one hell of a blowout," I assured him. "You sure know how to party, Moa."

"It's been a pleasure, I'm sure," Moa replied, shaking my hand warmly. "We were grateful to have you . . . Are you certain you won't stay here, just a little while longer?

"I'm sure," I told him. "Maybe do a little shopping, then hit the road." I eyed his uneasy demeanor suspiciously. "Why?"

"Well, we gotta little problem."

I had heard equivocation like that hundreds of times in my life, and the follow-up explanation was never good news. "What *kind* of little problem?"

"Oh, nothing big," Moa began. "Just that one of my guards just reported someone who looks like your friend doing card tricks in the atrium near Doorway A."

It took a moment for the words to penetrate all the way through the leftovers from a keg of Old Banshee, but my outrage meter pinned on overload.

"*What?*" I bellowed.

The sound of my voice brought Eskina running.

"But we got the impersonator," Massha interjected. "He's still in custody, right?"

"He sure is," Moa promised us. "He's locked in a box in Will Call. No way he's getting out of there."

My headache came back full force. "So, who's out there?"

Moa let out a heavy sigh. "It looks like there's another copy of Skeeve's card."

The Ratislavan investigator looked horrified.

"This is a total perversion of the process," she gasped. "Rattila is even a greater villain than we knew."

A rumbling sound disturbed our conference.

"Excuse me," Moa apologized, and reached into his pocket for a globe.

Inside the glass sphere we saw Parvattani's agitated face contorting. Moa set it down, looking shocked.

"We got more sightings," he informed us.

"More sightings where?" I demanded.

"Everywhere," Moa sighed. "Captain Parvattani says he's dancing with customers at Doorway R, he's pulling rabbits out of people's hats in Atrium N, he's taking candy from babies in Corridor B. In other words, either your Rattila's shapechangers can either teleport, in spite of The Mall's magik that is supposed to protect against it, and believe me, we paid a lot of money for that spell system, five hundred gold pieces a month just to maintain it—"

"Or?" I interrupted him forcefully.

Moa looked smaller and more forlorn than before. "Or all of them can turn into Skeeve."

Chumley's and Massha's mouths dropped open. I felt outrage bubble up in me.

"No!" I bellowed. "I don't believe it. I will not *stand* for a dozen impersonators dragging my pa—my friend's name through the dirt. We are going to take down this out-of-town rat!"

We stormed out toward the nearest Skeeve sighting. Corridor B, a few blocks' walk from the hotel. An outraged

crowd had gathered. Mothers comforted crying infants and
toddlers, all of whom were pointing over their shoulders
toward the jungle-gym climbing frame in the middle of the
atrium there.

A squadron of Par's guards had the structure surrounded, firing stun-pikes through the bars. I'd given them a
short course of basic training with the weapons, but evidently, I had forgotten to explain the futility of the circular
firing squad. Several guards were out for the count,
knocked unconscious by their own fellows' bolts.

Inside the playground I could see a shadowy figure
bounding from one side to the other. I wasn't in the mood
to wait for him to come out on his own.

"Come on," I gestured to my companions. We spread
out and marched on the monkey bars.

The impostor had to know we were coming. The crowd
noticed us right away, as you would notice a tank bearing
down on you, and parted like the Red Sea.

"Nyah nyah nyah NYAH nyah," chanted Skeeve's voice.

My dander, already up, hit new heights. I lunged into
the underhang of ropes and climbing poles.

WHAM! And promptly got a swing in the mouth.

I felt my teeth with my tongue. None were broken. The
people who weren't comforting crying babies laughed at
me. I snarled back at them.

Charging in was a miscalculation on my part. I stood
back, my head ringing. I shouldn't have done it. That was
dumb. I had not adequately scoped out the scene. That was
my own fault. I was a better strategist than that.

My judgment was clouded. I was furious because when
Moa had dropped the bad news on us I had been ready to
go. I was done. I was out of there. I could imagine that
Moa himself had suffered a setback, finding out that the
ring of thieves plaguing his Mall was still as much of a
nuisance as before. But I had come with only one task in
mind: take out the Skeeve impersonator and go home.
Success had been whisked out from under my feet like a
rug, and the anger about that was making me careless. I

stopped where I was and took a couple of deep breaths. Start over. Watch what the enemy's doing, not what you think he ought to do.

What he was doing was jumping out of the jungle gym whenever he saw a kid carrying a lollipop or licorice string go by. Light on his feet as the original Skeeve, he whisked out, snatched the good, and dashed back into his hiding place again. Chumley's assessment was that Rattila gathered power based on value of the stir that the impostors caused, one way or another. He must have been getting a big charge, so to speak, out of this performance. I beckoned over the nearest guard with braid on his sleeves.

"Hey, bellhop," I called.

"Yessir!" the kid barked, nearly knocking himself unconscious with a salute.

"Clear the area," I ordered. "Mr. Moa will back me on this. Get everyone away from here. Use force if necessary, but in two minutes I don't want anyone looking this way. Got it?"

The officer looked puzzled, but he obeyed. He pulled his crystal ball out of his pocket and gave the order. The guards, those of them still on their feet, reversed course and started shouting at the crowd to clear the area.

A collective moan of disappointment went up, but the people cleared off. Good. No more paying attention to the fraud.

At the back of my mind was the annoyance that several more impostors were carrying on like this all over The Mall, but I liked my chances of dealing with this one. He had limited his territory, always a mistake, and though his points of escape from this structure were numerous, they were finite.

Chumley, a security expert who had worked a lot of tricky engagements like popular band concerts and financial transactions, tipped me a signal that he'd counted seven exits. I just started bending the bars around one nearest me.

"Aahz, what are you doing?" Moa demanded, rushing over to me.

"Put your finger there," I instructed, keeping half an eye on the moving shadow.

Moa obliged. I tied the bars in a handsome bow knot and moved on to the next egress.

"Taking apart the infrastructure wasn't really part of the deal," Moa bleated, hopping up to try and get my attention as I walked.

I examined the next archway. It was too wide to stretch the soft metal alloy bars across, but The Mall administrator was just about the right width. The curving uprights groaned as I pulled them down and wound them into a ring. With one hand I lifted the slight Flibberite and tightened the metal bars around his waist.

"Stay here a minute." I instructed him. "Don't let him leave this way."

"Aahz, wait! Get me down from here!"

Moa's partner Woofle had been drafted, as had a few minor magicians who worked as clerks in The Mall. Woofle didn't like the idea of working with me any more than I liked working with him, but I needed the firepower to supplement Massha. What with the magikal arms and other gizmos being carried by the guards, we stood a chance.

"How are you on illusion?" I asked him.

Woofle eyed me with distaste. "Why?"

"Because he's staying out of our way, but he's a sucker for a sucker. Can you create the image of a helpless-looking kid with a big, fat, red lollipop?"

"Certainly I can!"

"And plant it over me."

Woofle's eyebrows went up, but he nodded. "That could work."

I waited while he closed his eyes. Illusion's one of those useful spells. You call down a hunk of power while at the same time picturing in your mind the face of the person in front of you being replaced by another image. I had taught the technique to Skeeve, who had passed it along to Massha, but she wasn't as good as he had been with non-gizmo magik. I was hoping Woofle was more advanced.

"You're done," Woofle announced. "The lollipop's in your right hand."

"Good," I replied.

Chumley glanced over, having sealed all the entryways but one, and did a classic double take. I gave him a hearty thumbs-up, and skipped off toward the open door. My companions hustled to take their places behind me.

I mimed licking the sucker as I skipped. I couldn't do anything about the sound effects of my footfalls booming on The Mall floor. I hoped the faker would miss them in the ambient noise, which would have covered the sound of a jet taking off. I didn't dare open my mouth, because there was no way he could mistake my deep, masculine voice for the pipings of a preadolescent. I felt like a moron. I had to remind myself this was for a good cause. I might be saving Skeeve's life.

Out of the corner of my eye I saw the shadow stalking me. I covered a grin and slowed my hippity-hop to a shuffle just as I crossed the opening to the jungle gym.

The figure darted out and made a grab for my lollipop. His hand closed on empty air, at about the same moment my hand closed like a vise on his wrist. He gawked at me for half a second, then plunged his teeth into my wrist. The texture of my skin surprised him into staring up at me out of his big, round, blue eyes. My heart sank. What if *this* one was the real Skeeve under a spell? I hauled my heart up out of my boots and wrapped my other arm around his neck. We could figure that out later. The Mall guards marched in to take their prisoner.

The impostor turned into a tornado. He made as if to gouge out my eyes, then kicked for my crotch. It wasn't the oldest trick in the book, but it was on the same page. I let go of his wrist, grabbed his ankle, and picked him up over my head.

I forgot how good Skeeve's reactions were. He stretched out his free hand and snatched away a stun-pike from the advancing guard. He blasted the nearest two, knocking them unconscious, then turned it on me.

I ducked my head, but not fast enough to miss the entire blast. My head rang, and I suddenly discovered I was grasping nothing.

He leapfrogged over the short Flibberites and tore into the crowd. Massha flew right behind him, zigging when he zigged and zagging when he zagged.

"Outta my way!" I bellowed.

I had to enjoy the expressions on the faces of the onlookers when they heard my voice coming out of a child's body. For the ones who didn't get the message, I elbowed them aside. The guards poured into the breach behind me.

Chumley had been a little closer to the crowd, but he moved slower than we did. I kept my eye on Massha overhead. She must have been getting closer, because her hands stretched out in front of her as if to grab something. Closer. Closer. Then she stopped, looked right and left, and arrowed back to me.

"Got a problem, big guy," she informed me.

FOURTEEN

"What do you mean, you didn't see which way he went?" Moa repeated, for the hundredth time, as hordes of shoppers filed by on every side. "You were flying right over his head!"

"Yes," Massha asserted patiently, though I could tell she was embarrassed. "I almost had him, when he vanished, right there in front of Cartok's. Two strangers ran off from that point in exactly opposite directions. I didn't know which one to follow."

"He had a confederate in the crowd," I reasoned. "Wily. I might have used a tactic like that myself."

Moa glanced at me, then shook his head as if to clear it.

"Woofle, could you—" He made some passes with his hands.

Woofle performed a gesture or two. The others looked more comfortable when he finished, but a couple of passersby nearly jumped out of their skins at my apparent transformation.

"Thank you. I prefer to talk to you face-to-face. It's very disorienting."

"But effective," I pointed out. "It worked. We almost had him."

"But we didn't," Moa reminded me. "He got away clean, and we don't know any more than we did before."

"Nope," I corrected him. "We learned something very important: whoever they are, these impostors don't know what they're doing."

"Huh?" Chumley asked.

"What do you mean, Aahz?" Moa pressed. "They're just as much of a pain in the you-know-where as before. More, if we have to put up with them harassing innocent customers!"

"Nope," I corrected him. "They're less. We were wrong. We thought Rattila had employed a bunch of shapeshifters to gather power for him. I proved last night that the cards themselves make you change, not magikal talent. Those impostors, whoever they are, know how to use those cards, and they make use of some of the abilities of the people whose personalities they're stealing, like charm or strength, but nothing that doesn't rely on instinct. That's why I think they're not magicians. I'm betting none of them are. They don't know what they're doing. Otherwise, we wouldn't be able to get close to the Skeeves. The kid may not be the most experienced magician in the world, but he packs one hell of a magikal punch, and he knows how to fly as well as a bunch of other things that I taught him. None of them have an instinct for magik. We're lucky. I wouldn't be surprised if they were all mall-rats, or something else of a low order of evolution."

"Notta chance—" Parvattani scoffed. Then he glanced at Eskina. "I suppose-a it's possible," he conceded.

"It is likely," Eskina exclaimed, energetically. "Those would not challenge Rattila for his power."

"So what's our next move, Green Genius?" Massha asked, looking more enthusiastic than she had before.

"We could use some more firepower, but I don't want to involve anyone else," I thought out loud. "I don't want anyone else finding out that these crooks are making a fool of Skeeve."

"Woofle will help," Moa stated. Reluctantly, the financial Flibberite nodded.

I lifted a finger. "Good. That's one."

"Aahz! Hey, Aahz!"

A female voice calling my name attracted my attention. I glanced over my shoulder.

"And that's two," I added with satisfaction.

The owner of the voice bustled toward us in a rustle of green satin, Chloridia was another old friend, a major hunk of gorgeousness, who had a popular variety show on the Crystal Ball Network in her dimension, Kall.

Her four arms wound around me passionately, and she kissed the air within an inch of each of my cheeks. Her large purple eyes, all four of them, were lined in bright green shadow, and her lips were painted green to match. "Oh, Aahz, it's been so long!"

"Hey, baby," I purred, enjoying the greeting. "What are you doing here?"

"Shopping!" She laughed, but the sound was brittle. I eyed her.

"What's the problem?" I asked.

She let out a tinkle of laughter. "I just had a bill collector appear at the studio, interrupting my show, and demanding the most outrageous sum!"

"No kidding," I replied, with interest. "Hey, sweetie, let me introduce you to some friends of mine. Massha, Chumley, this is Chloridia, an old friend."

"Nice to meet you," Massha greeted her, with a hearty handshake.

I had to give her credit. The old, pre-Possiltum Massha might have exhibited some signs of insecurity, but this Massha, court magician and friend of queens, acted like she saw Chloridia as an equal. I was pleased.

"Any friend of Aahz's is a friend of mine," Chloridia assured her, liking what she saw, too. "And who's this big handsome fellow?"

Chumley lowered his eyes abashedly and scuffed his toe on the ground. "Big fan," he muttered.

"Really?" Chloridia exclaimed. She gave him a thorough hug, which embarrassed him all the more. "I am always happy to meet my fans! Thank you! Where do you watch my show?"

"Trollia."

"Fabulous! We're number one in our time slot across the ether in Trollia."

"This is Eskina," I added. The little Ratislavan received another air kiss. "And this is Moa."

For the first time the grand Kallian charm turned off. "We've met," she stated coldly.

I raised an eyebrow. "Credit card problems, huh?"

"Why, yes," my old friend replied, surprised. "How did you know?"

"Why in hell did you get a card?" I asked her, as we headed toward the next field of battle, a Skeeve impostor selling raffle tickets in Corridor J. I brought her up to date on what we were doing there and what had happened so far. "They're nothing but trouble."

"Oh, you know," Chloridia tossed off airily. "The same old reasons. Exclusivity. Status. It impresses people so much more than producing fireworks or a rodent out of my hat, which is so hard on one's clothes or the upholstery, depending on where you are. And," she admitted, with a coy smile, "laziness. It was lighter than carrying around a lot of gold. Our kind of purchases can be pretty expensive, as you know, and those bags of coins throw the line of one's clothes just all out of whack."

I agreed, having pride in my style of dress. "But it's easier. No paper trail back to you, no data miners dropping sale flyers on your doorstep."

Chloridia sighed. "It was a mistake, I know it now, but it just seemed so . . . fashionable when I whipped it out in a crowd. 'Charge it,' I'd say, and people would *jump*. It was better than the Felidian hotfoot. *You* know."

I grinned. We'd had some good times together, me and Chloridia, and a bunch of other magicians about the same age . . . but I digress.

"So what's the trouble?"

"I started feeling . . . funny one day. Do you know, I thought I saw myself coming out of a boutique, one that I was about to walk into. I put it off to foreknowledge. You know."

I whistled. "I sure do."

Once in a while clairvoyance happened to all of us. You tried not to get involved in it, since there were thousands of possible futures to follow any single event. The ones who started to believe in their own prescience ended up drunk or insane or with their own talk shows, none of which fates I wished for myself. Though, with rare regret for my own lost powers, I wouldn't have minded *having* to look out for flashes of intuition.

". . . I went in anyway. I started looking through the racks. I found this absolutely *divine* magenta blouse, but my size wasn't there. I found one of those ever-hovering Djinni clerks and asked her to look for one in the back or size one to fit. She made a face. I was on the point of asking to speak with her manager when she told me that I had just been in, and made the *exact same* request, with which she had complied. Was I . . . having a little memory problem? She could show me my credit card receipt. And she did. That was when I went to the management." Chloridia glared at Moa. "They were sorry—they couldn't do anything. All they suggested was that I get in touch with the Bank of Zoorik people, have a new one issued, which would stop the old one. But it hadn't been stolen. I have very good spells to protect my valuables."

"I remember," I leered.

"Oh, Aahz!" She pushed me with all four hands. I stumbled. " 'But what about my face?' I asked *that man*." Chloridia threw a disgusted gesture in Moa's direction. The administrator looked abashed. " 'My face is my fortune.' He said they couldn't do anything about that. The guards said they'd be happy to tell the stores not to permit credit purchases by anyone wearing my face, but where does that leave me?"

"Paying cash?" I suggested.

She waved it away.

"Get with the century, Aahz. You're more fun when you're not being sanctimonious."

"But now we know it wasn't clairvoyance. You really did see someone who looked like you. We're trying to catch the people responsible." I glanced at her speculatively. "Do you have time to pitch in? It's in your own interests."

"I'd love to help," the Kallian gushed. "If I can work with *you*. Or this big hunk of fuzzy maleness." She cuddled up to Chumley and put a couple of hands through his arm. "Not those unsympathetic Flibberites."

Massha raised an eyebrow. "Don't you know any *male* magicians, Aahz?"

"Yeah," I countered, a little defensively, "like Cire."

Chloridia recoiled in shock. "Cire! Is he here?"

"Same reason you are, apparently," I replied. "I'm hoping we can get him to help, just like you offered to."

"He's likely to be more hindrance than help, you know."

"I know," I growled.

"I'll do what I can," Chloridia promised, fanning her face with one of her free hands, "but I've been feeling so tired lately. Out of it. I get very distracted by sales, for example. When I hear that music . . . I just forget where I am. I have to go to the sale!"

Eskina and I exchanged glances. "That is bad," she stated. "The mall-rats are wearing you, but you are wearing them, too."

Chloridia turned her nose up. "I never wear rat fur!"

"Ticket?" a voice asked, as a pasteboard was shoved practically up my nose. "Win a pegasus-drawn carriage!"

"No, thanks," I muttered, scanning the crowd in

Corridor J for that familiar face, when my eyes met the owner of the voice.

It was the phony! We recognized each other at the same time. He darted away toward a wall, where a rope had been left for his convenience in making a quick escape. I got tangled in the many legs of a multijointed insectoid who had been waiting its turn when the impostor saw me.

"Massha!" I bellowed.

The Lady Magician of Possiltum rose up from the confab she had been sharing with Eskina and Chloridia and shot after the impostor. Chloridia, who didn't need a belt for the spell, flew behind, Eskina clinging to her neck. They reached his escape route before he did. Eskina wriggled out of Chloridia's grip and slid down the rope toward the impostor. Immediately, he dropped off and ducked into the crowd, dashing directly between a couple of Parvattani's finest, whom I was beginning to equate with the Keystone Kops. The Flibberites grabbed for each other, both getting in my way.

"That one?" Chloridia asked, pointing. "That Klahd?"

"He's not a Klahd, he's masquerading as one," I shouted.

The Kallian shook her head. "You've been slumming since we used to hang out, Aahz."

She shot after him effortlessly. A bubble of light began to form between her hands.

"Watch it," Eskina warned. "They are tricky."

The impostor knew he was surrounded. I stalked him warily, hoping he wasn't going to be able to call on Skeeve's power, his downright astonishing luck, or, I had to admit it, his really surprising common sense. No, the fake continued to act like a scared animal. I congratulated myself. These weren't magicians, or even very smart beings.

But they were wily.

Chloridia's bubble arrowed after him. He dashed into the nearest storefront, and emerged with a smug look on his face. A wail sounded from inside the door. I glanced in as I went by. A very fat Imp was suspended in a blue balloon like the jelly in a doughnut. He sputtered, waving his hands for help. Chloridia immediately alit to undo her sorcery. The rest of us kept after the fake.

Our quarry stayed low, always ducking in between other people so we couldn't just dive on him or pick him up. Eskina followed him gamely, leaping up to catch at his legs. She didn't have a chance of nailing him, but I admired her persistence. Massha doubled around in the air, hauling her big ring out.

Mall guards poured out of a doorway, pikes at the ready. The impostor saw them and windmilled his long arms as he slid to a halt, then started running back the other way. Massha doubled around in the air. She aimed a finger at the Skeeve.

I saw Chloridia coming out of the store with the Imp. His pink face was even pinker than normal, and he wore a sheepish grin. Another fan. I had to grin. Chloridia stopped to sign autographs for a few others who had recognized her.

"Hey, Chlory!" I yelled. "He's coming your way!"

Chloridia glanced up, and her four eyes widened. She threw up her hands, a spell growing between them.

"I've got him now!" Massha crowed.

A brown blob shot out of her ring. The Skeeve spotted Massha over his shoulder and dove over the head of a Gremlin waiting her turn for an autograph. Massha's net missed him by a mile. Instead of winding him up, it enveloped Chloridia, tying the star up with the cluster of adoring fans. Her spell misfired. A bolt of golden fire blasted up and illuminated the ceiling as it burst like fireworks, stunning three pigeons.

"Ha ha ha ha HA!" the phony cackled, derisively.

He jumped up on top of a freestanding stall and stuck his thumbs in his ears. Then he disappeared down behind the stall. By the time I got there, he was gone.

I stomped my way back to the storefront.

Chloridia, with her usual aplomb, severed the strands of the net binding her with one hand while signing autographs

and shaking hands with the other three. Massha alit forlornly beside me.

"He got away from me," I told Parvattani, who rushed
over when he saw us.

The captain shook his head vigorously. "There is
another-a sighting, very close to here in Atrium G. We
must get there at once!" He set off at a clip. His men fell
in behind him. We waited until Chloridia had paused for a
few shutterbug portraits with her admirers and floated over
to join us.

"I'm so sorry, Aahz," Massha apologized, her face red.
"I don't know what's the matter with me. My gadgets are
misfiring all over the place. Maybe I'm just too involved in
this stupid case because it's all about the Boss."

"I doubt it," I replied, maybe more tersely than I
intended. "You're good at what you do. You know it, and I
know it."

"But I just blew a capture for the second time! Those . . .
creatures have really got me rattled."

Chloridia sailed closer and peered critically at Massha.

"It's not you, darling," Chloridia told her. "You're running some kind of overload. Are you taking some kind of
new supplement, or something? An alternative-witch-
doctor potion? Pep pills?"

"No," Massha fretted. "It's the same old me. I'm not
eating or drinking anything different. It couldn't be these
pants, could it?"

I glanced at the upturned seat of the rose-colored jeans
with the gold pocket on the back. "Not a chance. No Djinn
would waste a spell on something he was going to sell to
Klahds."

"Thanks!" Massha sputtered.

I scowled. "You know what I mean. They're mass-
produced."

"So are half the joke items on Deva!"

"True," I admitted. "But would you trust a magik item
in the hands of a Klahd?"

"Well, not just any Klahd—"

"That is new," Eskina interrupted, pointing to one of the dozen or so bracelets on Massha's meaty arm.

"Yes, it is. I bought it yesterday. You certainly are observant," Massha praised her.

Eskina shrugged off the compliment. "It is my job. Is it new enough that the problems started after you bought it?"

"I—yes," Massha exclaimed, and enlightenment dawned on her face. "That's right, I never found out from the shop what it did. That's not like me."

"It might be making you misfire, darling," Chloridia pointed out.

Massha's face reddened. "I think one of the shapechangers waited on me. The store owner said she didn't work there. It's probably a magikal booby trap of some kind." She took off the bracelet and handed it to the first person she saw going the other way, a blue Dragonet female laden with bags and packages.

"Here! It'll look beautiful with your scales," Massha asserted.

The pyrosaurian didn't know what to say. "Er, thanks!" she threw back as she was swept away in the stream of fellow shoppers.

"There," Massha announced, dusting her hands together. "*Now* I'm ready to kick some shape-changing tail."

FIFTEEN

"Everybody was kung fu fighting—hyah!"

The skinny figure under the spotlights executed a few side kicks as he pranced about the small round platform over the heads of the crowd.

"Retuuuuuurrrrn to me, and always be my meeee-lody of looooovve!"

I winced. I had always suspected the Imps of inventing karaoke. It had a way of taking innocuous music and rendering it so tasteless and painful that it induced hopelessness, even suicidal tendencies, in its listeners.

The gadget could be set to hover almost anywhere, providing a slate showing lyrics, backup music, and, naturally, a mirror ball for atmosphere. Not surprisingly, Klahds were another big market for the gadgets, so no one thought twice about the fact one was making a fool of himself by singing in public there at The Mall.

"At the Copa! Copacabana!"

Chloridia's face wore a more aghast expression than mine.

"Is that your friend?" she asked. "I'd advise him not to quit his day job."

"He did," I retorted, "but not to sing."

The impostor on the stage hit a sour note.

"I can't stand that anymore," Chloridia insisted.

She raised her hand, and a lightning bolt exploded from her joined fingertips. The mirror ball over the phony's head exploded in a burst of shards. The music halted, and the lights died away.

"Thanks," I growled.

I appreciated it, but time was when I didn't need that kind of help. At least Chloridia wasn't inclined to rub it in.

"Glad to oblige."

The security force mustered from several sides, pikes at the ready. Parvattani was among the group to my left. He looked tired. He must have been chasing Skeeve sightings since morning, same as we had.

To my surprise, the impostor didn't flee when his magikal music box blew up.

"Any requests?" he shouted.

The crowd, as usual, loved a spectacle. They didn't want the show to end either, and began to yell out the names of songs. The impostor got them clapping in rhythm and burst into song again.

"Oh, I wish I was in Dixie! Hooray! Hooray! In Dixie Land I'll take my stand—Come on, everybody sing!"

I understood what he was doing. If the crowd dispersed, he had no cover. I had to raise my assessment of the intelligence of Rattila's shapeshifters, or at least this one up one notch.

Massha, now confident that her gadgets were going to behave normally, launched a burst of blue light toward the figure on the stage. It enveloped him in a beam of light that pierced right to the back of one's eyeballs. Whether they wanted the show to go on or not, the audience had to stop looking at him. I thought it was a pretty clever move on Massha's part. The people started to drift away, leaving only a few standing and staring.

"Wait, everyone!" the impostor cried. "Look!" He held up his hands, and began to make fire-shapes on the ceiling. "Look! A duck! A horse! A rabbit!"

Chloridia threw a whammy of her own, and the phony froze in place, his hands making a birdie.

I grinned ferally. He had nowhere to go and no way to get there.

Now we had him. All around us were Parvattani's guards, halberds at the ready. I gestured to them to follow me in case the impostor suddenly figured out he didn't need a voice or hand gestures to defend himself magically, using Skeeve's talent. We couldn't be too cautious.

We closed in on the fake. I took the time to decide what I was going to do to him first. Punch him out? Pull out his fingernails? Make him invoke each of his cards one at a time and snap them while he was still wearing the faces? For a change I didn't have the visceral reaction, thanks to Massha's blue fire spell hiding Skeeve's stolen face.

The nearby bards had stopped playing. It was so eerily quiet that I could hear the sound of my own breath, that of my companions, and the sound of exhalations coming from just behind my shoulder.

I spun.

Hundreds of faces surrounded us, all with red-rimmed eyes, pale complexions, and gaping mouths.

"Who are you?" I asked.

The zombie faces didn't respond. I shrugged, headed for the burning figure on the platform. The closer I got, the closer *they* got. The nearest one was a Troll with long, pale gray-blue fur that smelled like an old sofa.

"Bathe much?" I inquired. It didn't answer.

Massha waved a hand in front of their faces. "Aahz, I don't like this. They're not conscious."

"So what?" I asked. "Describes most talk-show audiences. What matters is what they do."

The impostor was still burning like a Roman candle. I kind of hoped that the spell hurt. I reached for him.

Before my hands could touch the sparkling flames, two big, hairy hands reached around and grabbed me.

A Troll in good condition is no match for a Pervect, in the sense that a dragon is no match for a Zippo lighter. I was lucky. This one was under autopilot, or at least remote control. I shook him off. A couple of Imps jumped on me from behind. I hauled one of them over my shoulder and beat the Troll over the head with him. When I was done with those two, I launched the other Imp into the crowd. A female Deveel, a slimy, yellow slug with two heads and six arms and a werewolf, all with half-lidded eyes, launched themselves in my direction. Their eyes looked *bored,* while their fists, feet, and even teeth attacked me.

"Yow!" I howled, as the werewolf latched onto my ankle with his fangs. I kicked out. "Back off, Lassie! Hey, Chumley!" I called, no longer able to see my friends in the throng. "Massha! Anybody!"

A loud roar sounded from my left. Out of the corner of my eye I saw a squidlike creature flying in a low parabola, followed by a red lizard, an adolescent Gargoyle (you could tell by the punk patterns chiseled on its skull), and a batwinged beast with bright red fur.

The guards were outclassed and outnumbered, but they fought pretty well. Though they might not have been used to weapons of Mall destruction, they were used to working in teams. Two or three would stun a shuffling shopper unconscious, then an officer with bamboo finger traps would leap on the body and immobilize the arms. In short order, they put away three Deveels, four Klahds, and a flying shark-creature.

Massha kept trying to get close to the dais, but she was in a dogfight with another of the red-winged bat-birds. Eskina galloped by, clinging to the ear of a howling Bugbear whose ear she was biting. I looked around for Chloridia. She had to make this capture. Each of us had agreed on the priorities during the briefing: get the impostor. I flipped a Klahd over onto three Kobolds. They collapsed under his weight. I fought my way one more step. Then another.

"Aiyeee!"

A body dropped on top of me. I came up fighting, grabbing my new opponent around a furry middle.

"Aagh!" a familiar voice cried.

I halted just in time to keep from throwing Eskina into the face of an oncoming Dragonet.

"They are too many," she panted.

"Naw," I insisted. "We'll get through. Stay with me." I knocked out another Imp, and she accounted for a crazed Gnome.

Where was Chloridia?

At last I spotted her. She rose straight up out of the crowd, her bright green dress gleaming.

"How dare you?" she shrieked, pausing to slap a zombie Flibberite in the face.

I watched her float toward the pseudo-Skeeve. A fold of her long dress swished over my head, covering my eyes, but I didn't have a hand free to brush it away. It whisked off, and I glanced over where she had the impostor in a headlock.

But she didn't. She was gone. And the spell she had put on the shapechanger was wearing off. There wasn't time to wonder what the hell had happened to the Kallian. I threw myself toward the Skeeve-clone. The zombies surged in on me, their blank eyes rolling as if they were auditioning for *Night of the Living Dead*. I pushed one after another out of my way, but the sheer numbers overwhelmed even my strength. The weight pushed me to the floor, pinioned my arms and legs.

"Can't breathe," Eskina gasped, her tiny figure almost invisible under the Klahd who had tackled her.

I could keep breathing, but I really couldn't move. The zombies seemed to have fallen over on me like so much cordwood. I looked up into the blank eyes.

"Coffee," I choked out.

"What?" Eskina asked in disbelief.

"They're in a trance. They need coffee. We need Sibone."

"She cannot hear you here!" she squeaked.

"She can," I insisted. "She's a seer. She's watching out for us. Sibone!"

I felt my back flatten farther and farther into the floor. My physique was more resistant to crushing than the diminutive Ratislavan, but I was reaching my limit. Suddenly I smelled that unmistakable, delectable aroma.

"Oooo-oooooh!"

The zombies were entranced beings of few words, but their meaning was obvious. Little by little the weight started to lift off my body. As soon as I could, I flipped over and crawled to Eskina's motionless body. I listened to her chest. She was only unconscious. I hoisted her over my shoulder and stood up.

Bubbles tumbled out of the sky like spherical snow. The zombies ignored us now, pursuing the iridescent bronze spheres. As the cups of life-giving brew materialized in their palms, the zombies gulped them down, then held out their hands for more. I never saw anyone who wasn't pulling an all-nighter before an engineering final drink so much coffee at one time.

Soon, consciousness returned to the diverse faces. Most of them looked confused, others angry, and the rest embarrassed for their current behavior. One large Whelf female actually had the grace to apologize for having her foot in my face.

"I am so sorry! I don't usually step on people I don't know!"

"No problem," I assured her. "Go back to your shopping."

"Oh, yes!" she exclaimed, as if the opportunity had just occurred to her. "I was looking for a new wand for my husband's birthday!"

"Pay cash," I warned her, as she minced away.

All but one of the former zombies departed. Of course, the Skeeve was long gone.

I found Massha sitting on the stairs of the dais wrapping herself around a mocha lattecino with double whipped cream. Chumley was lying on the floor with an ice pack clutched to one big eye.

"What happened back there?" Massha asked.

"We were ambushed," I stated grimly. "Chloridia poofed out, so we don't even have the phony under wraps."

"Where'd she go?

"I don't know," I replied. "But we're still at a net profit, magicianwise."

I dragged the last zombie survivor, a half-conscious Walroid, away from his extra large cappucino. He goggled at me, his wiry mustache puffing out indignantly.

"We found Cire."

"They almost got me," Strewth panted, tearing back toward the Rat Hole.

In the cover of the riot he had switched identities, assuming that of a bicycle messenger he had once encountered in a bar. He jingled his handlebar bell. Shoppers jumped out of the way of his front wheel, diving into fountains or behind bards if they had to. He pedaled grimly.

"But they didn't get you," Rattila's voice echoed in his mind. "Hurry back! I need the power you gathered."

Strewth slithered into the hidden entrance and divested himself of the bicycle messenger's form. He scrabbled on all fours into Rattila's presence and lay panting at the huge rat's feet.

"They got all the raiders," Strewth gasped. "They're no longer out of it. They're back to normal."

He expected Rattila to be furious. Instead, the Big Cheese looked jubilant.

"Why aren't you mad?" he asked.

"They're rejuvenated," the Ratislavan gloated, his red eyes gleaming. "Don't you see the benefit? We can milk them *all over again*. The magicians! The technicians! The artists! The inventors! Everyone! Their special talents will be mine. And when we've drained them again, we can restore them, and start the process all over. I shall have more power than any magician has ever dreamed of!"

"Oh, I dunno," Wassup put in, speculatively. "I bet when you get right down to it they all want the same thing. Yeowwww!"

Rattila blew out his smoking finger as the brown mall-rat hopped around trying to put out his burning foot.

"There is nothing I hate more," he hissed, "than a minion who doesn't understand hyperbole."

SIXTEEN

"Outnumbered," Chumley grunted, staggering back to our suite. He unlocked the door and stood aside.

"Only physically," I grumbled, throwing myself into an armchair. I was more dismayed than I was letting the others see. "If I didn't want to kill them, I'd have to admire their tactics."

"Yeah," Massha added glumly. "The way that one Skeeve-impersonator ran into the crowd and two of our Most Wanted split off from there. The hesitation blew my catch. I didn't know which was the fake Skeeve. I couldn't decide which one to go after."

"We want all of them," Eskina argued. "We must capture all of Rattila's workforce, so he cannot gather any more power. Who knows when he will accomplish his goal?"

"We'll have to wait until we see the Skeeve again, then make sure he cannot escape us," Chumley suggested. "But how to ensure his appearance? And how can we cut off all routes of egress?"

"I don't know," I growled. "I've got to think."

"So, man," Cire asked, throwing himself into a chair near me and letting his flipperlike hands hang over the arms, "why did you hit me?"

"A better question might be," I snarled, raising my eyes to his, "why did I stop?"

"Hey, you're not still mad about that scam back on Pokino, are you?" Cire inquired, trying on an expression of injured innocence.

"I liked you better as a zombie," I grumbled.

Cire looked embarrassed. "Thanks, pal. I really appreciate it. You know what it's like, wandering around with someone's voice in your head telling you what to do?"

"No."

"We're going about this all wrong," Massha exclaimed, throwing up her hands. "He's got us running around all over this place. It's too big! We can't cover it all. We knew that from the beginning."

"We put the ball into his court," I realized, in annoyance, tossing the atlas onto the table. "It didn't work out the way it should have. Instead of cornering him and making him give up the impersonation, we've liberated him."

"You made him come up with some new innovations anyhow," Massha pointed out.

I grimaced. She was trying to be kind, but it stung.

"That is not what I have in mind. I hope word never gets back to the kid about being seen diving naked into a fountain full of guacamole, or cavorting drunkenly with a host of ugly females."

"Or singing," Eskina added. "He is very bad at singing."

"He won't hear it from me," Massha promised.

"Or me," Chumley agreed.

"What happened to Madama Chloridia?" Parvattani asked. "She leave-a so quickly."

"Probably had another appointment," I replied. I was a little torqued that she had taken off in the middle of things like that. "She's a busy woman. Probably had to conduct an interview. I hope she'll check in with us again soon."

"In the meantime you have me," Cire interjected brightly. "That's more than a fair trade."

"Yeah," I stated curtly.

"Oh, come on, Aahz," Cire wheedled. "You're not still sore about the time I landed you in the Hoppenmar jelly mines, are you?"

I eyed him. "Let's just say you're off my holiday list for the foreseeable, okay?"

Cire opened large green eyes in play wistfulness. "Make it up to you any way I can. C'mon, we used to be partners!"

"No!" I shouldn't have shouted, but that word set off associations in my mind.

"Pals, anyway," Cire continued, not at all put out by my protest.

Truth be told, I wasn't displeased to have him on our team. He was a pretty good magician. Not in the class I had been when I had my powers, or even in Chloridia's, but adaptable and teachable.

"We cut off all the stores too soon," I began, thinking hard. "We ought to have left one outlet where he could make purchases unmolested. Something small, but irresistible. The merchandise would have to be unique and attractive, and just costly enough that the value feeds into Eskina's formula for power reward. A shop that he can't resist coming into, where he wouldn't see the trap until it sprang closed on him."

"But which of these stores fits your specifications?" Chumley asked, pointing at the atlas.

"None of them," I replied, a long, slow grin pulling the corners of my mouth outward toward my ears as my idea coalesced into shape.

Massha's eyebrows went up. "But if it doesn't exist, then how can he shop in it?"

"When we open it, he'll shop there. If we build it, he'll come. I guarantee it."

"*We* open a shop?" Massha echoed. "Aahz, you're insane."

"No, it's the only logical step," Chumley contradicted her. "He's right: we narrowed our options too quickly, what. It is in our interest to create a shop to our own design, using our specialized knowledge and what information we have so far been able to glean about Rattila's power-collection tactics."

Eskina shook her head, admiringly. "I cannot get used to you talking like a professor."

Chumley lowered his head modestly. "It's very kind of you, but I had only a brief academic career. It made more sense to go into the personal-security business. Teaching pays so poorly in comparison."

"Can we table the mutual admiration society?" I demanded, now on fire with my idea. I pushed everything on the table to one side and spread out the map. "What we need is a smallish shop, but with some room to move around, plus a space we can use to set the detention spell. It needs to be situated close to one of the big attractions, like the cinema or the most popular restaurant."

"Or one of the anchor stores," Massha interjected.

"Yeah." I started to scrutinize the listings and circled the biggest and most popular.

As usual, stores moved around a little, but the big ones tended to stay where they were. From my experience, the best prospects seemed to be the Gnome Life Department Store, The Volcano, Beezul's Club, a membership-only warehouse stocked directly from Deva, Troll Music, Hamsterama, and a shop that made me gag even from across the hall, Adorable Tchotchkes.

"I'm crossing off Beezul's Club as a neighbor," I informed the others. "If the fake gets away from us, there are just too many places to hide. Beezul's sells everything from potions to dragons."

"Not Hamsterama, please," Massha begged. "The end-less cheebling would drive me out of my mind."

"Troll Music is good," Eskina piped up.

"Too loud," we all retorted in unison.

We'd gone past Troll Music three days before while a visiting band performed a demo from its current offering, and my ears were still ringing. Massha's cone of silence amulet had begun to collapse in on itself because of overload.

"Which one do you prefer?" Parvattani asked me.

"As much as it pains me to suggest it," I mused, looking over the list, "Adorable Tchotchkes attracts a hell of a lot of shoppers, all day, every day. The Volcano is good. So is the cinema. A lot depends on what Moa will let us have at short notice. I don't know what's vacant where."

"Where?" Moa echoed, when we visited the administration offices to ask him about a vacant space. "Where is never a problem, Aahz. We move stores all the time. I'll have a word with the shops on either side of the big ones you list-ed here and see who's willing to shift. It won't be for very long, will it?"

"I hope not," I told him.

I wasn't willing to commit to a definite time frame. This enterprise had turned out to be a much longer safari than I thought coming in. Now I wasn't leaving until I had the fake Skeeve's head on a platter.

"S'all right," Moa acknowledged. He reached into the right-hand drawer of his desk and pulled out a sheaf of paper. "So, if you'll just fill these in, I'll start asking a few people. I promise that even though we're talking about a short-term lease, we'll be very reasonable about the rent."

I eyed the stack with distaste. "What's all that?"

Moa regarded me with surprise. "You're opening a store, Aahz bambino. All the right paperwork has to be filed. Lease applications, credit checks, a short essay about how you came to decide on The Mall as your target location, a copy of your personnel files, blueprints of your layout with elevations and color swatches, signed copies of Mall rules affirming that you have read and understood them, and, of course, a detailed description of what you're planning to sell." He pushed the heap toward me. "Do you need a pen?"

"I—uh . . ."

"Me do," Chumley announced, dragging the heap toward him. He glowered at Moa. "Pencil. Pleee-eeze."

"Of course, of course!" the administrator agreed, hastily going through his desk. He handed a pencil to the Troll, who gripped it awkwardly in his fist and began to form letters laboriously.

"About the merchandise," I began, "we haven't decided absolutely on what we're going to sell."

Moa's eyebrows climbed his bald forehead. "You'll excuse me for staring, but that's usually the first thing a prospective tenant knows when he's coming in here."

"I know that," I scowled. "I'm not doing this for the long term. This isn't really a retail enterprise. It's a trap. All we want is to set up a plausible-looking outlet that'll attract the pain in the butt I'm trying to catch. He comes in the door, we slam it shut behind him, and you don't ask any questions about what happens afterward. Later, we clean the place out and leave. My problem is solved, and you have your retail space back."

Moa's eyes went wide. "I shouldn't have asked. All right! Leave that part of the contract blank. You'll let me know, right?"

"Naturally," I agreed.

"Works of art," Chumley suggested, from his desk near the hearth in our room.

"No," I stated.

"Handwarmers," Eskina offered. She and Parvattani sat across from one another at the table where I tried to make a list of merchandise to sell.

I turned a blank look her way. "In here? It's hot as an armpit in The Mall. Who would buy handwarmers?"

"It was an idea," the Ratislavan exclaimed, throwing up her hands. "I have not seen anyone selling them."

"Cheeble-pets," Chumley proposed. "They're cheap and cute."

"No way," I snapped. "If someone's going to start that fad here, it's not going to be us. Have you ever spent any time in a room with one of those? You'd go nuts!"

Chumley shook his head and bent to the list he was writing. "That lets out birdcalls, too."

"You bet your furry behind it does!" I agreed.

"Candles," Eskina suggested.

"Pocket knives," Parvattani added.

"No and no."

"Garters," Massha put in, tapping me on the head. She floated above us.

"Garters?" All four of us stared up at her. She shrugged.

"Same excuse as Eskina," she apologized. "I haven't seen anything like that here, either. Garters are sexy and fun. They started out as unisex stocking fasteners, you know, not just a female accessory. In some dimensions males still wear them. But, hey! What if they weren't just garters? What if they had gizmos attached to them? Noisemakers, or a little purse you could hide your house key in, or a magikal hourglass to remind you of your appointments? It could give you a little pinch to tell you you're going to be late to the doctor's."

"That's the most ridiculous thing—" I sputtered, then my initial rage petered out as I considered the impulse habits of shoppers. "That's just stupid enough to be unique. Good thinking, Massha. All right, let's add that to the list."

Unfortunately, it wasn't a long list. Chumley had suggested novelty candy. I had rejected the novelty angle as not being enough of a big ticket, but quality goodies might just pull in a broad range of clientele. Skeeve liked candy, so if the impostors were picking up his personal traits, they would be starting to get a real sugar jones at some point. Eskina's previous ideas had included scooters with anti-crash spells on the bumpers, a pet store selling flying mice, and magic feathers that gave you the power of flight. The last was so far-fetched I laughed out loud. Eskina wasn't dismayed. She had just kept on tossing out ideas. I had to give her credit for her perseverance.

Parvattani tried hard, but he didn't have much imagination. He suggested weapons, armor, healing charms, safety devices, antitheft gizmos. If I ever wanted to open a safety-products shop, I'd put him in charge of purchasing.

Massha's offerings had all been items of personal adornment. Hats that kept telepaths or wizards from reading one's thoughts sounded like a good idea, but they were too expensive and way too delicate. I wanted to be able to return for credit any merchandise we didn't sell. Jewelry would mean we were going head to head with at least a fifth of the stores in The Mall, and we were already courting resentment for going straight to the top of the list for a vacant store, ahead of at least sixty vendors who'd been waiting, sometimes years, for a spot.

Chumley's first notion was a bookstore, wishful thinking on his part. I had said no for two reasons: one, it was unlikely to attract the thieves, who liked flashy, expensive items, and books didn't really fall into that category; and two, he might become engrossed in reading some of the stock and miss that psychological moment to grab our impostor. Truth be told, so might I.

My own mind had gone blank. Over the years I had bought plenty of goods, but my specialty was selling services, magikal or protective or both. My mind was so focused on luring the card-carrying impostors into a small place that I didn't much care what we sold.

I had already made one trip back to Deva, for a talk with the Merchants' Association. After some heartfelt bargaining they were willing to give me pretty good terms for bulk buys with allowance for return of unsold merchandise, if only we could make up our minds what we wanted to buy.

"I give up," I grumbled, crumpling another list and tossing it into the nearest corner. "Give me your best idea. I'll see what I can do with the Merchants' Association."

"Board shorts," Chumley led off.

"Cheeble-pets," Massha put in. At my dismayed face she burst out, "Well, you know they sell!"

"Bottled water," Eskina insisted.

"That is too stupid for words," I snarled. "Who outside of a desert would buy water? Par?"

The guard captain looked up shyly, glanced up at Massha, and blushed. "I, uh, I like-a Madama Massha's idea, Aahz. The garters. The romantic-a angle is very nice. Many ladies would like-a to buy them, to make their legs pretty, or a gentleman might-a enjoy buying one to adorn-a the leg of a lady he admires."

Another glance, this time toward Eskina, and Par's cheeks burned more bronzely than ever before. This time Eskina joined him, her face going pink. I couldn't help beaming. Par was a good kid. So was Eskina. If we could knock out Rattila and his henchcreature, who knew what might develop between those two?

"Okay," I breathed. "All in favor of Chumley's suggestion?" No hands went up. "Massha's?" Nothing. "Eskina's?" Bravely, Par raised his hand.

"Do not vote for mine," the Ratislavan chided him, though she looked pleased. "It was stupid! All in favor of Parvattani's?"

All of us, except the abashed guard captain, put up our hands.

"All right," I concluded, rising from my seat. "I'll go see what kind of a deal I can do with the Deveels."

SEVENTEEN

The razzing from the Merchants' Association over my order for fifty dozen assorted garters, a mix of magikally endowed and non, lasted just long enough for the assembled business owners to speculate on how fast they could get the same item into their shops, and how much they could undercut their neighbors.

"Of course we can help you, Aahz," Frimble, head of the Devan Marketing Association, insisted. He was a scrawny, middle-aged Deveel with a slick little black beard, which he stroked with a speculative thumb and forefinger. "Naturally there will be a surcharge for rush delivery—and set-up fees—and a percentage to ensure exclusivity for a period of say, oh, seven days—"

"Add it up," I agreed, "and cut the total by fifty percent."

Frimble screamed. "What? You'd be cutting the throats of your friends! What kind of ingrate are you? For top quality you would have to pay double!"

"I wasn't born yesterday," I argued back. "And I doubt I'll be getting top quality anyhow."

"How dare you!" yelled Ingvir, a potbellied Deveel who

sold dry goods. He hoped to supply the twill ribbons and buckles, but I intended it to be on my terms, not his. "You son of a skink! I should know better than to try and do business with Perverts!"

"That's Pervect!" I roared.

"It's Pervert if you think I sell second-rate merchandise!"

"It's Pervect, and you do sell second-rate merchandise!" I exclaimed. "Maybe I should take my business elsewhere?"

"Who'd do business with *you?*" His voice rose in a shriek.

I started to relax. Deveel negotiation was always conducted at the top of their lungs. After several days of the genteel hum of The Mall I had started to forget how real trading was done.

"Ten percent discount," Coulbin shot at me.

He also manufactured small metal objects. The buckles he displayed were a little better looking than Ingvir's, and Ingvir knew it.

"Forty-five," I countered.

"Fifteen," Ingvir argued. "And I will cut you a deal on gold plating."

"Forty."

"Twenty," Coulbin shouted. "Gold-plating included!"

I was starting to enjoy myself, and Frimble hadn't even gotten into the fray yet. He held back, though, until the other two had made me identical offers at thirty percent off the original offer.

"Thirty," Frimble stated, "delivery included."

"You can't undercut us!" Coulbin shrieked. "You'd be buying the product from us anyhow!"

The argument started up afresh.

"Shut up!" I roared, over their voices. "Why not form a consortium?" I suggested, reasonably. "If this takes off, everybody could make a ton of money. And after a week, you can start selling them for yourselves. I won't need to have an exclusive for longer than that."

The Deveels all shot one another the kind of looks that never kill when you need them to. Frimble nodded curtly.

"All right, it's a deal," he stated. "Delivery in three days."

"Fine," I assented.

Without a word of thanks or farewell they all turned their backs on me and started the argument up all over again. I wasn't offended. I had known Deveels for over a hundred years, and they were like that. Once a sale was done, you were off the radar. They were already onto the next moneymaking effort, which in this case was deciding who would get what piece of my pie. I didn't care. The goods only had to be priced so I didn't lose my shirt and pretty enough and functional enough to attract the shapechangers' attention. If the garters fell apart the day after we captured them, I didn't care.

Leaving the Deveels to their argument, I *bamfed* out for Flibber.

"No!" Massha yelled, hanging overhead like a huge, gaudy mobile. "Paint the walls before you put down the carpet. I thought you people did this all the time!"

The Flibberites rolling out the mauve rug rolled it back up again and returned to the buckets and brushes near the walls.

"She tell-a us to do it the other way," one of them whispered to the other.

"Yeah, but she tell-a us to do it the first way the first time!" They glanced at me over their shoulders and hastily bent to their task.

Massha noticed me and floated down to my level. "How'd it go?"

"We're all set," I assured her. "The stuff will arrive in three days. Once we get this place fixed up, all we have to do is open the door and wait."

"What kind of bags did you get?" she asked.

"Bags?" I inquired blankly.

"To put sales in."

"We don't need bags!"

Massha gave me a hard look.

"All right, what about tissue paper? Tags? Gift cards? Antitheft devices? Receipts? Stationery? Business cards? And have you hired any clerks yet? I think I can train them, but it wouldn't hurt to get someone with real retail experience in here first."

"Hey!" I bellowed. "What are you trying to do here?"

Massha put her hands on her hips. "Set up a shop, sugar pie. I may never have run one, but I've been in thousands of them. Take the Bazaar. Most deals there are verbal, but even the Deveels wrap up small goods when you take them out of the store. Otherwise, how do you tell the shoppers from the shoplifters? Also, it's a courtesy for merchandise that's easily broken, soiled or"—she grinned—"a little embarrassing, like underwear. And what we're going to put on the walls falls into that category."

"I—er—I didn't think of bags," I admitted.

"Do you want me to take care of it? You'd have to take over here."

I looked around at the workers plastering, painting, and papering. The smell was already making my eyes water. "I'll do it."

I headed for the door. "And what about music?" she called behind me.

"I'm already on it!" I assured her.

"Naturally, naturally," Moa remarked, when I laid out the situation for him. "We can take care of everything for you. We do it for hundreds of the stores here. A lot of them are sole proprietors, don't have the time or expertise, or access to the right resources. I'll send a Djinn around to you at your hotel. He'll get everything you need."

"Marco at your service!" exclaimed the cheerful, portly Djinn in purple robes who appeared at the door of our suite. He bowed.

"Another Djinnelli?" I asked, showing him in.

He beamed at me. "My cousin Rimbaldi said you were a sharp observer! We are so happy you decide to join our little community! Now, come, let me show you all the things we can offer."

Marco waved his hands. The room filled with huge, hardbound sample books.

"Shall we begin?" he inquired.

"The visitors are doing what?" Rattila asked.

Garn timidly extended a paint chip to his master. "They're opening a shop. This is the color. I just spent three hours painting the walls. There was nothing else to steal yet except this. They don't even have a name."

Rattila rubbed his paws together. "How fitting!" he cackled. "They are going to assist me in draining the essence of their own friends, and I can use their own merchandise to do it! What are they selling?"

Garn rubbed his nose with a paw. "I dunno."

"Then go back! I want a full report. I want to see it," Rattila added greedily, "with my own eyes."

"Boxes," I decided finally, after going through dozens of packaging options.

"Good choice, Master Aahz," Marco congratulated me. He threw a hand toward the hovering examples. "Now, flat square, cubic, flat round? You have all these choices because this handsome little item"—he flourished one of our sample garters—"would look beautiful in all of them." He kissed his fingertips. "Now, which one would you like best, if you were bringing a present to a beautiful lady?"

I have always prided myself on being able to scope out the psychology of people I was dealing with. In this case, I had to guess how people I didn't know yet would think. The factors that went into the decision were subtle. Now, subtle I could do, no problem, but I wasn't sure about generally popular.

"Flat round," I announced at last.

"Very nice!" Marco agreed, jotting a note on the notepad that followed us around the room. "Out of the ordinary. I recommend two sizes, for a single item, and for two or three."

"No," I corrected him, narrowing my eyes at the floating boxes. "Just the one size. We're trying to go for the special, one-of-a-kind look."

"Then you need ribbons, or bags to put multiple boxes in."

"Ribbons," I decided at once. "Three colors. White—no, silver boxes, three colors of purple ribbon. Pink's too namby-pamby. If we're going for solid sex appeal, then let's go for it."

"It's a pleasure to do business with such a decisive personality, Aahz!" Marco exclaimed heartily. "Except for my cousins, everybody is so timid; and then they are so unhappy with the results."

"You oughta set up shop in the Bazaar," I suggested, with a grin. "We get the screaming out of the way in advance there."

"And, now," Marco went on smoothly, "a catalog?"

"No," I stated flatly. "We're gonna change styles all the time."

Truth was, I had given the Deveels a fairly free hand, and I wasn't sure what they would come up with. Also, the less of a paper trail I could leave, the better. The last thing we needed was to have a catalog turn up ten years from now, and have someone bug us in the middle of an important operation in search of a size eight blue left-handed garter with marabou.

"Ah!" Marco exclaimed, enlightened. "You are an exclusive boutique. I understand."

"Yeah. A boutique." I was picking up all kinds of vocabulary as I went.

Marco made notes. "So you will want purple-and-silver tissue. Business cards—magikal will cost you a gold piece per hundred. Paper, a thousand per gold piece."

"Paper. Er, silver ink on deep purple card. Shiny." I began to picture it in my mind. "A little frilly ring in the upper right-hand corner. The store number in the bottom right."

"And the name?" Marco asked, pencil poised.

"Uh." He had me there. I hadn't even considered what we were going to call it. "Garterama?"

"Not a boutique name," the Djinn declared firmly.

I wasn't really the marketing specialist. "We Are Garters?" I grinned evilly as a thought struck me. "Garter Snake?"

Marco wiggled a hand. "Not really family appeal. A few species would respond to that favorably, but some won't. Cute is what you want. Perky. Make the buyers think they're in on something special."

"Not bad," I mused.

Good advice. But what could we let the punters in on? I had to admit that I was surprised that Massha had suggested garters in the first place. Not that she was body-shy; her normal attire was a modified harem-girl outfit. And she had a healthy attitude about love and marriage. She'd waited long enough for them, after all. I don't know why her idea took me off guard. I guess it had been a long time since I'd thought about the little things that made a relationship romantic. She knew them, and she was willing to share.

"How about Massha's Secret?"

Marco kissed his fingertips. "The delectable lady? Perfect, perfect! Yes, that will attract the visitors, you wait and see! Shall I prepare a lovely portrait of her to hang on the wall over the counter? It can wink at each person!"

I cringed. "I don't think that's what she's got in mind. But, uh, you could put a winking eye on the receipts."

Marco waved a hand, and a nice line drawing of a long-lashed eye appeared on the notepad.

"Thicker line there, and more curve in the lashes. Yeah. Substitute that for the garter on the cards, too. And you mentioned in-Mall ads. A simple line drawing in purple on white or silver posters. No text, at least not at first. Let them wonder. Then add the store number in the second round. Then add a slogan, 'Do you know Massha's Secret?' Yeah. I like that."

"You are very subtle for a Pervect!" Marco exclaimed.

I nodded with satisfaction. "I've been around. Now, what about key chains? And maybe lapel pins? Bumper stickers?"

"T-shirts?" Marco asked, writing furiously.

"No!" I exclaimed. "I don't want to go crazy on this. I'm just trying to sell garters."

Marco and I quickly agreed on the rest of the designs, colors, and quantity of each item. I thought Massha and the others would be pleased, and the intrigue ought to bring in the punters on the run. Everyone loved a mystery. Half the fun was becoming an insider before the other people you knew.

"And to prevent theft," Marco concluded, with a flourish, "the very latest in deterrents!"

He presented me with a very small wooden box. I opened it, to behold a second lid, this one of glass. Beneath the glass was a small, very angry-looking black-and-white bee. It threw itself at the lid, trying to get out at us.

"They are very hard to kill, they cannot be bought off

with honey or other sweets, and they cannot be removed without the correct spell. Anyone who carries a piece of merchandise past the alarm belt, which you will place around your door, will be stung repeatedly. The bees also have a very loud buzz, which can be heard for several feet."

"Perfect," I acknowledged, handing the box back. "We'll take a hiveful."

Marco tossed the box into the air. It vanished.

"Then we are finished. Thank you for the order. You are much easier to work with than many of your species."

"Thanks, I think," I replied sourly.

"I just wonder—" the Djinn began, with a pensive look on his broad face, "because you came here to catch a thief—my cousins and I hope that your new interest in the retail industry will not take your attention away from that ambition."

"Hell, no," I assured him. "That's still our primary focus. All this is to help out with the hunt. Keep that under your turban, though."

"Of course, of course!" Marco exclaimed, overjoyed. "Then we give you the best service, and the fastest delivery!" He kissed me on both cheeks. "I will see you, tomorrow by noon! You will be very pleased, I promise."

"You look happy," Massha declared, as I strutted back into the shop.

Chumley was hammering racks into the wall with his bare hands, aided by Eskina, who passed him nails as he asked for them. The décor was about finished. Three of the walls were mauve, and one was about the same shade as Chumley's fur. The Flibberite painters, looking pale and tired, staggered out with the buckets, ladders and drop cloths. I waited until they were out of earshot before I replied.

"Come and see what I've got," I invited them.

The small back room had been divided into two
spaces. One of them was the storeroom, for back stock.
The other was a cozy mirrored room where customers
could see how they would look in a garter without having
to try it on

"It's my own spell," Cire explained smugly.

"And it has nothing to do with that hairdresser on Imper
who was using the same idea more than twenty years ago,
huh?"

Cire looked hurt. "Mine has a lot of new wrinkles!
Really!"

"Like?"

"Like," Cire echoed, a crafty expression on his broad
face, "that Imp hairdresser didn't have anything in her
spell that compared the customer in her chair with the list
of Rattila's victims."

"If one of the misused faces enters," Chumley added,
"the door will refuse to open. The room is quite secure. I
have tested it myself."

"Nice. Nice," I assured them, nonchalantly. "Now, I've
been doing really important work."

I spread out the boxes, ribbons, papers, sample posters,
and other items on the table in the back room.

Cire goggled. "This is important?"

"You can't just throw open the doors without the right
ambience in place," I snarled. "It'd look too amateurish."

I hoped Massha wouldn't toss it back in my face that it
had been her idea. But she was turning over the boxes and
cards with a look of delight on her face.

"Oh, Aahz, honey," Massha cooed. "They're beautiful!
'Massha's Secret'?" She went scarlet, but she leaned over
to kiss me on the cheek.

"Don't get soft," I snapped. But inwardly I was glad she
liked it. "Think all of this will lure the thieves in?"

"They will not be able to resist," Chumley assured me.

Massha looked it all over again, holding up the ribbons
and other little knickknacks. I felt a surge of pride.

Everything was coordinated and professional-looking, and, I was sure, guaranteed to appeal to the chosen market. But an expression of faintly puzzled discomfort crossed her face.

"Aahz, honey," Massha remarked at last, holding a ribbon up next to my face. "You clash."

EIGHTEEN

With pride and trepidation I stood at the entrance to the shop two mornings later. Our hired musician, Gniggo, a Gnomish pianist whose keyboard hung suspended in midair, played old standards, vying desperately against the disco beat blatting from the bards just outside in the corridor and the sale music piping out good and loud from above the store façade. In spite of the protection of Massha's amulet, my ears were killing me.

The Mall itself had opened only ten minutes before, but I was not surprised that hundreds of shoppers had already found their way to the newest store on the block.

Moa himself had agreed to be present at the grand opening. We also had a full contingent of security personnel on guard in case any of the counterfeits made an appearance. Though, after Sibone's intervention the other day, we had to be careful that we intercepted real phonies, not the originals whose identities had been hijacked by Rattila and restored from zombiehood by the emergency infusion of coffee. Most of the rescued shoppers were back in The Mall, making up for lost time.

Parvattani, in full uniform, caught my eye from the edge of the crowd and waggled a finger unobtrusively. I grumbled to myself. It meant neither he nor any of his guards had managed to spot any of the impostors coming into The Mall. I knew they were there somewhere; I could feel it.

To deafening cheers, Moa walked out in front of the crowd with his arms raised. He turned toward the store entrance and beckoned.

Massha, decked out in a brand-new outfit of purple silk gauze trousers and abbreviated harem-girl top with silver trim and with her orange hair in a knot on the top of her head, floated casually on her side with her head propped casually on her fist to hover beside Moa. The right leg of the trousers was slit from ankle to hip, letting a lace-and-silk silver, purple-and-pink garter with a tiny silver pouch on the side peek out.

"Mwah!" Rimbaldi Djinnelli threw her a passionate kiss from the front of the crowd. "*Bella donna!* She is one of my best customers, you know," he told the Imp next to him.

"Massha, will you do the honors?" Moa asked.

Massha reached into the tiny pocket of the garter and drew out a gigantic pair of silver shears three feet long. The crowd gasped, then cheered. She slapped them into Moa's hand.

Moa, an old pro, stepped to one side, allowing the center of the ribbon to be visible to the crowd. "I now declare this store open. You should shop here in good health."

He cut the ribbon and ducked hurriedly to one side as an avalanche of buyers thundered into Massha's Secret.

"Ooooh! Aaaah! That's beautiful! I must have that!"

I allowed myself a wide grin, listening to the murmurs, cries, and howls of approval as the visitors perused the new merchandise.

"Mine!" shrieked a female werewolf, hanging on to one side of a powder blue feather garter adorned with a golden jewel.

"Mine!" bellowed a female Gargoyle, firmly attached to the other end.

The werewolf took a swipe at the Gargoyle, and blunted her pink-painted claws on the Gargoyle's stone flesh. The Gargoyle rose into the air, trying to take the disputed item with her. The Djinnies we had hired from one of Marco's cousins started to move in to separate the combatants. Chumley waded in from his post near the wall. I relaxed. If I had any doubts as to whether this place was going to be a success, they were dispelled. We were off to a great start.

Massha plunked herself down in the violet-upholstered "husband waiting chair" under the ostrich-feather fan to the left side of the door.

"I have never been so worn-out in my life!" she declared. "Well, maybe once or twice," she corrected herself with a grin. "This was almost as much fun, though."

"No details!" I protested, trying not to let pictures pop into my head as I counted out the cash box. "That's a secret you can keep to yourself."

The Djinnies, popping gum, finished tidying up what was left of the display, and departed. The guards Par had left on duty sat against the wall next to Chumley.

"Ni-iiice," I drawled, letting coins run through my fingers. "We've already got enough here to pay off the Deveels and about half of Marco's bill. By tomorrow we ought to be running in the black."

"We did very well!" Chumley exclaimed.

"Not really," I grunted, perturbed, as I totaled sums in my head. "It means our prices are too low. If the items are jumping off the shelves like that, it means we're under the threshold of what we could be charging. Let's raise everything fifty percent by tomorrow."

"You're kidding," Massha goggled. "We made a fortune."

"We've got an exclusive here," I argued. "We've got it for one week before the Deveels start copycat operations. Let's make the most of it."

"All right," Massha responded, dubiously. "You know what you're doing."

Eskina moved around the walls, poking here and sniffing there. She stopped, one foot still in the air, her eyes wide.

"What's up?" I asked her.

"It's his scent!" she replied. "I smell him! Rattila was here!"

"When?" we all asked at once.

The Ratislavan investigator closed her eyes and concentrated. "Not long before the store closed. The scent is still warm."

"Can you follow it?" I asked, but she was already on the move.

Par jumped to his feet to follow her. I tucked the bag of coins in my pocket and ran along behind.

Baying low in her throat, the Ratislavan investigator ran out into the corridor. The last few stragglers were being herded toward the nearest exit by a few of the guards. The bards had already packed up. All the noises that usually filled The Mall had died away in the distance. Eskina picked up speed. I had to run to keep up with her. The little figure in the thick white fur coat had stopped looking cuddly and harmless. We saw her in full police mode, the equal or better to Parvattani and his security force.

Cire scrambled alongside me.

"I was going to tell you, we had a few false positives in the chamber today."

I frowned. "Why didn't your trap work?"

"Well, the people proved they were the real thing," Cire explained. "Their credit was good. They didn't act like impostors."

I smacked my forehead. "Half of the identity victims cleaned up their credit rating as soon as we pulled them out of their trance! As for acting like the real thing, the impostors are *really* good at letting the personality in the card overwhelm their own. I'm sure when they were pretending to be you they were pretty convincing, too!"

"Oh," Cire murmured in a very small voice. "I guess I should have told someone."

"Never mind," I spat out. "If Eskina can lead us to Rattila, the whole mechanism's going to collapse anyway."

Walroids! It was all coming back to me in clear and lucid memories why I had stopped hanging around with Cire. Too bad Chloridia had split. I thought of sending a message bubble to Kall to ask her when she was coming back.

Eskina reached the big intersection in front of Hamsterama. She ran back and forth in zigzags, stopping before the metal gate that barred the door. Her eyes were fixed on something very far away as she concentrated on keeping the scent in her mind.

"Open up," I ordered Par.

"The master key!" he ordered. A guard sprang forward with a magik wand and touched it to the gates. They popped open. Eskina let out a howl and snuffled her way inside. We followed into the twilit shop.

"Cheeble cheeble cheeble cheeble cheeble!" the small, furry denizens of the shop greeted us in their high-pitched voices from their little wooden hutches. Some of them put down the poker hands they were playing, others looked up from their knitting or books. I eyed them suspiciously. Were they harboring a fellow rodent somewhere? We didn't know where he might have gone to ground, so I signaled to Chumley to hang out by the door. Massha levitated to the ceiling, and I took a position against one of the turquoise-painted walls, where I could see the rest of the store.

Eskina quested among the habitats, with Parvattani on her heels, his pikestaff at the ready, presumably in case Rattila sprang out at her. Every so often Eskina would glare over her shoulder at the captain. I grabbed him as they passed me.

"Give her a little space," I whispered.

Startled, he stepped back two paces. Eskina's shoulders relaxed, but she kept her nose near the floor. Around and around she went. The cheebling rose to a deafening squeal as the resident hamsters caught her sense of urgency.

Abruptly, Eskina turned around and snuffled her way toward the door. Baying, she ran out and turned right, continuing on down the hall. I sniffed the air: hamsters, disinfectant, a faint whiff of sulfur, the lingering body aromas from a million weary shoppers. A Pervect has keen senses, especially hearing and sight, but my nose must be no match for a Ratislavan raterrier. She could pick out one subtle scent from the overwhelming smell and follow it.

"Awoooo!" she howled, by then pretty far ahead of us.

Rattila had covered a lot of ground since he had left Massha's Secret. Was Eskina moving fast enough to catch him?

"Rooooo!"

I cringed. We didn't stand a chance unless he was deaf as a post.

Faster and faster she ran. We stayed right with her, past the empty bandstands, past the shuttered pushcarts, and block after block of empty, dark showcases.

"The scent is fresh here!" Eskina called to us. "He was here only moments ago!"

I felt my blood rise. When I got my hands on that Rattila, I was going to take him to pieces. Chumley's big jaw was set so hard the fur on his face bristled. Massha had a handful of jewelry ready. We were loaded for bear.

"Awoooo!" Eskina howled, and swung around the next corner, past The Volcano.

It was always too hot around there. If I saw Jack Frost, I was going to remind him to turn up the air-conditioning. The scent led her around the next bend, past a row of tents. Eskina was panting with excitement.

In and out of the canvas jungle we wove, following the eager tracker. She let out a delighted cry.

An echo of the shrill sound came from just ahead of us. We all shut up and listened. Someone was whistling.

Around the tent occupied by Potpourri King came a squeaking cart drawn by a knee-high ungulate. Behind it

an elderly Flibberite swished a mop from side to side across the shining floor. He looked up at us, and the whistle died away. He squinted through the gloom

"Eskina, isn't it?"

"Treneldi?" Eskina inquired.

The old janitor grinned and swashed forward with his mop. "What're you doing out so late, eh, dearie? Thought you'd be in the bed shop by now, turning around three times."

"Did you see anyone come through here?" I demanded.

Treneldi peered up at the ceiling ponderingly. "Not since the doors closed, no."

Eskina quested around frantically, roaming from side to side of the corridor. "The scent is gone."

"Damn!" I growled.

"C'n I help you find something?" he asked.

I looked at the huge pail aboard the ungulate's cart. "No, it looks like you have already taken care of it for us."

"Good night to you, then, sir," Treneldi replied. He resumed whistling and mopping, elbowing his way past Chumley and Parvattani.

"That's it," I declared. "We lost it. Come on. We'll check out the next hundred yards. If we don't pick it up again, we'll call it a night."

"So close!" Eskina wailed.

"Very close, my little countrywoman," Rattila muttered happily to himself, pushing the mop across the floor as he watched all the swagger droop out of the visitors' stride. He yanked back on the ungulate's tether. "Slow down. I am missing spots."

"Strewth!" the little beast said. "Why do we have to do it at all?"

"Never slack off when someone is looking," Rattila replied. "Isn't that your own rule, you mall-rats? Besides, they are not gone yet. Hush!"

The big green one called Aahz came charging back as though his feet were on fire.

"One side, blueface," he snarled.

Idly, Rattila drifted to one side. The other visitors came along swiftly behind, dodging the beast and bucket as the mop licked around their feet.

"So observant they think they are," Rattila murmured smugly. "They don't notice the humble floor cleaner is hovering several inches above the floor."

"Now can we go back?" Strewth whined. Rattila kicked him.

"*When* we finish the floor." He smiled. "I am enjoying myself."

NINETEEN

"I suppose we could have lost the scent at some other point, what?" Chumley suggested wearily, as we sat slumped against the entrance to Massha's Secret.

Massha had dropped off long ago, snoring in musical tones. Eskina had been game as they come, rechecking all the points we had gone over, in case Rattila had doubled back at any point and disappeared into a wall or something. She had nodded off, too, curled up against Massha's side. Cire lay on his back, out to the wide, domed belly upward, his flipperlike hands flat out at his sides. Par had had to go back to the barracks to check over the graveyard shift and maybe get a few winks. I couldn't get comfortable on the shiny floor, but my pride wouldn't let me give up and go back to the hotel.

"We missed something," I acknowledged, going through the memory of the night before. "Where? What?"

"I say, don't berate yourself, Aahz," Chumley offered sympathetically. "If Rattila is so emboldened as to venture out, into our very environs, it means that he thinks he is becoming stronger, or that we are vulnerable."

My keen ears picked up the rustle of footsteps. I looked around. They seemed to be coming from everywhere. They became louder, multiplied. I sprang to my feet and braced myself.

Suddenly, the owners of the feet hove into view: the shopkeepers and clerks returning to The Mall.

"Good morning, Aahz!" The Faery owner of Adorable Tchotchkes threw a smile our way as she waved a wand and disenchanted the night lock.

The big pink-and-blue doors flew wide, and tinkly music poured out of the store. Others called out greetings to us as they opened for the day.

"False alarm," I grunted, sitting down again.

"Aren't you opening up today?" asked Pitta, the Impish owner of Pitta's Petite Pitas, the food shop two down from ours.

"Huh?"

Pitta blushed pinkly. "I want to get a garter to surprise my boyfriend."

"Oh," I replied, feeling a little stupid. I had been concentrating so hard on how we failed to track Rattila that it slipped my mind that we had a perfectly good trap already armed and set. "Yeah. Of course, we're opening up."

I nudged everyone awake.

"Mine!"

"Mine!"

"Get your claws off it! It's mine!"

A three-way brawl in the middle of the shop between two Deveels and a Dragonet didn't faze the shoppers bumping one another to get to the wall displays. In The Mall it was just business as usual. I kept a close eye on Cire to make sure he didn't let any more "false positives" go by.

"They all look nice," Eskina insisted impatiently to an Imper female who stood in front of a mirror unable to make up her mind among half a dozen garters she was modeling on each leg. "It doesn't matter which one you choose."

"Well, I don't know . . ." the Imp dithered.

Eskina reached out and pulled out a loop of black lace and yellow ribbon roses, and let it snap back against the Imp's pink thigh. "Take that one. Don't argue."

I sighed. It wasn't worth it, trying to turn a lifetime, hard-bitten investigator into a tactful and patient salesperson.

To my surprise, the Imp beamed with gratitude. "Oh, thank you! Yes, that's the one I like best!" She peeled off the others and put them back.

Eskina turned away with a smirk.

Marco Djinnelli floated in. "Everything looks so wonderful!" he exclaimed, gesturing at the decorations. "All of the little touches . . . you have good taste, Aahz."

"Not just me," I grunted, though I was pleased. "My team likes to get down to those little details."

The Djinn beamed effusively. "And you have made them. Er—as we agreed, half my payment today, please?"

"No problem," I assured him, leading him to the counter. We had counted out his share into a small bag that I left in a box with the remaining security bees. They hummed fierce-ly at me as I retrieved the bag, but we had had words earlier, and they didn't even come close to stinging. "As we agreed."

"Thank you, my friend, thank you!" Marco declared, winding the bag into the sash that went around his ample middle. "I will be back in a few days, also as we agreed. I wish you a profitable day, eh?"

"Thanks, pal," I grunted.

Marco floated off, and I locked up the box. That was out of the way. Now to earn the other half of his fee and clean up a little profit for ourselves.

"Now, when you fasten the buckle it turns on the alarm on the grouch bag, honey," Massha informed an eager pur-chaser as she folded a zebra-striped leg bangle into a box. "If you forget to disarm it before you take it off, it's going to howl bloody murder and deafen everybody for three blocks around. Let me get the bee off there. Enjoy it."

She tucked the money into a bag.

A Deveel woman stepped up with a stack of frou-frou items and the light of battle in her eye.

"How much?" she asked.

Massha tucked the bag of coins into her generous cleavage and started out from behind the counter.

"Hey!" the Deveel protested.

"What?" Massha asked, startled. Probably a little dazed from lack of sleep. I sidled in beside her.

The customer pursed her lips. "You're not going to tell me the prices are fixed here. Not when they're so high!"

Massha seemed to snap out of it and smiled sweetly at the Deveel.

"They're fair. I defy you to find lower prices for this quality anywhere else in The Mall."

"You know perfectly well no one else in The Mall is selling garters!"

The smile became tooth-achingly sweet. Massha was fine now.

"Of course I do, honey. Now, do you want them gift-wrapped?"

The Deveel wouldn't have been a Deveel if she hadn't tried one more time for a bargain. She gave a friendly, woman-to-woman grin.

"Discount for volume?"

I showed all my teeth. "Priced as marked. If you don't want them, the broads behind you will grab them the second you put them down."

The Deveel gave me a look of disgust and clapped the items into Massha's hand. "All right! *Perverts*."

"Pervect," I corrected her, but I didn't really care.

She was counting out coins, resentfully but accurately. More sales in spite of the jacked-up prices meant we were really making a splash. In a little while I was going to have to head back to Deva to pick up another shipment.

A flipperlike limb emerged from the gap in the purple curtains at the rear of the store and signaled frantically. I glanced at Massha.

"I'm fine, Big Shot," she assured me, elbowing me in the ribs. "I just took a little standing nap. I'm going to sleep well tonight. Better see what he wants. Don't worry about old Massha."

"If you're certain . . ." I began, leaving her an out if she wanted one.

"Yes! I'm just not as young as I used to be. Hustle. Cire's getting a little wild there."

She was right. The hand waved more energetically. I signed to Chumley, who moved up a little to support Massha, and headed toward the back room. As casually as I could, I slid behind the curtain into the recessed niche. There wasn't much room beside the excited Walroid, and he nearly whacked me with his flipper.

"What's up?" I asked.

His broad face came up from the magikal black-rimmed lens, a commercial spyglass that we used to monitor the goings-on in the dressing room.

"I've got two," Cire whispered. "The alarm spell went off, very strongly. I wasn't going to let you down again, Aahz. This time I'm sure. I got accurate facial overlays from the globes that the Djinni merchants are using. These two are the goods!"

"Let me see," I growled.

I peered into the lens. I recognized the two-headed female and the sharklike being as two of the bodies I had tried on.

"They've stuffed about eight garters into their handbags and clothing," Cire explained over my shoulder. "They brought about twenty apiece in there with them. They're still trying them on. After that they're going to figure out they can't get out. What do you want to do?"

"Let me think a minute," I breathed, staring into the magikal peephole.

We could just tear in there and interrogate them, but that would kick up a fuss and maybe scare off any other shapechangers moseying around the store.

"Can you throw a silence spell on the room, keep any-one out there from hearing through the walls?"

Cire frowned. "The detection spell needs constant attention, Aahz. It's pretty intricate. You don't want me to have to rebuild it from scratch. It takes a lot of concentration."

"And you can't concentrate on more than one thing at a time?" I asked.

Cire folded his arms. "Okay, big mouth, you throw the silence spell!"

"All right, all right," I growled. I hated being powerless. Chloridia wouldn't have given me such an argument. "I'll go in and chat with them. Disguise me as one of the sales-girls. You can multitask on a simple disguise, can't you?"

"Yes!" he responded peevishly. "Boy, anyone would think you'd remember the last time we were together in Miniam."

"I DO remember the last time we were together in Miniam," I rejoined.

"All right, there's no need to be huffy about it," Cire replied, more subdued. He closed his eyes and concentrated. "Okay. You're done. You make a cute Djinnie."

"Thanks a heap," I grumbled.

"Which one of you is Massha?" a harsh voice bellowed over the music and the usual screaming of the customers out in the showroom.

"That's me, Tall and Indigo. What can I do for you?"

I listened with half an ear while I studied our prey.

"We've got to separate them from their decks of cards," I told Cire. "Where do you suppose they're keeping them?"

"I didn't notice them in the two-headed gal's handbag. The one with the teeth's got a bigger bag, but she's not wearing any clothes."

"You're operating in this Mall illegally," the rough voice exclaimed.

"No, we're not," Massha replied, still friendly. "Got a business license and a lease, right up there on the wall."

"That isn't enough, and you know it!" the voice growled, low and threatening.

"No, I don't know anything of the kind," Massha answered, patiently but more firm than cordial.

"Trouble," Cire muttered.

I glanced out between the curtains at the speaker. The athletic-looking Flibberite in the dull plum-colored tunic reminded me a lot of Woofle, with businesslike mien, and the big guys behind him reminded me of Woofle's muscle men, or maybe the Mob that held sway in Klah. It occurred to me that there might be an equivalent to Don Bruce's boys in The Mall. Maybe we hadn't greased all the palms we had to.

"Change of plans," I snapped out. "Drop the disguise. Now!"

"Make up your mind," Cire grumbled, but he shut his eyes. As soon as he opened them, I hustled out into the showroom, wearing a conciliatory grin.

"Couldn't help overhearing you," I informed him. "Can I help you?"

"I was just talking to the owner of this establishment," the Flibberite stated dismissively, and turned away.

I grabbed his arm and turned him back. The two muscle men started forward.

"She is the owner, but I'm the business manager. Name's Aahz. What can we do for you?"

The speaker shook off my hand and plunked a card down in front of me.

"Inspector Niv Dota, Flibber Revenue. Have you filed for a tax identification card? The department has no record of an application from any firm doing business as Massha's Secret."

Taxes!

"Er—" I glanced at Chumley, who raised his hands to his shoulders. "I thought so. We filled out a whole ream of forms with The Mall's administration." I grinned even more amiably, which caused him and his escorts to backpedal a few paces.

The inspector recovered his aplomb faster than Woofle had, but, then, tax people had to have ice water in their veins.

"The Mall is not empowered to issue tax identification

cards. You must apply in person at a licensed Flibber Revenue Office."

"Really?" I asked, my eyes wide with innocence. "We weren't informed of that fact."

"Any business, especially demon-owned, must have proper documentation," Dota snapped out. "And that information is part of the language of any commercial lease issued anywhere in this dimension, so I am sure you were informed. So I have to ask myself," he continued, leaning toward me, his eyes slitted dangerously, "did you skip over reading all of the fine print in the papers you signed, or did you decide you might . . . get lucky? Maybe we wouldn't . . . notice?"

"Of course not," I replied smoothly, coming around the counter and dropping an arm onto his shoulders. He cringed. I held on. "Inspector, I am sure that we can work this out to everyone's satisfaction. Naturally we want to be law-abiding members of society—"

"Hey! Let us out!" a shrill female voice howled.

"The door's stuck!" two more voices joined in, as the two-headed woman added her complaint.

I looked innocently at the inspector's frown. "Malfunction in the dressing room. We'll take care of it in a minute."

"You're going to have to close down," the inspector gritted.

"Sure!" I agreed. "At the end of the day. You see, we're not really—"

"No. Now."

Eskina moved up, protest in her eyes. I shook my head surreptitiously.

"Excuse me a minute."

"What'll we do, sugar?" Massha asked in an undertone.

I leaned over to her and Eskina. "Go shut them up if you can. Let Chumley take the register. I'll take care of this." I turned back to Dota. "Now, about that card—like I was trying to tell you, we're not really businesspeople trying to run a store."

"No kidding," the inspector replied, with the air that he'd heard this story before. I felt my temper rising, but I pushed on.

"Look," I stated flatly. "We're interdimensional investigators tracking down a ring of dangerous thieves in this Mall. My colleague over there has a badge from the dimension of Ratislava. All we need is a few days."

Dota interrupted me. "Even if such a wild story was true, it's not my jurisdiction. You ought to have applied for the correct credentials in the first place. You can't operate this place without it. I'm padlocking this place until you fill out the correct paperwork."

"What?" I bellowed. "No!"

At that moment, the door of the dressing room exploded outward.

The shoppers in the store scattered, screaming, and the inspector's two sides of beef hit the floor and rolled, coming up with cocked and loaded crossbows, not unlike Guido and Nunzio's Iolo Specials, but the tips of these quarrels were glowing.

"The door was locked," the shark explained coyly, swimming on the air rapidly toward the exit.

The two-headed woman minced beside her, holding a handful of tasteful, pink, pocket-sized grenades. Out of her open handbag peeked a black satin legband and a stack of rectangular cards.

"Clear the store!" Inspector Dota shouted. "You, ladies, out the door. Now!"

The two impostors were happy to oblige, making for the door as quickly as they could.

"Stop those two!" I yelled. "They're stealing our merchandise."

I shoved toward them. Dota's muscle grabbed my shoulders and yanked me back.

"It's illegal to operate here," the inspector insisted. "Let them go."

"The hell I will," I snarled, shaking their hands off me. The two had nearly made it to the door. "Massha! Cire!"

Cire flung himself out of the alcove and leveled his hands at the two females, who doubled around a display. The rest of the customers still in the store started screaming. Cire let fly. The thieves doubled around a rack near the door. The orange ball of flame hit the rack head-on. It blew up, sending garters flying everywhere. The thieves found themselves pressed against the backs of frantic shoppers, all trying to get out of the store at the same time. Massha took to the air, her hands fumbling for a necklace pendant.

The shark tried to wiggle her way into the crowd. Now was not the time for niceties. With a flattened hand I chopped upward at the wrist of one of Dota's goons. The crossbow went flying. I seized it out of midair and leveled it at the shark's tail. She saw me and went low. I took a bead on the two-headed broad. She shoved hard into the crowd.

BZZZZZZZZ! BZZZZZZZZ! BZZZZZZZZ!

The alarm around the door went off. All the customers jammed there started screaming and slapping at themselves as the theft-control bees installed on the unsold garters realized they were being stolen and went into action. The frauds couldn't escape now. Grinning fiercely, I dropped the crossbow and dove after them.

And hit the ground sprawling with a ton of weight on my back. I wrenched my head around. One of the goons was sitting on me. Dota came around to loom over me.

Chumley saved the day. In two quick strides he reached the doorway and grabbed each of our subjects by the nape of the neck.

"Let 'em go," Inspector Dota ordered.

Chumley turned his moonlike eyes disbelievingly toward the tax man. "Huh?"

Dota nodded to his goons, who leveled their crossbows on him.

"Let 'em go *now*," he repeated, in a voice of quiet menace.

At that range the quarrels could not miss, and whatever

the glowing arrowheads meant, it couldn't be good. Very reluctantly, Chumley released our prisoners.

Dota turned to point at Massha and Cire. "The rest of you employees, freeze!"

"But they're ripping us off!" I protested from the ground. "I, er, want them to come back and pay for those items."

Dota was unmoved. "It would be an illegal transaction. You can't be selling this merchandise anyhow until you have an identification certificate."

I gave in and flopped on the purple carpet. "How long's processing time?"

"Three to four weeks."

"Three or four *what?*" I bellowed.

The jam at the door cleared. The shoppers fled, most of them dabbing at stings. The shark and the two-headed broad paused just long enough to wave sweetly at me before disappearing into the usual thick crowd wandering The Mall's corridors.

Dota's goon got off of my back. I didn't bother pursuing the two impostors. We'd lost that round. I turned to the inspector.

"Look, we're investigators trying to clear up a ring of thieves in this Mall. We've got the cooperation of the administrators and half the shopkeepers here. This is our best shot at capturing the criminals!"

"You'll have to find some other way to do it," Dota insisted. He glanced at his enforcers. "We're done here. Have a nice day."

Massha settled down next to me.

"It's not your fault, Hot Shot. Moa must have forgotten to mention the tax forms. He's not the finance guy."

I felt steam shoot out of my ears. "But Woofle is. I bet he deliberately kept the facts back. I'm going to have a word with him."

Chumley patted me on the back. "Forget about it, Aahz. You can't prove it. Really, it's my fault, what? I could have read through all of those documents in full detail, but truthfully I would still be there now if I had tried. I thought I had noticed all of the important provisions."

"We will find another way to catch them," Eskina assured me.

I looked around at the shop. Most of the displays had been torn down by the hysterical crowd. The dressing room had been destroyed. What was left of the merchandise was scattered across the floor. Acrid smoke rose from the burning rack near the door. The place was ruined.

"What the hell else could go wrong?" I asked.

"Hello?"

Marco Djinnelli floated through the buzzing doorway.

"What happened here?" he asked, sympathetically.

"A riot," I replied, shortly. "It's gonna be a while until we can give you the second half of your money."

"Understandable, understandable," Marco agreed, soothingly. "We are friends. But the first half, as we agreed? I have come for that."

"What?" I demanded. "We paid you."

"No, of course not," Marco demurred politely. "All on credit, I ordered all these items for you. So beautiful they were." He kissed his fingertips. "Alas for such destruction!"

"No," I corrected him. "I mean, we paid you the first half of what we owe you about an hour ago."

"No, no! An hour ago I was enjoying a cappuccino with my cousin Rimbaldi at the Coffee House. The divine Sibone sends her best to her beloved Aahz." Marco narrowed his eyes at us as we all stared at him. "You are telling the truth, aren't you?"

"Marco," I began slowly, "what kind of credit account do you use?"

"Gnomish Bank of Zoorik," Marco replied. Light dawned on him as he studied our faces. "No. No, it is not true."

"I think it must be," Chumley rejoined. "How closely do you scrutinize your statements, Marco?"

Marco waved a hand. "Oh, you know, debits and credits

come and go—but you are saying that I am being stolen from, in my very own account! I must go and look. What a terrible thing!"

The Djinn flew off, muttering to himself.

"What do you think, Green Genius?" Massha asked.

I frowned. "I think that the rat we captured wasn't carrying cards for all the bodies they can change into. They probably have hundreds each, maybe more." I crunched across the debris on the floor. "Let's lock this place up. We need to question the rat and find out where the rest of them are, and how many different identities are circulating."

TWENTY

We couldn't get near the Will Call office. Yellow tape stretched across the corridor, and the guards bustling back and forth behind it refused to let us through. I showed the Flibberite sentries the IDs that Moa had issued us.

"Look, we've been deputized by Captain Parvattani," I argued. "We have to talk to his prisoner."

"We haven't got a prisoner, sir," the guard replied stoutly.

"Fine," I grumbled. "Have it your way. Use whatever politically correct term you want. Detainee, intern, person helping you with your inquiries."

"I mean, sir," the guard corrected me, his eyes forward but his cheeks glowing blue like a cheap television screen, "that the person you seek is no longer in our keeping."

"The hell he's not! Where's Parvattani?" I pushed past the guard station. Chumley, Massha, and Cire followed in my wake, plowing forward like "his" and "hers" and "his" humvees.

"Please, sir, sir, madame, stay behind the line!" the guards squawked. They didn't have a chance.

"I'm busy!" I bellowed back.

"I'm with them," Eskina stated perkily, trotting along behind us.

Parvattani greeted us, rings under his eyes as deep as the ours from a sleepless night.

"I should have-a sent word," he apologized, showing me the empty cubicle where the mall-rat had been sequestered.

It was furnished like a studio apartment, with a convertible sofa bed, a bookshelf and a reading light, probably used most of the time by hamsters waiting to be picked up.

"But it has taken all my attention."

"No problem," I assured him. "We've been having the day from hell ourselves. Any signs of forced entry?"

"Magikal," Parvattani replied. He held up a translucent gel in a frame. We looked through it at the temporary cell. The whole thing danced with deep violet light. "A huge expenditure of very powerful magik, like-a we have not seen here before. Much too much to undo a single locking spell, such-a as held this room shut. The Djinns are very worried."

I was, too. It had to mean that Rattila had sprung the prisoner, either before or after he paid us that little visit last night. He must be feeling pretty cocky, to expend a ton of energy on, as Par said, a cheesy little B&E job.

One of the guards ran up and saluted.

"Here is the crystal ball, sir," he snapped out. Parvattani took it from him.

"This-a was planted in the ceiling. It will show everything that-a happen during the night."

We all bent over it to watch. Par tweaked the spell so the night unfolded before our eyes in a matter of moments. Most of it was black, except for a burst of blinding light. He ran it back and started it over, much more slowly. The glare, when it came, illuminated not one but two bodies silhouetted against it. Two thieves, breaking open the Will Call box where the mall-rat had been staying. Then a face filled the globe's surface. There, thumbs in ears so all the fingers could be waggled at us, tongue stuck out to the roots and eyes squeezed shut in playful disdain, was Skeeve's face. My blood pressure shot through the roof.

"I want this guy's hide!" I roared.

"My loyal subjects," Rattila announced to the cheering mall-rats. "Our company is complete again."

Mayno twirled his long black whiskers as he bowed low before the Throne of Refuse.

"Thanks to our gran' patron," he declared. "To be freed from such petite quarters eez a plaisir. Zere was nozzing to steal in zere. It was bor-*ring*."

Garn was the last to return to the Rat Hole. He had been spying on the visitors.

"You should've seen them," he gloated. "Running around in circles trying to figure out how we did it. How did we do it?" he asked Rattila.

"Stupid!" the Ratislavan sneered. "My new power exceeds everything they have at their disposal!"

He threw out his paws, and lightning sprang from them, ricocheting around the room. The mall-rats threw themselves to the sweating floor. Piles of clothing and baby toys burst apart, showering them with plastic shards and fabric tatters.

"Just think what it will be like when my talent is complete!"

"Uh, Ratty, you gotta get some control on there, dude," Strewth mentioned, from the foot of the throne.

"DON'T call me Ratty!" Rattila raged. Fire burst out of his mouth in a torrent. It splashed against the nearest heap of luxury goods and set it ablaze. "Say, I like that. When I am angry I am much more terrible." He loomed magnanimously over Strewth. "You may call me Ratty when I tell you to."

"Sure thing, R—I mean, Master."

"In the meantime, you will recite my titles, *all of them!*" He glared at all the mall-rats.

"King of Trash, Marquis of Merchandise, Collector of

Unguarded Property, Magikal Potentate Extraordinary, Rightful Holder of the Throne of Refuse, and Ruler of All Rats and Lesser Beings."

Rattila's eyes slitted with pleasure. "Again." Strewth sighed and repeated the litany. The others joined in. "Good. Now, we celebrate!"

With a mere flick, Rattila drew enough power from the lines of force that crossed over The Mall to draw a nearly clean white damask tablecloth out of the bag where it had rested untouched for two years. Candlesticks came from every quarter of the Rat Hole and set themselves in the center. Candles inserted themselves into the sockets. Rattila lit them with a thought. He almost laughed at the ease with which he created fire. This was the life! This was worth five long years of gleaning power from mundane, pedestrian shoppers. And he had the visitors to thank. If Aahz and the others had not drawn attention to Skeeve, Rattila would have treated his card like all the others, not delving deeply into the knowledge that the Klahd had amassed over the years. What advantages he had missed!

Bottles, cans, baskets, and boxes assembled themselves on the cloth, with Rattila conducting them like an orchestra leader. The mall-rats' eyes were wide with amazement and greed at the sight of sweetmeats, sausages, jellies, biscuits, and condensed cream of tomato soup. They gathered around the cloth, rubbing their paws together.

"And now," he announced, with a sweep of one claw, "we feast! First, the caviar!" At his direction the tiny jars opened, and their jewel-like contents spread themselves onto round crackers, which dealt themselves out to the assembled mall-rats. They all exchanged nervous glances.

"Uh, Rat—Rattila, we don't like caviar," Strewth ventured.

"You have to like it!" Rattila boomed, his red eyes gleaming. "It is *expensive.* Think of all the poor mall-rats who *don't* have caviar!"

"Oh, okay, dude," Strewth replied, resignedly.

With a shrug to the others, he took a bite, trying not to

gag. The others followed suit. Rattila could feel their distaste. He rather enjoyed it.

Perhaps the grand celebration was premature. He
should have saved it for when the gauge in the Master Card
had reached the top of its potential limit, but it was close.
He really felt his power now. It was wonderful. The Massha
cards were feeding him nicely.

"The day is coming soon when I shall be all-powerful,
omnipotent, all-encompassing!" he informed the rats as he
served them pressed pheasant, another costly delicacy. "I
lust for that moment."

"Whatever," the mall-rats murmured, shoving unfinished
caviar under the tablecloth and hoping he didn't notice.

"It is! It's whatever I say!" He let loose with another
blast of power that shook the foundations of The Mall.
"You see! I control everything!"

From a nearby heap he caused a Massha's Secret box to
fly to him. The contents spilled out, feathered garters flit-
ting around in the air like round butterflies. Yes, and in his
future, butterflies *would* be round!

"Pretty, pretty!" Oive and Lawsy crooned.

"Yes, they are," Rattila acknowledged.

He squinted at the garters. They were full of magik. It
must be his! He reached for them and touched them with
the Master Card. The feathers drooped as the power was
drained from the garters.

"Awwww!" the mall-rats chorused. "Why'd you do
that?"

"What do you care if they work?" Rattila snarled,
throwing the silk wisps away from him.

"Well, they're cool that way," Oive argued. "I like the
one with the lunch box on it. You can keep a sandwich
fresh all day in that little pouch."

"Don't worry," Rattila declared, crushing the last garter
in his clenched paw. It burst into flames, but he didn't seem
to notice. "Soon all the power in this Mall will be mine,
and you will have all the working toys that you could ever
want. Everyone's lunch will be yours!"

Strewth and a few of the others started to edge backward. They were terrified of him. They thought he was going insane. He caught a whisper of the ringleader's thoughts: *Power corrupts.*

"No!" he thundered, letting loose a blast of magik that shook piles of merchandise down all over the vast chamber. "Power is good! It can be dangerous, yes. *Knowledge* is power," he slavered. He started to flip the box aside, then laughed at the name. "Massha's Secret. We've learned a lot of Massha's secrets, haven't we?" he asked, holding the image of the Jahk in his mind.

Lawsy had done a good job of gleaning truths out of her. Honestly, she could have obtained a real credit card with less information than she had unwittingly given Lawsy. Rattila luxuriated in it.

"She doesn't use all the power she has at her disposal, preferring to rely on all that jewelry. If she did, I would be already over the mark. But this will do," he insisted, fondling the Master Card. "This will do nicely. I'll add the Pervert and the Troll to my collection after I have become the most powerful magician in the world. In the meanwhile"—he turned to glare at his trembling workforce—"eat up! There are rats starving in Brooklyn!"

"We can wait until the next Skeeve sighting," Chumley suggested, as I stomped out of the Will Call office.

I didn't know where I was going, but if I had stayed there, I would have started breaking heads, and none of the heads I wanted to break were there.

"What do we do now?" Cire asked, glumly. "Our trap is gone, and so is our subject."

"I don't know. I have to think," I replied, moodily.

I was torqued by the invasion of the tax agents and the disappearance of the mall-rat, but what really irked me was the expressions of deep and sincere sympathy on the faces of the merchants. Our humiliation had become com-

mon knowledge. I figured the shoppers who'd been in
Massha's Secret when the explosion came had spread the
word about the riot. The merchants almost certainly
thought we were complete screwups. So much for
M.Y.T.H., Inc's reputation.

A plump female Djinnie came sailing out of a shoe boutique and whisked around us in circles.

"Oh, you lovely people," she gushed. "Marco told us all
about what happened! He told all of us, and we have told
everyone else in The Mall!"

"Yeah, yeah," I grunted, with an embarrassed wave,
hoping to stave off the recitation. I didn't want to live
through it again.

But the Djinnie and I weren't on the same page.

"Thank you, thank you, thank you!" she beamed, zoom-
ing in to kiss me soundly on the lips. She seized Chumley
and Cire and planted one on them, too. "We are all now
checking for discrepancies in our expenditures! You may
have saved many of us from that horrid Rattila!" She
hugged Massha and picked Eskina right off the floor. "You
are wonderful!"

"Yeah," I agreed, realizing now what she was talking
about. I should have guessed. The Djinnie would be a lot
more interested in not getting ripped off than in our tax
shutdown. I straightened up a little. "We are."

"Come, choose *anything* from my shop," she invited,
guiding us toward the shoe displays. "Each of you. Please."

"We were just trying to do a job," I argued. "But I
noticed how my companions perked up at the Djinnie's
gratitude. "Well—okay."

Not that I needed shoes, of course, but the proprietor,
name of Tarkeni, had snappy accessories, including belts
and personal-grooming kits, one of which was made of
scaly leather not unlike my own fetching skin, except in
bronze. I found myself turning it over in my hands a dozen
times until Tarkeni stuffed it in a bag and pronounced it
mine.

"It is the least we can do!" she exclaimed.

By the time we left the shop all five of us had more of a spring in our steps.

"You see, big guy?" Massha declared with a wink. "Retail therapy definitely helps."

"This is the life, huh?" Cire asked, admiring his new shoes.

Flippers like his were hard to fit, and the boots the Djinnie had pressed on him must have been worth dozens of gold pieces.

"Rather!" Chumley agreed, enjoying his new ParchmentMan automatic book scroll.

Other grateful merchants were eager to help us recover from our run of bad luck. I hardly had time to think about the Skeeve impostors or our own humiliation as we were dragged out of the corridors every hundred paces by another shopkeeper or booth owner.

"You are good people," a Gourami remarked, kissing us all as she urged us to try on the glass finger and toe rings she sold.

"My mother would want you to have this," a teenage Whelf insisted, pressing a bag of candles on us.

I even found myself wandering around a furniture store with the Djinni owner hovering at my heels promising a deep discount on anything in the store.

"Or anything you choose to order," he added, hospitably, smiles wreathing his broad blue face.

I browsed a selection of recliners to take the place of my burned-out armchair, thinking what pleasure I'd get out of handing Woofle the receipt and insisting he pay the balance.

Thanks to one of Massha's gadgets, what parcels and boxes Chumley couldn't haul floated along behind us on our way back to the hotel.

"If we don't get the alarm to chase a Skeeve-clone, I'm going to take a nap," I informed the others.

Massha cupped a huge yawn behind her broad hand. "Good idea, Short and Scaly," she responded.

"There you are!" Rimbaldi Djinnelli came flying toward

us through the crowd. He seized Massha's hands. "I love you even more today than before, you beautiful lady! Come to my shop!" He herded us all along with him. "You must all see the outfit that my wife has designed for this so generously made lady, whose body matches her heart. It will fill you all with delight!"

I caught sight of a familiar quartet of purple eyes on the other side of the hall near an art gallery.

"Hey, is that Chloridia?" I asked, pulling the gang to a halt. "Let me catch up with her."

"Of course!" Rimbaldi boomed. "You shall bring her along, too."

But by the time I turned around again, she'd disappeared into the crowd. I was relieved to see her back in The Mall again. We would cross paths again sooner or later.

TWENTY-ONE

As we entered The Volcano, Jack Frost, elemental building engineer, glanced up from a conversation with one of the Djinnelli cousins to tip us a friendly wave. The store was steaming hot, as was the discussion.

"I fixed this spell yesterday," Jack insisted, his cheeks and nose more than usually pink.

He threw up his hands, and the familiar white cones of cold came radiating out of his fingertips.

"But you feel how it is now?" demanded the Djinn, his face blue with outrage. "It is too hot again! Your spell failed."

"I don't get it," Jack admitted. "It really should not be this hot in here. It's not natural. Hey, Aahz!" He nudged me as we passed. "Sorry about the shop. It was a really nice place."

"Well," I tossed off noncommittally, "easy come, easy go. It is pretty warm in here. Anything wrong?"

"This whole place, she is over a live volcano," the Djinn exclaimed, giving us a distracted nod of greeting. "Of course sometimes it gets too hot! You are failing at your task, and do you know what I say to that?"

Jack blew a cloud of white condensation. "The elemental under that volcano's a friend of mine. He keeps it down to normal most of the time. Moa and I have already worked out when he can have the next eruption, and it's not for eight years! So, don't tell me I'm not keeping on top of this!"

"Then, tell me why it is always *my* customers fainting from the atmosphere?" the Djinn demanded.

Jack shrugged in exasperation. "I dunno. Maybe it's your prices. Look, let's keep a cool head over this. Your floor *is* solid, right?" He stamped on the glowing orange floor. "There isn't a good reason more heat's venting up through here."

A bleebling sound interrupted their argument. He pulled a snow globe out of his pocket, and his sandy brows went up.

"Oops! Gotta skate! Fire in the corn-dog shop. See you all later! Take it easy, Aahz!"

"Later, Jack," I called, as the elemental froze the floor before his feet and whisked gracefully out into the corridor.

"This way, this way!" Rimbaldi urged, his arm still firmly around Massha. "My wife has been racking her brains for the very best design that would suit you, and she has done it! Every stitch, painstakingly made by fairy hands, every silk thread spun by the very most expert spiders! Our gift to you!"

"A gift?" Massha asked. "You really shouldn't have."

"But I must, dear lady. In, in!"

At Rimbaldi's urging, Massha went into one of the larger dressing rooms with two of the Djinnies.

"Watch it, honey," her voice came through the thin walls. "No, that's me! I can't—oh, oh, boy! Yes, that does do something for old Massha!"

The curtain swished open. Head held high, the Court Magician of Possiltum swished into the room, followed by yards and yards of marine blue silk. The bodice was cut

low over her bosom, full sleeves encased her arms, opening to a smooth flare at the wrists, and the skirts, flat in the
front and full in the back, swirled all around her legs.

"Oh, I say!" Chumley exclaimed, overcome.

"Gorgeous," Eskina declared.

Massha beamed. "Thanks. I feel great. What do you
think, Aahz?"

"Very nice," I said, honestly.

The color of the silk went well with her mop of orange
hair, and the fabric flowed over her more-than-generous
curves like water over smooth rocks. Massha stared into
the glass almost in a dream, turning this way and that.

Rimbaldi was beside himself with delight. The Djinni
tailor floated around her several feet off the floor, declaim-
ing, "It's you! It's you!"

Bemused, Massha turned to me. "But who am I?"

"What do you mean, who are you?" I asked, puzzled by
the expression on her face.

Her pupils had disappeared into her irises. "Who am I?"

"Uh-oh," Eskina groaned. "Massha, look at me."

The tiny female climbed onto a chair so she was face-
to-face with the puzzled magician. She took Massha's face
between her hands. Massha tried to bat her away, but she
kept staring blankly at her own reflection.

"She's been issued," Eskina explained. "Somewhere in
this Mall they're using up her essence. Probably pretty fast.
Rattila must have his shapechangers shopping everywhere,
and likely for very expensive items."

"Rot!" Chumley declared. "How could they have gotten
to her? We have been near her every minute."

"I do not know," the Ratislavan spat. "But they have."

"How come we haven't heard from any of the people
she's been ripping off, then?" I demanded. "She's a store
owner now. They'd probably have shown up by now wanting to cosponsor advertising throughout The Mall."

"That is exactly what I wanted to talk to you about,"
Rimbaldi replied, popping back with his arms full of
brightly colored clothes. "Madama, she shops here every

day. I thought perhaps I could say that Massha's other secret is that she loves The Volcano! Alas for the beautiful store." He kissed his hand to her. "And such a good customer. She always pays cash, every moment. That is why we are making this gift to her."

We all looked at each other. I shook my head.

"The sneaky bastard. He's been keeping the Massha impostors off the radar by having them buy things *legitimately.*"

At that moment I hated Rattila more than I'd ever hated a living being, but I had to give him credit, so to speak.

"Rattila would love to get his hands on someone like her," Eskina agreed. "He wants her power. With it he might actually make it to full magician status. We've got to stop him very, very soon."

"How?" Chumley asked, wrinkling his brow.

I smacked one fist into the other palm. "We're going to have to put out an APB on her. Rimbaldi, you've got a communications spell to the guards?"

"Yes, of course I do," Rimbaldi averred, glad to have something to do at last. "I can also alert the shopkeepers to prevent her—however many of her there are—from making any more purchases."

"Better than that," I began, with a raised hand, as a thought struck me, "if anyone's masquerading as her, tell the shopkeepers to hold them, keep them busy, or just sit on them until we get there."

Rimbaldi pulled out his little globe to inform his many relatives of the new development.

Before Rimbaldi had finished speaking, Parvattani and a quintet of guards appeared in the store and surrounded us.

"This is-a terrible!" he announced. "I have just heard the news. All eyes are watching out for Madama Massha."

I gave him the rundown that Rimbaldi had just given me, of Rattila's latest dodge.

"It's clever," I admitted. "We've been concentrating on fraudulent purchases to gather energy. He kept it on the up and up, and no one paid attention."

"He is a true adversary," Parvattani stated, shaking his head. "Madama Eskina, if I have denigrated your efforts in the past, I apologize with all my heart."

In spite of her worry, Eskina was touched by the handsome apology.

"I understand your skepticism. The important thing now is to save Massha as well as the friend Skeeve."

"I obey," Parvattani acknowledged.

He brought out his own crystal globe. Tiny images of uniformed guards deep inside it turned to look out at him.

"Now hear this, now hear this," he intoned into it. "Be on the lookout for this Jahk, name of Massha." He held the orb up to her face, and her image appeared inside it. "If found, apprehend. The suspect will be using magik. Approach with caution. I repeat, approach with caution."

He nodded to me, then shook the globe. Particles flew within, then re-formed as the faces of Djinns, Deveels, mermaids, and countless other species.

"This is Captain Parvattani. Fraud alert. Do not allow this female Jahk to make a purchase in your establ—" His voice was cut off suddenly. He clutched his throat.

I spun. Massha, her eyes fixed on nothing, was squeezing an invisible object between her hands. I marched up to her.

"Stop that!" I bellowed. Startled, her hands flew open. Her eyes changed.

"What's the problem, Green Stuff?" she asked, pursing her big lips in a grin.

"Nothing, Massha," I assured her. I looked back over my shoulder at Par. "Go on. Hurry up."

"Right, sir—Repeat, do not allow this female to make a purchase in your establishment. Notify a guard as soon as you can, preferably before she exits the store. That is all." He shook the globe once more and put it back in his pocket.

"That was me in there," Massha whispered, aghast, pointing at the little sphere in Par's hands. "Why?"

"They've got your facts," I stated bluntly. "You fell into a trance for a minute."

She fumbled for her magik detector. The red jewel was glowing.

"How'd they get through my defenses?"

"You must have let them," Eskina explained. "Think! Did you talk to anyone? Give anyone personal details?"

"Beyond shooting the usual bull at the inns, no," Massha mused. "No, wait! I answered a couple of questions the clerk asked me when I bought that bracelet, the one I gave away."

She held up one thick wrist. I remembered the blue stone-encrusted bangle.

"You took a consumer survey?" Eskina demanded, horrified.

"I was just chatting with the clerk—*who was a shapechanger.* Right." Massha's broad face turned scarlet. "That's it," she stated. "When I get home I'm quitting my job. I am not fit to be a court magician, or any other kind of magician. I knew we were under attack from every direction, and what do I do? I walk right into the enemy's hands. Me and my big mouth."

"Stop that!" I ordered. "You can hold a pity party when you get home, but in the meantime, if you haven't noticed, we have a job to do. Skeeve's still in danger!"

Massha was so embarrassed that she wanted to turn down the gown Rimbaldi had had made for her. I insisted that he wrap it up and hold on to it for her, along with all our other gifts.

"We don't need the excess baggage right now," I reminded them both. "We need an intervention. Can you direct us to the nearest witch doctor?"

"It's a case of possession," the female Flibberite explained, taking the tubes of her diagnostic device out of her double-pointed ears, "but the manifestation is unlike anything I've ever seen before. It's more like repossession, where someone's taken you over like a thing."

Massha was frantic. "What can you do?" she pleaded.

The doctor frowned. "I'll do my best to corrupt this spell. You know, as a fellow professional, I can't undo it without knowing the spell that made it possible, but we'll fit you out with a firewall spell that will keep any more attacks on your psyche from getting through." The doctor rummaged around in her pocket and came up with a little white pad. She scribbled on it and handed the top sheet to Massha. "Take that to the nearest alchemist and have it filled."

The alchemist, a gnarled male Gnome in a white jacket, attached a little gold box to Massha's necklace. We all crowded around them in the small shop, trying not to brush the myriad of little gadgets crammed onto the shelves lining the walls.

"This is a very powerful spell. It needs to be renewed about once a month, but I hope you won't need it for longer than that. Keep it on you at all times."

"Thanks." Massha sighed heavily, clasping the charm. "I feel better already."

"How's it work?" I inquired.

"Reflexively," the Gnome replied. "If anyone tries to read her mind or put any other predatory spell on her, the firewall rebounds on them."

"Like this?" Cire asked. He whipped up his hands and pointed them at Massha.

Luckily, Cire's back was to the door. A ring of fire sprang up around Massha, gathered itself into a huge mass, and kicked outward, sending the Walroid sprawling into a cluster of shoppers. He staggered to his feet, shaking his head to clear it. The shoppers picked themselves up, gave Cire a resentful look, and went back to their browsing.

"Whoa!" Massha exclaimed, as the fire subsided back into the little box. "That's some gizmo!"

"You want to take a break?" I inquired solicitously, after we paid the alchemist and left.

"No. Now I want revenge," she insisted, sailing above our heads with renewed confidence. "It's not just for Skeeve, but a little bit for me, too. How do we get this Rattila?"

I thought for a minute. "We need an attraction," I decided. "One that will pull in as many of the thieves as possible. Something they can't resist. An event that Moa can publicize the hell out of. A promotion of some kind?"

"Oh, but there are sales promotions every day," Parvattani pointed out, marching along beside us.

He wore his uniform, since the subterfuge was now pointless. Everyone, including our opponents, knew who we were.

"Our customers see everything, and they want to be a part of everything. You'll get thousands of people participating. We will be no better off than we are now."

"Cardholders only, of course," I stated. "It'll be irresistible. A members-only event featuring a raffle. For a date with a celebrity."

"And where are we going to find a celebrity?" Massha asked.

I looked around at our party. "Eskina?"

She snorted. "You are joking, of course."

I changed my mind on the spot. No, she didn't have the kind of big personality a celebrity needed. "Yes. I'm joking. I didn't mean you."

"What about me?" Cire asked, hopefully.

"Yeah, right," I scoffed. "With your credibility and attention to detail."

Cire clutched his chest in mock outrage. "That was one time in Imper! Well, maybe a few times. Who else are you going to ask? The purple bath mat here?"

"Not I," Chumley interjected at once. "If I employ unaccustomed loquacity to make a good impression, I shall spoil my marketability as a hired threat."

I fixed my eyes on Massha. She levitated away from me in alarm.

"Oh, no, Big Spender! We just spent a load of money and magikal energy putting up a firewall around me. And aren't they going to recognize me as the owner of Massha's Secret?"

Parvattani cleared his throat. "Madama, you would be surprised. To the shoppers, you can-a put on a pair of glasses, and you are disguised. Different clothes, a different hairstyle, and you are another person!"

She played her final, desperate card. "What would Hugh say?"

I advanced on her. "He'd be proud of you, stepping into the face of danger to save a friend. We're doing this for Skeeve, remember?"

She stopped floating backward. "Of course I remember, Green and Scaly. That's why I came. But what good will it do if Rattila gets my soul because I put myself up where he can take another crack at me?"

"Because he won't get anything real out of you," I assured her. "In fact, if we can get him to overload, maybe we can contaminate some of the talent he's already gathered, set him back a ways."

Massha looked dubious. "And how are we going to do that?"

I grinned. "Lie."

TWENTY-TWO

"No push!" Chumley cautioned an overeager Deveel who tried to climb over the velvet ropes surrounding Massha's lush throne inside her scarlet silk pavilion.

Gold-plated standards shaped like medieval trumpeters held banners with her picture on either side of the doorway. It didn't surprise me at all that The Mall had a huge supply of set pieces and furniture to support every kind of promotional activity under the sun. It'd be a good investment, if you had the space to store it, and space galore was one thing The Mall had.

In the days we'd been there I had seen raffles, drawings, talent contests, concerts, circus acts, square dances, formal dances, sock hops, animal acts, makeovers, caricaturists, fortune-tellers, food tastings, and product demonstrations of every kind, as well as the endless and ongoing hall music. The latter convinced me that whoever held auditions Moa—or his agent—had a tin ear, to make sure they were getting the worst possible performers in the entire universe. I knew street musicians in a hundred dimensions who played on homemade instruments who were a thou-

sand times better. I needed my concentration intact. After
an hour or so of persuasion, I had managed to convince the
Mall manager to silence the bands within a half-block
radius of Massha's encampment. Otherwise, I was going to
go crazy, and I needed my wits at their sharpest. Even with
the full complement of security guards sprinkled through
the crowd, it still looked like a disaster bubbling toward
overflow.

I admit that I had underestimated the number of cardholders, or maybe word had spread to other dimensions
over the three days we had had the posters up advertising
Massha's appearance.

MEET THE RED FAIRY! the one-sheets screamed. WIN A
DATE—AND A WISH!

In smaller print below the rules of the contest had been
set out: only holders of credit cards would be allowed to
enter the drawing, one entry per person, winner must be
present to collect the prize. We intended to winnow out the
duplicates; all of those would be frauds, whom Par
couldn't wait to arrest.

In the meantime, each of the lucky contestants would
get a chance to meet the Red Fairy. Massha sat in her tent,
sprawled a little uneasily on a pile of cushions in the triple-
wide throne intended to be roomy enough for any kind of
pseudoroyalty from the Lollipop Queen to the King of the
Elephant Gods. What remained of her harem costume had
formed the inspiration for her present getup, filmy red
robes covered with rhinestones and sequins. On her feet
were shining ruby slippers, a crown adorned her freshly
coiffed, newly dyed scarlet hair, and on her back, the cause
of her uneasy posture, were a pair of huge, filmy wings,
tinted garnet red, iridescent as soap bubbles but more
durable than fast-food condiment packets. She had gotten
over her initial discomfort and was now dispensing beatif-
ic smiles and gracious nods to the awed passersby through
the fine veil over her face.

"I look like the Ghost of Christmas Hangovers," she
murmured to me, out of the corner of her mouth.

I stood at her side, dressed in a spiffy herald's uniform.

"You look terrific," I shot back. "Hugh would be crazy about you in that outfit."

She paused, as Chumley roughly escorted a family of Imps out of the tent. "You think so?"

"I know it," I flipped off, with airy confidence.

Her husband, retired General Hugh Badaxe, had fallen madly in love with Massha a few years back. The two of them had taken to disappearing together whenever possible. In their case, getting married seemed like an almost unnecessary afterthought. They made one of the most stable couples I knew.

I leered. "He'd like you in nothing better."

"I *know* that," Massha replied, with a giggle.

A Deveel female in a chic shirtdress with a notebook floating beside her was the next to enter. Her pointed ears were almost perked forward. Clearly she had heard a little of our exchange. She went forward to take Massha's hands, but a growl from Chumley stopped her at a respectable distance.

"Dear Red Fairy, I'm Somalya. Love the color scheme, baby! I write a popular column of who's hot and who's not for the *Hottenuf Gazette.* You're definitely hot, so we want all the dish from you. Who's he? Is he your significant other? My readers would love to know."

I cleared my throat. Massha didn't really need the warning.

"Well, I don't really like to give personal details in public," Massha began in a conspiratorial undertone, "but Guthlab's a real looker from Capri."

"A Capricorn?" The Deveel signed to her pencil, which wrote avidly in the notebook. "Is it true what they say about Capricorn males—"

"Oh, yes," Massha assured her, settling back on her cushions with a luxurious wiggle. There was a *crunch!* from her wings. Gamely, she ignored it. "Horny all the time."

"Really! Well, are you going to, er, tie the knot at any time in the future?"

"Just as soon as his divorce is final," Massha stated, with a wink.

"Give our readers just a few more personal facts," Somalya urged. "What is your favorite food?"

"Er, chickalick stew."

I kept my face from breaking into the grin that hovered just below the surface. Massha hated chickalick stew. She always said the beans made her break out. She was doing a good job under pressure of pulling fibs out of thin air.

Somalya was delighted that our "star" was willing to share. "What do you like to do on the perfect date?"

"Skee-ball."

"What's your shoe size?"

"Seven and a half."

"When's your birthday? Paper or plastic? Boxers or briefs?"

"Dat enough," Chumley uttered suddenly. He dropped a heavy hand on the Deveel's shoulder and turned her toward the exit.

"Oh, please," Somalya begged, hopping up and down to be seen over Chumley's huge arm. The scribbling notebook hovered over her head. "Just one more statement for our readers."

Massha fluttered her fingers in farewell. "I love you all."

"Whew!" she whistled, as the flaps sagged closed behind the reporter. "I thought my mind would go blank if she asked me anything else. Thanks, Chumley."

"My pleasure," the Troll replied, with a gallant bow. "Your prevarications were most glib, I must say."

"We're not going to fool Rattila, though." She sighed. "He already knows who I am."

"We're not trying to fool him," I reminded her in a low voice. "We're trying to cut down on his workforce. If we can get him, too, all the better. Cire's standing by outside with his spell on 360-degree reception."

A gentle "ahem" from outside reminded us that more people were waiting for their brush with greatness. I signaled to the guard to let the next punter in.

"Lady, look at you!" a Klahd exclaimed loudly, shepherding his wife into the tent. He held up a camera. "Go and pose with the Red Fairy, honey. D'you mind? One more, with the kids, okay? Hey, that's great!"

Massha and Chumley had things under control so well that I decided to go and check out the crowd. Moa and his fellow executives, in fancy brocade tunics that were so heavily padded they could hardly get their arms out in front of them, sat checking credit cards at a carved wooden table flanked by guards just outside the ropes that surrounded Massha's tent. Moa had insisted on being part of our subterfuge.

"I want to see these pains in the waddayacallit face-to-face," Moa told me.

They were doing land-office business. Thousands of eager faces lifted toward me as I flung open the flaps of the tent, then dimmed slightly when they realized I wasn't the Red Fairy.

The kiosk plastered with posters just behind the executive table was actually hollow. Inside, Cire deployed his spell. He had a gizmo to snap the walls of the tent closed if any of the impostors made it inside. The guards were ready to pounce if and when the signal came.

Moa himself was waiting on a female Gnome with fluffy hair and a turned-up nose who reminded me a little of Eskina. I glanced around to see where our sawn-off ally was hanging out. No sign of her. She was just too short to be seen over the heads of the crowd. Her magik sniffer must be on full alert, though.

The fancy credit cards these individuals were carrying were just a single sign of a well-to-do, if not opulent, lifestyle. I saw dozens of beings from multiple dimensions carrying on conversations with personal-sized crystal balls. One female Deveel stared into a compact mirror while changing her features with enchanted cosmetics. She couldn't make up her mind for the longest time which nose to go with, but finally decided on an aquiline design with flared nostrils. She caught me looking when she glanced up, and I gave her a nod of approval. Bridling with pleasure, she snapped the compact shut.

Moa accepted the entry form from the Gnome, and the next customer ambled forward. My eyes nearly popped out of my head. My Pervect shapechanger!

Behind me, the kiosk started rocking furiously back and forth. Cire had detected her, too.

I poked the guard at Moa's left in the ribs.

"That one," I whispered. "Get her."

He glanced back at me, curiously.

My whisper was too quiet for a Flibberite to hear, but it was more than loud enough for a Pervect. Her gaze lifted. Our eyes met and locked. In one smooth move she leaped over the table, her claws going for my throat.

"She's an impostor!" I croaked, tearing one hand off my windpipe.

Then the guards reacted. Both of them grabbed the woman's upper arms and attempted to haul her off me. She backhanded the guards, knocking them into the tableful of executives.

Cire exploded out of the kiosk, spells blazing. The Pervect hauled up her skirts to reveal a black lace garter on her left thigh, flipped open the minute pocket attached to it, and hauled out of it a vintage Thompson submachine gun. Cire and I ducked for cover as she sprayed the immediate area with bullets. The air split with the deafening report. The tent behind me collapsed with a crash. Fifty armed Mall guards and I jumped on the Pervect.

The crowd went crazy. These were the power shoppers, the elite, the coddled buyers who were wooed with wine-and-cheese events and half-price coupons. When one Mall guard rose from the fray with a bloody nose and the gun, they ran away shrieking.

This woman was one dirty fighter and strong as a dragon. Whatever vitamins these thieves were taking, I wanted the formula so I could bottle it and sell it. We rolled together along the floor, knocking over people and tables in our wake. She went for my eyes with her talons. When I threw up a forearm to guard, she dug the heel of her hand into my windpipe. Gasping, I dragged in a deep breath, then let it out in a single bellow.

"Chumley!"

No answering roar. He must be protecting Massha from the stampede.

Parvattani jumped into the exercise. "All together-a now!" he shouted.

Working with the well-oiled precision I had admired in his troop the first time I'd seen them, the guards surrounded the Pervect and dragged her off me. She continued to struggle, gouging the Flibberites with her fingernails and punching them whenever she could work a hand free.

"Cire, freeze her," I choked out, as I got to my feet to help the guards.

The Walroid scrambled up and pointed his hands at her.

A bolt of bright green light hit him between the shoulder blades, knocking him over. I searched for the source of the attack. I turned around, expecting another invasion of the zombie shoppers, but the advancing force was an army of one. Chloridia undulated toward us, her four purple eyes glassy. Cire staggered to his feet. I threw myself at her, trying to distract her aim. She shot another solid bolt at me, and followed it up with another at Cire. The Walroid went backward over a table. I could hear him groaning.

"They got her," I groaned. We needed magikal backup, and quick. "Massha!"

"Help!" her voice came, muffled by the tent.

I looked around. The Pervect had thrown the guards off and disappeared into the screaming crowd. Parvattani nursed an eye rimmed with purple as he helped to pull the table off Moa.

"Consarn it!" shouted Skocklin, Moa's partner, as the guards pulled him free. "I never thought they'd attack like that."

"You thought maybe they'd give up like they were playing hide-and-seek?" Moa chided him.

"Someone's going to have to pay for all this damage," Woofle exclaimed, looking pointedly at me.

I turned my back on him and started fighting my way through the fallen tent's folds toward the writhing, kicking mass.

"Massha, Chumley, hold still!" I instructed them. "I'm right here."

"Mmmm!"

With a mighty heave I hauled the scarlet canvas away. A pair of crumpled gossamer wings quivered and lifted, followed by the rest of Massha.

"Whew!" she wheezed. "That's better."

"You okay?" I asked. She nodded, her chest heaving as she gasped for breath. "Good. Can you heat up one of your gizmos and help me lift the rest of this tent? Chumley's still in here somewhere."

"Aahz, he's not," Massha insisted, clutching my arm. "I tried fighting them off, but they cut a hole through the back flap and came in right past the guards. They seemed to know which gadget I would go for next, and had a countergadget ready. They zapped him with some kind of spell and carried him off!"

"Chumley?" I asked, disbelievingly.

"Yes," Massha replied. "I did everything I could to stop them, but I was outnumbered. I'm sorry, Aahz!"

"Who took him?" I demanded.

Massha looked me sadly in the eye.

"Eight Skeeves."

TWENTY-THREE

Not surprisingly, being carried by eight beings of less than average strength was bumpy at best. They dropped him again and again on the hard tile floor. Chumley would have protested if his mouth had been free, but two of the Klahds—he refused to call them Skeeve even in his thoughts—had wound sticky tape around it.

He struggled to get free, to no avail. How was it that eight puny beings were able to sap his superior strength? He suspected that it was not their doing; these were the worker drones—the queen, or, in this case, the king of the hive had cast an enfeebling spell and interfered with Massha's magik.

A ninth figure caught up with the group and hoisted Chumley's left shoulder. Chumley's heart leaped. At first he thought Aahz had discovered the subterfuge and was about to rescue him, but it was a Pervert—er, Pervect of the female persuasion.

"Zis is not fair! Why can I not match ze ozzers?" the Pervect asked, in a peevish tone.

"Because you lost your Skeeve card," one of the bland

Klahdish faces responded. "The Big Cheese doesn't remake them, remember?"

The Pervect grumbled. The group trotted on, rounding corners. Chumley tried to keep track of all the turns they made, but he was not accustomed to watching the ceiling.

"Whoops," the lead impostor gulped. "Patrol on the way! Hey, you, disguise us!"

Chumley caught another glimpse of green out the corner of his eye, this one dark and smooth. The newcomer was Aahz's friend Chloridia.

"Mmm!" Chumley exclaimed, trying to get her attention. Her four eyes never focused on him. Her expression was one of dazed obedience. He was shocked. She must have fallen at last under the spell of Rattila's card theft.

"There you are," the impostor lugging Chumley's left foot grunted. "We can't let go of him. Put a disguise on us."

At the impostor's order, Chloridia began to chant in unknown words. In a moment the Klahds bearing him became a host of meaty Djinns in coveralls. Chumley shuddered to think as what they might have disguised him.

"Good," the leader stated. "Now, go buy something. We'll call you if we need you."

"Mmmmh!" Chumley blurted, frantic to get her attention, but she had already turned and undulated away.

The Klahd-Djinns hoisted his limbs once more and continued their journey.

A good deal of the ceiling went by, with several more changes in direction, until the disguised horde finally carried him over a threshold. The scent around him was somewhat familiar, that of brimstone and sulfur, along with a sharper odor reminiscent of ammonia. Through the shoulders of the illusory Djinns around him, he spotted tall shelves supporting myriad pairs of the blue trousers that had so captivated the Klahds. Therefore, he was in The Volcano. Where, then, were they taking him?

Row after row after row of dressing rooms flashed past him in peripheral vision. Chumley tried to keep count of the doorways. He recalled from their early orientation that

The Volcano was extradimensional. It could be the reason they had never managed to discover the whereabouts of Rattila was that it lay not in this dimension but in another.

The answer, which surprised him, was not long in coming. A few hundred doorways had gone by when his escort made a sharp left through a gaudily dyed curtain and into dank, hot darkness. As soon as they were within, the disguise spell dropped away.

His eyes, more sensitive than many other species', adjusted very swiftly. Chumley became aware that the party trod a downward slope. Feeble lights issued from the ceiling, lending the Klahds a leprous cast. A howl sounded from far ahead.

"Uh-huh!" one of the impostors announced. "Sounds like the Big Cheese is home."

"Well, well, what have you brought me?" a squeaky voice asked with eager menace.

The Klahds dropped Chumley on the floor. The landing was not painful, as his fall was cushioned by an uneven pad of some kind.

A black-furred face imposed itself between Chumley and the ceiling. Before the Troll's eyes was one of the largest vermin he had ever beheld. Nearly the size of Eskina, this creature had a narrow, tapered head terminating in a quivering black nose with long, wiry whiskers that quivered when it talked.

"Welcome to my Rat Hole," the vermin chittered, showing sharp, yellow, rectangular teeth, a startling contrast to the ebon fur. "You've met all of my associates? I am Rattila, Lord of The Mall, and soon to be of all Ratislava. What do you think of my domain?"

The tape was ripped away from Chumley's mouth, painfully pulling out a good deal of facial fur. With his feet still bound, he attempted to stand up and banged his head on the ceiling. He toppled onto a heap of clothes and noticed that all of the garments still had the price tags attached. He wrenched himself into a sitting position. As far as Chumley could see, the sprawling chamber was filled with clothing, jewelry, books, musical instruments, large appliances, rolled-up rugs, and furniture, all in their original bags or containers, and all piled haphazardly, as if the getting was more important than the having.

"It's rather a tip, what?" Chumley blurted, then felt abashed. "I do beg your pardon. What bad manners, making personal comments like that. I believe it's the heat."

Rattila's eyes glowed red. "You are just jealous," he hissed. "You envy my collection. Well, you're a part of it now. You belonged to M.Y.T.H., Inc. So that makes you an absolutely priceless asset that my Skeeves here have acquired."

Rattila sprang away from Chumley, revealing a long, snaky, hairless black tail, which he cracked like a whip. The impostors scattered out of his way. Rattila ascended one of the heaps, this specimen greasier and more well worn than the others. At the top, Chumley beheld a seat of some kind. It appeared to be made out of items made of precious metals, such as watches and tableware, tied together at random. It could not have been comfortable to sit upon, but Rattila lounged upon it as if it was a throne.

That was it, Chumley perceived. This was the mania Eskina feared: Rattila had set up a kingdom right there underneath The Mall itself!

The gigantic black rat plunged his paw into the heaps of spoil underneath his throne. The paw reemerged, wielding a golden rectangle that gleamed as bright as a torch.

"Behold the Master Card!" the black rat announced. "Bring me the power you have gathered for me. All the identities you used!"

As Chumley watched, the impostors dug through their belt pouches. The Pervect female opened her purse. They all produced piles of cards, much thicker than the collection he and the others had confiscated from their erstwhile captive, and thumbed hastily through them. All of the Skeeve imitators came up with the same blue card.

"One Card to Rule The Mall, One Card to Charge It,

One Card to cruise The Mall, and in the darkness Lodge It," they chanted.

As soon as the spell cleared, Chumley spotted their erstwhile prisoner, the black-mustachioed mall-rat, as Parvattani had called him. He had been the Pervect. Chumley recalled the complaint that their captive no longer had a Skeeve identity to employ, and that Rattila wouldn't—not couldn't, but wouldn't—restore that power. Chumley was inwardly pleased. At least they had deprived Rattila of one ninth of his ability to drain Skeeve's identity. Yet, as the transformations went on, he made another surprising discovery.

"You're *all* mall-rats," he observed aloud.

One of them, a brown rat with white paws, jumped up on his chest. He was half Rattila's size, which made him perhaps a twentieth of Chumley's.

"You got a problem with that?" he asked, showing his long, white teeth.

"Why, no," Chumley insisted mildly. It was a game effort to intimidate, and though it was ineffective against his present target, Chumley respected it. "I'm not speciesist—just commenting. My goodness, my manners have just gone out the window today, what?"

"Listen to him talk, dude," a slender, pale-furred specimen remarked. "We sure he's not one of us? He doesn't sound like a Troll."

"Enough, Oive!" Rattila snarled. "Bring me my power!"

Obediently the mall-rat on Chumley's chest hopped down. All nine moved toward Rattila, clusters of cards held up. The black rat gathered them all up and touched them to the gold card.

A flash of light blazed from Rattila's scrawny paws. It enveloped the black rat and made him seem larger. Chumley disapproved.

The light died away, and Rattila flung the lesser cards away from him. "So close," he wailed, clutching the glowing golden card. "It's still not enough! I want to be a magician!"

He bounded down from his throne to Chumley.

"You shall give me your identity, too," he slavered, bringing his red eyes close to Chumley's mismatched yellow ones.

"I don't believe so," Chumley replied.

He hadn't much magik of his own, but he had been raised in a magikal household, where Mums and Little Sister were always slinging off spells, and woe betide the unlucky Troll who hadn't at least a shield spell to protect him! He concentrated on raising it, even as the drooling rat laid his mangy paws upon him.

He was shocked to feel that the Ratislavan's magik cut through his defensive enchantment as an axe through tissue paper. Chumley rolled away, trying to keep Rattila from touching him again. Alas, the room was too crowded to allow a meaningful escape. His energetic gyrations brought mountains of boxes cascading down upon him until he was well and truly trapped.

"Resistance is useless," Rattila hissed, drawing magik crackling out of the air.

"Oh, heavens, no, it's not," Chumley replied weakly. "You know, you can't build a decent circuit without it, what?"

The Troll fought valiantly, but his limbs had been struck powerless. "Oh, how distasteful," he exclaimed, as the black rat laid paws upon him.

"How could we miss someone kidnapping *a Troll?*" I demanded, pacing around the purple carpet in the ruins of Massha's Secret at about four the next morning. With the help of the entire Mall security force and about half the shopkeepers, we had split up and covered every yard of The Mall we could. My feet were killing me, but guilt drove me. I couldn't stop moving.

"You were concerned about me," Massha pointed out, looking embarrassed. "Who knew they would go after someone else? We all assumed that Rattila was going for the victims with the greatest magikal talent."

"Yes," Cire piped up. "I would have thought I'd be the logical next target."

I snorted. Eskina looked woeful.

"The trails go nowhere!" she reported. "I followed them all, every set of footsteps that led out from the tent, but the tracks are spoiled. Too many scents, then nothing. Chumley's is not there at all. They must have carried him."

"We have no witnesses," Parvattani admitted, wearily. He'd supervised the whole operation on the run at my side. His tall ears were droopy with exhaustion. "I have seen the crystal balls and consulted every lookout. They must have-a disguised themselves as soon as they left the tent. I followed several leads of groups carrying a large burden out of The Mall, but all of them check out. Grotti's Carpets had a special sale today."

"This is terrible," Massha moaned. "Should we go back and try to find Tananda? She could help."

I stopped pacing and rounded on her.

"Are you saying we can't handle this by ourselves?" I roared.

Massha was taken aback. "There's no need to jump down my throat, big guy! I just thought she's got the right to know her brother's been abducted. She might have some, I don't know, Trollish way of finding a family member."

"Not as far as I know," I informed her sulkily. "And I've known the two of them for decades. I'm as worried about him as you are. We've got a pretty good force right here. You've got my experience and brains, your intuition and talent, Cire's . . . we've got Cire—"

"Hey!" Cire protested.

"—Eskina, Par, and just about the whole population of The Mall willing to help us. Let's give it one big try. If we don't locate him soon, I promise, I'll go and collect Tananda, Guido, Nunzio and the whole Mormon Tabernacle Choir."

In spite of her exhaustion Massha's big mouth quirked

in a half grin. "It's not that I don't believe in you, Aahz, honey. Where my friends are concerned I don't really believe in myself."

"Well, you ought to," I insisted. "I might have been pissed off when Skeeve let go of that cushy job as Court Magician, but I think you bring qualities to it he never did." Massha floated over, threw her arms around me, and gave me a big kiss. "Hey, save it for Hugh!"

"You know, Aahz, you may have the teeth of a land shark," she smiled, "but your bark is a heck of a lot bigger than your bite. Okay. Let's brainstorm. How do we get Chumley back?"

I couldn't look at her for a minute. I turned to our local expert. "What do you think, Eskina?"

"It is not logical," she agreed. "I think it must be a slap in our faces. Rattila has never needed to take his victims away, only their identities. This is directed at us, to show that he can remove our strongest colleague, and there is nothing we can do about it! We cannot even find his hide-out, because we cannot trace the scent to where he and his servants go to ground."

"What did you say?" I demanded, ceasing my pacing in midstep.

"I—" she began, looking confused.

"Never mind," I waved it away, feeling like the sorriest neophyte ever to hang out a shingle. "You said *trace*. Why didn't we think of that before?" I smacked myself in the forehead, hard.

"What?" Massha asked. "What didn't we think of?"

"We've been trying to set traps for them here in The Mall," I explained. "Rattila's just sent us an engraved invitation to carry the fight into his own domain, only he forgot to put a return address on the envelope. We"—I indicated our little party—"are going to phone the reverse directory and get it."

Eskina's eyes widened. "What does that mean?"

"It means," Massha translated, her eyes shining with admiration, "that we're going to plant tracers on Rattila's impostors and get them to show us where he hides out. We tag them, then follow them to their lair. It can't be too far away. They are in and out of here too often. Good thinking, sugar!"

"Could be extradimensional," I reminded her, "but you've got your gizmo. I'm prepared to follow them to hell and back."

"Me, too, Aahz, honey," Massha agreed, patting me on the hand.

"But how are we going to tag them?" Cire asked. "They're not going to sit down obligingly and let us tie GPS transmitters to their collars."

"Oh, yes, they are," I insisted. "In fact, they'll pay for the privilege of having us do it."

"How?" Parvattani demanded impatiently.

I gestured at the room around us. "Massha's Secret is going to open up for one more round of sales: a *going-out-of-business* sale. We've got to promote the heck out of it. Put up posters, whatever it takes. Go wake up Marco and have him paper The Mall with advertising. We're going to reopen for one day only to let go of a little special merchandise."

"But we don't *have* any merchandise," Cire pointed out, indicating the bare walls.

"We will," I insisted. "I'm going to go pick it up on Deva. Get this place cleaned up and ready. I'll see you in a few hours." I pulled my D-hopper out of my pocket.

"Good luck, Hot Stuff," Massha wished me, blowing a kiss.

TWENTY-FOUR

Six hours later, Moa reopened Massha's Secret to great fanfare.

The rest of the team had done a terrific job cleaning the place up. A hastily deployed curtain took the place of the splintered dressing-room door. Where the décor had been too damaged to repair at such short notice, Cire had covered it with an illusion. Most of the displays could be resurrected and put to use. All that had lacked, up until one half hour ago, was something to put on them.

I stood behind the counter, ready, still smarting a little from my whirlwind visit back to Deva. In order to get merchandise with only a couple of hours' notice I had had to use that phrase that all Deveels love and no one with any sanity would use: price is no object. I spent half an hour on a brainstorming session with sleepy Deveel fashion designers. To cut the fee somewhat I negotiated partial credit with them, because within a few days all of them would be working for Deveel merchants waiting the remaining two days to break into our market.

That wasn't important. The whole idea, I kept reminding myself, was to get what I needed, immediately, to save Chumley, to break the influence Rattila held over Massha, and to keep Skeeve from falling into his power.

I got what I wanted: within a mere five hours they produced twenty dozen garters, all of them very, very special. I figured for my purposes that number would be plenty.

As soon as I had the boxes in hand, I hopped back to The Mall. Parvattani's guards could hardly hold back the crowds already hanging around outside the shop. The avid shoppers oohed and aahed as we hung up the garters. I gave a quick rundown to the Djinnies.

"Mood detector, snack dispenser, MP3 player, poison nullifier, poison ring, love philter, steamer trunk." I stated, going down the rows and pointing to each of the items in turn. "Baby monitor, burglar alarm, perfume bottle, portable safe, memo reminder—and don't forget, when Cire slips you the word"—I stopped behind the counter and showed them a box underneath—"push these goods on whomever he's pointing at. Got that?"

They nodded. These two, Nita and Furina Djinnelli had been hired for the day from The Volcano. Rimbaldi had promised me his two nieces were the smartest salesclerks he had. I was counting on that. Chumley's life might depend upon it. I knew this was our last chance.

At ten on the dot, I nodded to Moa, who cut the ribbon. Accompanied by the reedy strains of The Mall's sale music, the shoppers poured in.

"Ooh! I didn't see these the other day!" an Imp woman cooed, falling all over a powder blue baby monitor garter. "Oh, this would come in so handy!"

"These are absolutely great!" a Klahd agreed. "These are even better than the first shipments. Too bad they're going out of business!"

"Mine!" shrieked a Deveel.

"Mine!" a Gnome shrieked back, trying to haul a black lace love philter garter away from her.

"Mine!"

"Mine!"

By eleven, Cire had tipped the wink to Nita and Furina about a dozen times. I was pretty sure there would be some overlap, since we never could be sure which were the real shoppers in the database, and which were the phonies, but by the end I was certain the ground had been thoroughly seeded.

Take that, you son of a rat, I thought. No one kidnaps one of my friends without suffering the consequences.

And, right on schedule, about half past eleven, Inspector Dota and his merry stiffs arrived.

"Shut this place down," he ordered Massha. "You don't have a right to hold a going-out-of-business sale, because you never were in business in the first place."

I pushed myself in front of him.

"Yeah, *de jure* we weren't in business, but *de facto* we should be able to hold a clearance sale, since you're denying us sales during the preprocessing time, and we can't wait around for our identification card to clear."

Dota glared at me.

"Cease all sales at once," he ordered the Djinnies, who were wrapping boxes furiously.

They looked at me. I glanced at Cire, who gave me a meaningful nod.

"Do it." I turned to the crowd of waiting shoppers. The Djinnies backed away from the counter. "Ladies and gentlemen and—whatever: due to circumstances beyond my control the sale is suspended. Any further transactions are illegal."

"Awwwwww!" A woeful cry arose from the audience.

"So, since we can't sell 'em," I began, every syllable making my teeth hurt, but I reminded myself, this was for Skeeve, for Massha, and for Chumley, "you can *take* whatever items you wish, free of charge."

"Yayyyyyy!"

The woe changed to cheers and whoops of joy. Shoppers began pulling everything they could reach off the

displays and walls. The usual fistfights had started, mixed
it up, then broken up hastily lest the combatants miss any
chance to grab free swag. A group of shoppers got together and stormed the back room, pulling down crate after
crate of goods. I felt a wrench as each of them marched out
the door carrying merchandise I had paid for and for which
I now had no means of recovering the cost.

In no time the store was stripped to the walls.

"You brought that on yourself," the inspector informed
me. "I hope you feel satisfied."

I narrowed a baleful eye at him even though I did feel
satisfied at that moment. "You've ruined our day. I'm no
longer a merchant in this establishment, so I'm no longer
under your jurisdiction, so you get your indigo butts out of
my legally leased space, or I'm going to teach your bully
boys a new place to hide their crossbows."

Inspector Dota gathered his dignity and departed. I
slammed the door behind them.

"We are now officially out of business," I announced.

"How could the tax inspectors have gotten on to us so
fast?" Massha asked, bemused.

I folded my arms and leaned against the wall, very satisfied.

"Because I called in the tip myself. We didn't need a
whole lot of time, just enough to make sure our tracers
went out with the right people."

"Aahz," Massha remarked. "You are a genius."

"Save the compliments for when we get Chumley
back," I stated, slapping my hands together and rubbing
them hard. "Now, let's give 'em a while, and start running
down the traces."

"But of course, Aahz," Rimbaldi exclaimed exuberantly,
when I took him aside in The Volcano for a private chat.

The usual flock of Klahds were gathered, openmouthed,

around a salesgirl doing a demonstration on the Gold Pocket Djeans, so no one was looking at us.

"The entire fleet of Djinnelli family carpets will be at your service, whenever you wish. Gustavo has offered weapons. Marco has offered any security arrangements you might need."

"Thanks," I breathed. "I don't know how far or how fast we'll have to move."

"They are yours, though you have to fly to the ends of the dimension, my friend! We are so sorry about the Troll."

I winced at the notion of running all over Flibber. I was already regretting that I had let so many tracers go out. But I was playing the odds. I was betting that experienced thieves like Rattila's would have captured a preponderance of the tagged goods. I hoped we would only have to chase one or two concentrated signals. At the moment The Mall was still full of small traces, scattered in every direction.

"No one saw anything unusual around here yesterday afternoon?" I asked.

"Oh, no," Rimbaldi insisted. "Business was very brisk. Several hundred purchases, two shipments, many fights— it was a good day."

I turned to go. "Just keep your eyes open, will you?"

"Of course," Rimbaldi asserted. "Your mission is our mission!"

Everyone knew what we were doing. Marco, a total convert to our cause, had spread the word privately among his relatives, and Eskina and Sibone had made sure that each and every one of their friends was on board with us.

"Wait until The Mall closes," I insisted when anyone asked me. "Just hang on."

"It's an hour before the place closes down," Massha observed, kicking one foot impatiently in the "husband's

chair" in the empty storefront. She jingled her collection of
magikal jewelry, supplemented by a few choice purchases
she had made that day. "I don't know about your capacity
for shopping, but I couldn't have lasted from ten this morning until now. I'm too antsy to wait much longer. I'm worried about Chumley."

"I agree with Massha." I glanced toward Cire, who was
playing some kind of interactive game with a guy in another dimension through his crystal ball propped on the counter. "How about it? Are we ready to start running them
down?"

"Gotta go, Delos," he remarked to the face in the globe.
He snapped the atlas of The Mall down on the counter and
put the crystal down on top of it. He passed his hands over
its surface, and the ball clouded up. "Okay, I'm ready."

"I, too," Eskina added, showing her sharp little teeth.

Parvattani rose to his feet and saluted me. "The Mall
force is at your service, sir!"

"It's just Aahz," I corrected him, with a sigh. "All right,
let's move it out."

Cire flew out ahead of us, keeping his eye on the joined
orb and map. "My global-positioning system," he
explained, hovering about five feet off the ground.
"There's a lot of dispersal already," he continued, nearly
colliding with a couple of gigantic black insectoids rolling
their purchases down the hall with their hind legs. "A few
have gone ex-dimension."

"Uh-huh," I acknowledged. It would be a pain to chase
them, but we were ready.

"Hmm. A few of your hard-core shoppers are sticking
with it. I show a few big clusters of garter signal still here
in The Mall."

"Ooh, their aching feet," Massha offered sympathetically, flying alongside Cire.

"Might be the thieves," I suggested. "I figure Rattila's

got at least a dozen henchcreatures, and they will have snatched more of our special booty than anyone else. Let's check out the closest traces first. Which is the biggest?"

Cire changed direction at the next intersection, heading toward Doorway K. He and Massha picked up air speed. Eskina and I found ourselves trotting after them, with Parvattani and his troop quick-marching behind.

"This is a really big collection," Cire informed us, excitedly. "I wouldn't be surprised if we found the whole gang right here."

Cire indicated a spot ahead that I recognized as one of the indoor arenas. It sure seemed to be the kind of venue where pickpockets would gather in force. Music louder than usual ricocheted off the rafters, a hoochie-coochie theme. The usual crowd of gawkers formed a solid barrier.

"I'll go check it out," Massha offered, lofting upward, as Parvattani's guards started to clear a way for those of us stuck using ground locomotion. With Eskina clinging to my shoulders, I forced my way forward through a forest of shoulders as high as my head. Occasionally the crowd would hoot with laughter or cheer at what they were watching. I hoped it wasn't another Skeeve appearance. I was *not* in the mood to deal with it politely.

"Never mind, honey," Massha called down to me.

At that moment, I pushed my way into the center. A long-legged silver-skinned dancer gyrated past me and tipped me a wink with one of her huge, blue-lashed eyes. Her skimpy costume consisted of two large jewels and a floaty wisp of cloth in strategic places on her body, but her arms and legs were ringed with a dozen marabou-trimmed Massha's Secret garters. Once in a while she would peel one off and sling it into the appreciative crowd. She danced close and snapped one under my nose with a sultry expression. The watchers howled with delight. I snarled.

"This is not our problem," Eskina announced in my ear.

"No kidding," I agreed. I shoved my way out of the

crowd. Cire hovered on the perimeter, looking embarrassed.

"Honestly, Aahz, I had no way of knowing!"

"Never mind," I told him. "Where's the other one?"

"Corridor O." Cire directed us toward the next largest signal.

In the big open space not far from Doorway P, we scanned the thinning crowd looking for Cire's shopper, hoping it was one or more of Rattila's thieves.

"This one was really greedy," Cire chuckled, heading toward the inevitable music stand. "I'm getting at least twenty or thirty of the tracers on the other side."

We pushed our way past the musicians, now mauling Pervish dance music. I winced at the "Toothgrinder's Waltz" being rendered in 5/6 time and at least five different keys.

A trio of blue-skinned ladies—a Dragonet, a Djinnie, and a Gremlin—stood together amidst scads of shopping bags, mostly from lingerie boutiques. By their gestures they were discussing hats. Since they had three vastly differently shaped heads I couldn't imagine a single style they could possibly agree on.

"I beg your pardon, *bella donnas,*" Parvattani interrupted them with a cordial bow, "but I am with The Mall security force. May I inspect your purchases, please?"

"Certainly not," the Dragonet replied, clutching a small green bag protectively to her chest. "Why would you ask such a thing?

I stepped forward, snapping the credentials Moa had given me out of my pocket. "Pardon me, ma'am. Undercover agent Aahz. We have reason to believe that a notorious shoplifter is attempting to smuggle himself out of The Mall in a bag."

Their eyes went wide.

"In a *shopping bag?*" the Djinn asked.

I nodded. "Mini Mitchell is a dangerous felon from, er, Nikkonia. A Shutterbug. He's been known to snap candid pictures of ladies in their undergarments and sell them to newspapers—"

"Say no more!" the Gremlin stopped me. She pushed her bags at us. "Please, look, look!"

I took a cursory glance through the bags, while Cire scanned them unobtrusively from a distance. He was getting very excited. I held up one sack after another as I finished with it. He shook his head again and again. In the end, I ran out of parcels to inspect, and I had to let them go.

"Thank you, ladies. You're safe from the snoop. Have a nice day."

The three scooped up their shopping and retreated.

"Well!" I heard the Djinn comment, before they were swallowed up by the crowd. "It's good to know they're keeping a close eye out for our safety!"

I turned to Cire, who was still excited.

"What's the matter, did you get a false positive?" I asked. "Why did we let them go?"

The Walroid's face shone with excitement. "Because they weren't giving off the signal. It's still here."

"Where?" I demanded.

Cire pointed one thick finger straight down.

"Under the floor?" Moa asked, when we called him and the other administrators to the scene. "Impossible. This building is built on the slope of a giant volcano. There's nothing under The Mall."

"I don't mean to interrupt—no, sir!" Skocklin interjected, "but, boy, you're not thinkin'." We all turned to the bandy-legged Flibberite in surprise. "'*Course* there's somethin' under here. There's the cellar."

"But we abandoned it. It was never finished," Moa pointed out.

"How good do you think a ring of shoplifters need to have their hideout?" Skocklin asked, scornfully. "You think they care if we hung up drywall? Consarn it, that means they've been right underneath our noses all these years, and we never knew it!"

"Never mind the recriminations," I put in. "How do we get down there?"

"Well, now, you don't," Skocklin announced. "It was sealed up. We discovered a better way to expand, into other dimensions who had some space to lease."

"Someone, specifically *Rattila*, figured out how to break through your seals," Eskina stated, confronting the Flibberite. "How else do you explain this signal?"

"Well, little lady, you're just wrong. It's unlivable. We didn't bother to keep the spells up, tidying the place, or anything, since it wasn't going to be used."

I eyed him as something nibbled at the back of my memory. "What kind of spells?" I demanded.

"Oh, you know," Skocklin mused, "climate control and all. We're sittin' on top of a volcano, after all."

"The Volcano!" I roared.

"Why, dagnabbit, why is the scaly boy gettin' all riled up?" Skocklin's voice faded behind me, as I shot down the hall.

"What's the hurry, honey?" Massha asked. Her levitation belt let her overtake me with ease.

"You were pretty out of it the last time we were in The Volcano," I explained, pumping my elbows to get the highest turn of speed. "Jack Frost was there, arguing with one of the Djinnellis about how hot it always was in there. He said he renewed the cooling spell frequently, but it shouldn't be wearing out that fast unless they were getting a heat leak from below!"

Massha's eyes went wide. "So you think the way down is somewhere in there?"

"It has to be," I asserted. "Where would be a better interface for thieves? Rattila's people wear dozens of different faces. The Volcano's the busiest store in The Mall.

People are always coming and going, and they have about ten thousand dressing rooms. Who would notice if somebody went into one *and never came out?*"

"Pretty convenient, living right underneath your place of business, huh?" Cire wisecracked, huffing along behind us.

"Idiot," Eskina snorted, running past him.

TWENTY-FIVE

Rimbaldi greeted us with outstretched arms. "What news, Aahz?" he boomed.

"You're harboring fugitives," I rapped out, marching past him.

"What? What does he say?" He reached for Massha's arm. "Dearest madama, what does he mean?"

"You might be closer to your shoplifters than you think, honey," Massha explained. "Can we look around?"

"Of course! My shop is at your service."

"Spread out," I ordered the group. Parvattani was on the horn in seconds. Guards, both uniformed and undercover, started filling the gigantic store. "And be ready! They've been a step ahead of us all the way. They've *got* to know we're coming. Seal the doors."

The shoppers present, began to protest. Rimbaldi and his clerks hastened to assure them that nothing was wrong.

Eskina, more nimble than I, ducked past me and started sniffing the ground for familiar scents. Cire peered behind mirrors and displays.

With Parvattani at my heels, I started flinging open dressing-room curtains.

"Sorry, madam-a," he apologized to an Imp woman we caught trying to wriggle into a pair of djeanns three sizes too small for her. "Your pardon, sir," he offered to a multi-legged Scarab wriggling into a lapis-lazuli-colored pullover tunic.

"Quit apologizing to them," I snarled. "This is important."

"How far back should we go?" Massha asked. "This place is practically infinite!"

I started sniffing sulfur and brimstone. I knew we couldn't be far off.

"It's got to be in the Flibber half," I insisted. "The extradimensional section wouldn't have access to the cellars here."

"Good thinking," Eskina exclaimed. "But how far back is that?"

"Up there," Rimbaldi indicated, pointing ahead. "Just in front of where that werewolf is coming out."

"Good," I stated. "Let's cut to the chase."

I figured if I were Rattila, I would conceal the entrance to my lair where it wouldn't be easily uncovered, say in the midst of a thousand doors just like it. I wouldn't use the farthest door, because of the tendency people have, either in dressing rooms or lavatories, to use either the very first booth or the very last. Rattila had proved he was a pretty good psychologist, or *he* had learned a lot from the identities he had ripped off over the years. Well, today was the last day he was going to have the benefit of those identities.

I flung open the second-to-last dressing room. Instead of the usual cramped stall with two hooks, a mirror, and a wooden bench, it contained a long, black, downward-sloping corridor. Waves of sulfur-scented hot air rolled out, making us gag.

"Sacred lamps!" Rimbaldi exclaimed, bobbing up to the ceiling. "I never notice that before!"

"This is it!" Cire exclaimed, his crystal ball glowing
brightly.

"I smell him!" Eskina yowled. She shot forward, baying
loudly. "Rattila!"

We plunged forward into darkness.

"Welcome, Aahz," a chilling voice echoed all around us.

Pale phosphorescence picked out looming shadows in
the inky surroundings.

"Hell with it," I snapped. "Massha, light us up."

"Gotcha, honey," she replied.

A rosy orange glow issued forth from a charm in the
palm of her hand and spread out as far as the eye could see,
hundreds of yards! Thousands! The farther it went, the
more astonished I was. And the room was far from empty.

"There must be a million gold pieces' worth of merchandise in here," Massha breathed, looking around at the
heaps and piles everywhere that reached up to the low
ceiling.

"The stolen goods!" Parvattani announced.

"That's not all," I reminded them. "We're not alone."

Around us, dozens of pairs of beady little eyes reflected
the light back to us. And two unusual pairs side by side:
one odd-sized and moon-shaped, and the other slanted and
glowing red.

"Greetings, Aahz," hissed the voice we had heard
before. The pair of red eyes bobbed slightly. "Welcome to
my Rat Hole. I am Rattila."

"Yeah, I guessed," I replied, sounding as bored as I
could.

Massha increased her light spell, and I finally got a
good look at the creep who had caused all my current
problems.

Rattila lounged at his ease on Chumley's chest. The
Troll appeared to have been tied up with duct tape, a sub-

stance that, though it had its own magikal properties, should never have been strong enough to hold him. Rattila was a ratlike creature, similar to the host of mall-rats crouching around us in the Rat Hole, but much, much bigger. If he had been standing next to me, he might have come up to my collarbone. His yellow teeth and red eyes provided the only relief from a personal color scheme that was unrelieved black: fur, nose, tail, and claws.

"He has grown huge!" Eskina squeaked, taken aback for the first time since I had known her. "He should be half that size!"

"Yes, my fellow Ratislavan," Rattila gurgled. "I have finally attained stature befitting my status."

"Hah!" Eskina scoffed. She put her hands on her furry hips. "You are a night janitor. Now, you will give me back the device, and we will return to Ratislava, where you will face justice."

"You are all forgetting something," Rattila reminded us, holding up one skinny claw. Immediately, it was filled with crackling energy like a ball of lightning. "I have your friend."

"You okay, Chumley?" I called.

"Fine," he grunted.

"Good. All right, Rattila, what do you want?"

"Now you are making sense," Rattila crooned, with all the confidence in the world. Casually, he tossed the ball of lightning a few times, then shoved it in the Troll's face. Chumley recoiled, and we all smelled the odor of singeing fur. "I want all of you to leave here. Forget about me. Go away and let me complete my business. If you don't leave at once, then your friend dies. *That's* what I want. Do you understand?"

"Uh-huh," I nodded. "Oh, well . . . *sorry, Chumley!*"

With that, I leaped at them.

Rattila gawked at me for one second, then threw the lightning ball at us. I rolled to one side, ignoring blows from the pile of socks the lightning hit, and came up running. Rattila leaped off the Troll's belly and dashed away,

shrieking, into the malodorous hideaway. The rest of the
mall-rats scattered in all directions, most of them heading
for the exit.

"Get them!" I bellowed, as Parvattani and his people
stood frozen. "I'll get Rattila."

"*We* will!" Eskina shouted, running into the gloom after
the giant rat.

Par, Cire, and the guards started chasing mall-rats all
over the place. Massha sailed over to cut Chumley loose. I
lost sight of them.

"He must not escape," Eskina panted.

The dark figure ahead of us dodged around piles of
stolen goods. Lightning balls and tongues of flame crackled toward us. We threw ourselves into heaps of moldering
clothes and stinking upholstery to avoid them. Smoke
began to fill the low chamber as Rattila's missiles set more
and more swag on fire.

"He won't," I coughed.

The truth was, I didn't have a plan. I had hoped that
superior numbers would overcome Rattila and his followers. I was surprised but relieved that there were so few of
them. Par should have no trouble rounding them up.

The footing was unsteady. Bedsheets, T-shirts, tunics,
socks and stockings, hats and underwear had been tried
on and strewn all over them place in ammonia-scented
heaps. I tripped on a knot of scarves. A bolt of green
power sizzled over my head, incinerating a grandfather
clock.

"He is doubling back," Eskina stated.

I took a moment to judge my bearings and realized she
was right. The sound of a free-for-all was ahead of us once
again. I heard Parvattani bark out orders.

"He's heading your way!" I bellowed.

I hoped Cire and Massha could cut him off, but with all
the power he had at his disposal, he probably outgunned
them. I wondered how *we* were going to deal with him if
we caught up.

"Halt in the name of the law!" I heard Parvattani shout.

Another blaze of crackling power came in response. We saw the backwash of actinic white light and heard a yell of pain.

"We must get the device away from him," Eskina insisted.

"We will," I insisted grimly. "Split up. We'll flank him."

Eskina nodded sharply and ducked away to the left, between a pair of full-length mirrors.

Emerging into the area we had been in before, I spotted Rattila alone. He was clambering up the highest heap of junk, heading for a metal seat that looked like a science-fair project at a school for young torturers. I made straight for him. He spotted me about the same time I spotted Eskina coming up behind him.

"C'mon, ugly," I taunted him, walking toward him nice and slowly. "Give up. You don't know how much power we can raise against you."

"I know all about you, Aahz," Rattila snarled, scrabbling frantically at the debris with both paws. "Magikless freak! Big talk, but nothing to back it up. Your Skeeve had more talent than you will ever have!"

"True," I acknowledged, evenly. "The kid's full of promise. But so what?"

I was livid that he had been picking my ex-partner's memories like daisies. When I got my hands on him I'd tear him a new orifice, but Eskina was within a pace of making the collar. I couldn't blow it for her.

"No matter how good someone is, there'll always be a better one coming along in a moment. He's the real thing. You're just a pathetic wanna-be."

"I am the epitome," Rattila hissed. "I hold *all*—"

Eskina pounced. Her teeth snapped shut on the nape of his neck. In spite of the near parity of their sizes, she managed to lift him off the ground and shake him.

In a flash, he became a huge red Dragonet. Eskina lost her grip and tumbled down the mound. Rattila galloped toward the exit.

I ran to catch Eskina. "You all right?" I asked, setting her upright. She pushed away impatiently.

"Yes! Hurry! He is getting away."

We dashed out into the shop, but we couldn't spot Rattila right away. Chaos reigned in The Volcano. Though I had told Rimbaldi to shut the place down, dozens of his relatives and other shopkeepers had descended. I guessed that word had gotten out that we had uncovered the lair of the gang that had been ripping them off for years, and they all wanted a piece of the action.

Rattila's henchcreatures—henchrats, now that it looked like all of his associates were rats like him—weren't stupid. I watched an Imp, pursued by Marco Djinnelli, disappear into a standing rack of clothes and emerge on the other side as a Shutterbug, full of injured dignity.

"Get your hands off me!" it squeaked, as the Djinn teleported to the far side and nabbed him.

"So sorry," Marco apologized, letting him go immediately. "Did you see an Imp—"

"That's him, Marco!" I called, as Eskina and I dashed toward them. "Shapechanger!"

The Shutterbug didn't wait around for light to dawn on Marco. He fled into the melee. Marco gathered his wits and teleported after him. The mall-rat turned into a Djinn, too, and started *bamfing* around, trying to find a way out of the store. Luckily The Mall's security system prevented him from being able to hop farther than the door, where Cire was waiting for him with his back to the carved doors, which had been bolted and chained shut. The Djinn-thief popped out again, just a moment before Marco and two of his cousins converged on the same spot.

All around us Parvattani's officers chased the thieves, who morphed into various shapes in hopes of escaping notice. I thought I spotted Rattila's red-scaled form near the big three-way mirror halfway to the front. I pushed my way toward him.

"Leave me alone!" a plump Deveel matron shrieked, holding her purse to her. "I am not a mall-rat! I am a long-time customer!" Bisimo, Parvattani's lieutenant, tugged at the purse. "Oh, you brute!" The handbag flipped open, sending cosmetic cases, address book, black leather wallet, and a pair of sequined thong underwear flying. No credit cards.

Bisimo's cheeks turned sapphire. "I am so sorry, madama!" he stammered, helping her to pick up her belongings. She belted him over the head with the empty bag.

Chumley had made the first real capture. He held a mall-rat up by the scruff while he snapped its collection of identity cards one at a time in his teeth. Massha hovered over a gondola of clothes that writhed and gyrated. Every time a limb stuck itself out of the hangers, she zapped it with a little gadget that looked like a miniature lightning bolt.

Rattila was getting closer to the entrance. Guards saw him coming and threw themselves on him or tried to stun him with the pikes Massha had issued to them a few days before. Scales crackling with power, he threw off attacks and attackers with ease.

"Cire!" I bellowed. "Stop him!"

The Walroid saw him coming and braced himself. His huge flipperlike hands whipped out, producing a cone of cold white light. Rattila-the-Dragonet emitted a jet of fire sixteen feet long. I couldn't blame Cire. He dove to one side.

Eskina, baying shrilly, bounded up, trying once again to bring Rattila down. He swatted her away into three oncoming Djinnelli cousins. Before anyone else could get close to him, Rattila threw an enormous blast of magik at the doors. They splintered and burned. Rattila dove through the hole. I headed after him.

"Cire, Eskina! Come with me!" I shouted. I backed up, preparing my dive carefully. I hate fire. We Pervects are very vulnerable to it. I threw up my arms to protect my face.

"Aahz!" Massha called, just before I jumped. She hovered in the air, brandishing a kicking brown creature by the ear. She shook it at me. The creature struggled and whined. "What about these mall-rats?"

"Handle it!" I bellowed. "You can do it just fine!"

I leaped.

TWENTY-SIX

Cire flew up to the ceiling as soon as we were outside The Volcano and pointed in the direction of the fleeing Dragonet.

"There he goes!" he shouted. "He's changed again—he's a Flibberite, I mean she!"

Massha's salesclerk, I thought grimly. But Flibberites couldn't cover ground as fast as Dragonets. We stood a better chance of catching him now.

The Mall would be closing very shortly, which meant the crowds had thinned down a lot. Eskina and I pelted down the nearly empty corridors. Our prey was clearly visible ahead of us.

He knew we were following him, too. He turned and launched another powerball in our direction. I threw myself to the left behind the nearest obstruction, a cotton-candy stand. The cones of fluff blackened, smouldered, and went up like torches.

"I'm not hurt," I shouted, as much for my allies as for Rattila. "Is that all you've got, you pitiful little vermin?"

In answer, a cannonade of small embers followed. I

avoided almost all of them. One struck my arm like a foul ball. I batted out my burning sleeve and kept running.

"You are under arrest," Eskina shrieked. "Felony theft, conspiracy, receiving stolen goods, larceny, criminal damage to property, grievous bodily harm, kidnapping, fleeing and eluding—"

Another bolt roared toward us, this time aimed at her. She had been expecting it, though, and flattened herself behind an empty musician stand. The firebolt slammed into a wall, leaving a singe mark the size of a medicine ball.

"Is that the thief?" the gray-spotted Shire horse demanded, as we rolled past the oat shop.

"The master thief!" I shouted back.

"My friends and I will help!" he whinnied. He threw back his head and let out a long neigh. Shopkeepers and clerks poured out into the corridor. What guards had not already converged on The Volcano joined the throng.

"No, don't get in our way!" I yelled. All I needed was for innocent civilians to get hurt by this maniac. The shopkeepers paid no attention, falling in around us. Those who could fly caught up with Rattila, only to get pelted with magikal fire. A Phoenix was burned badly enough to burst into a pillar of flames. By the time I passed him he was reduced to a heap of ashes, out of which peeked the curved shell of the new egg.

Others weren't so lucky. Imps, Gnomes, Deveels, and Djinnies who weren't quick enough to dodge or magikally avert Rattila's attacks suffered burns and scorches. The corridor was getting crowded again.

"He's only got one idea," I hissed to Cire when he swooped low enough for me to hear. "Can you counteract those fireballs?"

"Think so," the Walroid stated. "I can extinguish them when I see them coming."

I groaned. "So why weren't you?"

"Oh, come on, Aahz! It's been a long time since I saw action like this."

In training or not, once Cire had the idea, he made good use of technique. Rattila snapped out missiles at the growing crowd as we followed him around corners, up ramps, and down stairs. Cire sailed along at a comfortable altitude, snuffing out the crackling spheres like birthday candles.

"Where is he going?" Eskina demanded. We passed through the center court of The Mall.

"The loading dock," I guessed. "That's where the other rat went to ground."

"I can beat him there," offered one of the Shire horses. Risking Rattila's attacks, she galloped past him.

"We must stop her," Eskina warned.

"We can't catch her," I retorted. "Besides, there's nothing there but garbage, unless it's the back way into the Rat Hole."

I couldn't have been more wrong.

We banged through the swinging metal doors into the unadorned space where the shop owners received their deliveries and dropped off their refuse. I spotted the Shire horse and the other clerks who had run on ahead of us. They were all standing stock-still, staring at a pair of figures at the end of the long chamber.

The one on the right was Chloridia. She had come back!

Just in time I recognized the shadow thrown up on the wall of the figure on the left. Rattila had turned into a basilisk! The still figures had been turned to stone statues.

"Don't look!" I warned Eskina and Cire, as they stumbled to a halt behind me. I pulled them down behind a crate. I couldn't warn the others, who piled into the room, took one glance at the sinuous figure wavering back and forth, and froze in place with surprised looks on their faces.

"Chlory!" I shouted. "It's me, Aahz! That's Rattila! Stop him!"

I peeked around the corner to see if she heard me.

She heard me, all right: a bolt of bright green light shot toward me. I ducked back as the magik came close enough to sizzle a few of the scales on my cheek. I glanced again. Chloridia marched toward us, a blank look in her eyes.

"Rattila has her in his power," Eskina hissed.

"Well, she's not as strong as I am," Cire insisted. He stood up and flung a double flipperful of golden light in her direction.

The four-eyed enchantress chanted a brief phrase, and the light dissipated. She leveled her hands at us, and the packing crate blew into pieces. Rubber Kewpie dolls went flying in every direction. We backed off. Chloridia advanced on us, with Rattila behind her, cackling.

"Take that!" Cire announced. A pit opened up at Chloridia's feet. She simply stepped out onto the empty air. "Uh-oh. Run."

We ran.

"Quick," Cire demanded, as the swinging doors swished shut behind us. "What are her weaknesses? What can I exploit?"

"Nothing," I spat out, after searching my memory. "She's a consummate professional. She teaches magik at the Kallian academy in the off-season from her daily show."

"Fishguts!" Cire swore.

We headed into the nearly empty midway. Behind us the basilisk's scaled belly hissed on the tiled floor. I couldn't hear Chloridia's footsteps at all.

That was because she had taken to the air. As we rounded the corner into the food court, she alighted in front of us, her four purple eyes as blank as poker chips.

"Chlory, snap out of it!" I ordered. "You're under a spell! Listen to me!"

A sneer twisted her lovely face as she waved an arm. The entire display of pies in a pastry-shop window came flying at us.

I dove for cover behind a caramel-corn wagon, pursued by a plank of lemon meringue pies. They all splatted harmlessly on the glass, showering me with blobs of filling. Cire yelped as a pot of soup dumped itself on his head.

"Ugh! I hate licorice!" Eskina wrestled with strands of black and red looping around her like whips. They knotted themselves, pinioning her arms to her body. She attacked them with her sharp little teeth.

"Chlory, it's mind control!" I called. "Think! I know you're in there somewhere!"

Chloridia's arms waved again, and more display windows burst outward, their contents flying to do her bidding.

"Aahz, look out!" Cire shouted.

He dove toward me just as a roasted chicken on a skewer arrowed toward my heart. He jumped in the way. The skewer missed me, but it went partly through Cire's arm. I dragged him into the doorway of the chicken shop and yanked it out.

"Ow!" Cire protested. "That hurt as much coming out as going in."

"Sorry," I offered. "I never knew you'd take a pullet for me."

Cire's face screwed up in a pained grin. "What are friends for?"

The blinding glare of a warming light gave me an idea. I picked up the nearest heavy object, a rolling pin used for making the shop's celebrated pot pies, and put it in Cire's good hand.

"Take this. When you get the chance, *use it!*"

"For what?"

"Hey, Chlory!" I called, standing up. The blank eyes turned toward me, and the hand flew up to throw another spell. "The media is here! They want to interview you!" I turned the light so it shone in her face. "Look! The cameras are rolling! Come over here for your close-up!"

Somewhere, deep in the controlled mind of the enchantress, the need to seek publicity overrode Rattila's spell. She hesitated, then tottered toward me.

"That's it," I crooned. "Come on. The reporters all want to talk to you. Come right in—"

Clunk!

Cire whacked her across the back of the head with his rolling pin. She sagged bonelessly to the ground.

"She's out for the count for the time being," I announced. "Now, for Rattila."

I stepped out into the hallway, just in time to see the basilisk's tail disappear around the next corner.

"He is running away! He is cowardly without his minion!" Eskina crowed, taking off after the fleeing snake.

"Well done, Cire," I remarked, grudgingly.

The Walroid smirked, clutching his wounded arm.

"So you finally forgive me for all those other times when things didn't exactly go right?" Cire asked.

"When you screwed up," I corrected him. "It's a start. Now we've got to fix your arm and snap Chlory out of her trance. Sibone!"

"I am here, darling Aahz," came the sultry voice. Sibone undulated to me and wound a couple of arms around me, while one sinuous arm extended to charm golden bubbles out of thin air. When the heady aroma of fresh coffee began to percolate down to us, Chloridia's four purple eyes fluttered open. She reached for the nearest iridescent sphere. It turned into a substantial pottery mug full of ink black liquid.

"Oooh, my head!" she moaned.

"I will take care of them," Sibone assured me, turning her lidless eyes my way. "Go!"

I took off in the direction of Eskina's energetic baying.

The sounds of battle echoed from the high ceiling when I got to Atrium K. Eskina ducked and wove between the examples of statuary that adorned this particular intersection, all the time trying to get closer to her quarry. He had changed form again. I spotted him as he dove behind a granite plinth holding the image of a gryphon rampant. He was now a Deveel, but his ears still retained the double point of a Flibberite. Something was going wrong with his magik!

"Hey, ratface!" I shouted. "I'm over here!"

Rattila turned my way and threw a chunk of energy at me. I flattened myself on the floor as it went sizzling overhead. Not sizzling, really, but fizzing. I rolled over in time to see the bolt hit a bar table at a nearby inn. It made St. Elmo's fire dance in the ribs of the umbrella, but after that it dissipated harmlessly. I thought it looked more like static electricity than lightning.

He had lost his connection to the lines of force! We had him now!

Rattila saw me get to my feet with a broad grin on my face. He must have known he was history now. Even his disguise slipped. No longer a Deveel, Dragonet, or Djinn, he was reduced once more to being a plain old black rat. Fear huge in his red eyes, he eluded Eskina one more time and started running down the hall.

"He's wearing out," I panted to Eskina, as we jogged after him.

"He must not be carrying the device," Eskina pointed out. "He must seek it again, or the new power will desert him. If he succeeds in getting to it again, he will become as powerful as he was before."

Tired as I was, that news galvanized me. I started pumping my arms to make my legs move faster. I wished Cire would catch up with us again. We could certainly use his flying ability.

"To The Volcano!" I puffed.

TWENTY-SEVEN

When we reached The Volcano it looked markedly different than it had only minutes before. All the fighting had ceased. The Djinnies and the mall-rats seemed to have been cooperating to put the merchandise back on the shelves, but now they all stood, gawking, in the direction of the entrance to the Rat Hole. Massha floated on the air toward the back of the store.

"He went thataway, Big Spender!" she called, as I thundered down the orange aisle.

"He seeks the device," Eskina explained. Massha swooped down to join us.

"He doesn't have it?" she asked, surprised.

"He's running out of gas," I stated. "We can knock him out once and for all if we can get to the device ahead of him."

"But where is it?" Massha inquired.

"Under the throne," Chumley exclaimed, an enlightened expression on his face. "He calls it the Master Card. I saw him stow it there after he had used it."

The glowing aisle under my feet felt hot, as if the volcano under the floor sensed the turmoil going on above it.

We hammered down the ramp into the Rat Hole.

"One Card to Rule The Mall, One Card to Charge it . . ." Rattila had reached the mound ahead of us. Chanting, he dug his paw into the rotting trash and came up with a gleaming rectangle of gold. Suddenly, the black rat was replaced by a glowing golden wyvern. It spat a stream of acid at us. Chumley caught a whole load in the chest. Howling in pain, he beat at the spreading blob of blackness in the middle of his purple fur. Massha flew to his aid.

Rattila let go with another gob. It splashed at my feet, burning a few holes in my pants hems.

I was too furious to care. This whole adventure started with me getting fireballs thrown in my general direction. This was the being to blame for my partner's damaged reputation, for the trouble we'd all been through. I wasn't about to let him get away again, no matter how much punishment I had to take to get to him. I stepped over the acid and advanced on him.

Massha was ready with a few tricks of her own. Like trying to see one tree in a thick forest, I had never noticed one particular piece of jewelry or another in her formidable ensemble. The solid gold lemon was new to me.

"Here comes the spoiler," she called. She waved it, and the spurting acid turned into huge potted plants, which landed with a thud on the cluttered floor. I laughed. Rattila snarled and changed shape. I growled now; he had transformed himself into the attractive Pervect I had first seen in Rimbaldi's shop.

Evidently the original had had a purseful of heavy-duty hardware. Rattila dipped into the handbag and came up with a fully automatic repeating crossbow. We all dove for cover as the armor-piercing rounds sprayed out.

I took advantage of the muzzle flash blinding my adversary to start crawling, commando fashion, to my left. Once his sight cleared Rattila was looking where I had been, not where I was. He let the enchantress's image drop. I was glad; the mangy SOB didn't deserve to wear a Pervect face.

I figured two or three or four could play at the identity-theft game.

"Massha," I hissed, "disguise me as him. All of us!"

"One special coming up!" Massha announced.

I couldn't see the change in myself, but suddenly there was a big black rat hovering in midair, one lifting an end table to use as a missile, and another one sneaking up behind Rattila.

Eskina had entered the field of battle now. She had a pair of handcuffs dangling from one hand as she crawled up the mound. I stood up, making as much noise as I could. Rattila stared at me, then at Chumley and Massha. He looked shocked and angry; then he grinned, showing all his teeth.

"So, you like my face," he smirked. "Well, I like yours, too!" Beginning the interminable chant again, he changed into the image of Massha. "Don't I look pretty? An over-sized Jahk with garish taste in clothes?"

"Not everyone looks good in basic black, you scum," Massha retorted furiously, clasping her hands together.

Rattila's face contorted as he started to choke. Abruptly he recovered, and an evil grin spread across his face. "How do you like turnabout, *Jahk?*" He closed his/her hands, and the floating rat that was Massha began to cough, clutching her throat. "And your pathetic little toys—those aren't real power!" Her necklaces and bracelets began to shatter. The fragments rained down. "Yes, that one, too!" Her flying belt disappeared. She thumped to the ground.

Chumley heaved the end table at him. He dodged it. I flung myself forward. Eskina scrambled the rest of the way up to the peak of the mound.

Rattila heard the jingle, and spun. Massha stopped coughing. Now Eskina was suffocating. Her handcuffs went flying. I closed the rest of the distance.

Rattila couldn't keep his mind on more than one thing

at a time. I put him in a judo hold and tripped him over on his back. As soon as I grabbed him, Eskina fell down, gasping for breath. Chumley joined us, holding on to the figure's kicking feet.

"Some world-ruler you are," I scoffed in Rattila's face. "You lose focus too easily. I bet all your spells fall apart like that." I reached for the gold card.

Roaring out his rhyme, Rattila squirmed out of my grasp in the shape of a gigantic serpent. Chumley reached around with both arms and locked my arms in the corners of the serpent's jaw so he couldn't sink his fangs into anyone. I spotted the Master Card on a tiny chain around the snake's neck, and started to shinny up the writhing, muscular length toward it.

"Mmmph mmmph mmm mmm mmm mmmph, mmmmph mmm mmm mmm mmph," Rattila-the-snake muttered around my arms.

In the next second I was grasping a bright yellow, six-foot fish covered with five-inch-long spines.

"Yeowch!" I yelled. It was an effort, but I held on.

"I'll take care of it, honey," Massha called. I don't know how she did it, but the spines became rubbery and soft. We wrestled Rattila to the ground by his fins and dragged him by inches down the slope toward Eskina and the handcuffs. His flukes flopped furiously, trying to make me let go.

"No way, vermin," I snarled. Eskina jumped on top of him and fastened the cuffs around one fin. The open mouth goggled a few times. We collapsed on top of a nest of thin tentacles like pink spaghetti. They whipped around us with astonishing strength and dragged us up toward a maw filled with incurving teeth.

"You don't know the power of the Master Card," Rattila slavered.

I braced myself off a bundle of the writhing tentacles and came around with both hands joined in a double fist. I smashed it into the grinning face. The tentacles contorted painfully as the face collapsed in pain.

"I don't believe in credit cards," I informed him, giving

him a solid kick, and followed it up with an uppercut.

Eskina sank her teeth into the tentacle holding her. Chumley, uncommonly furious for a being of his temperament, knotted the writhing legs together in a gigantic macramé plant holder.

"Gives other people too much power over you."

Rattila wailed in pain. I recognized the chant again.

"I no longer need to control you," he yelled, changing into a Troll the exact likeness of Chumley. "I've got power over all your friends!" He lifted each of us in one hand and threw us down the mound. "Where are my mall-rats?" he roared, stomping toward the showroom.

Massha staggered to her feet. "They're not coming," she announced, dusting herself off. "They got a better offer."

The Troll spun on his heel, gawking in astonishment.

I wanted an explanation from Massha, too, but it would have to wait.

Chumley was there and ready for him.

"You do not deserve to wear my face," he informed Rattila, wrapping one meaty arm around the other's head.

If you've never seen two Trolls fight, let me tell you it is not a lot different than watching two avalanches rolling toward one another. The collateral damage to the location, furnishings, and anyone unlucky enough to be within range of a limb or thrown object is usually considerable. Most insurance policies written in dimensions where there is a lot of D-hopping specifically exclude damage sustained involving a Troll, a lot like the dragon-fire exclusion. I had always found it amusing that insurance never covered anything that was likely to cost the most to repair.

Massha, Eskina, and I followed the battle as it progressed around the overstuffed Rat Hole and up the ramp out into The Volcano. Roars, howls, and thuds warned the curious listeners in the store overhead to get the hell out of the way and retreat to a safe distance by the time Chumley and his impostor rolled through the curtained doorway.

"Should we not help Chumley?" Eskina inquired.

"We're far more likely to get in the way," I informed

her. "If Chumley needs our help, he'll ask."

One Troll was clearly flagging. He heaved up a low platform, brought it down on his opponent's head, and stopped
to pant. The other staggered backward, then came running
at the first one with his head down. The first went flying
back into a rack of clothes.

I figured Chumley had gotten enough of his own back
by now. Moa and The Mall guards watched, wide-eyed,
with the shopkeepers and Jack Frost, who must have been
called in about the heat leak again. As soon as my way was
clear, I beckoned to the Djinnellis.

"Give us a hand!" I shouted, miming pulling two
objects apart.

The Djinnellis understood and held up their folded
arms.

Suddenly, the two Trolls were plastered on the air like
huge, shaggy paper dolls. I realized then that the exhaust-
ed one was Chumley. The other, a glint of gold showing
through the fur near his neck, seemed fresh as a daisy.

To the amazement and consternation of the Djinns,
Rattila shook off the suspension spell. He seemed to grow
larger as he marched toward me.

"That was refreshing!" he boomed. "I am nearly at full
power! And I am going to use your friend's identity to do it!"

The Troll vanished. In his place was a tall, skinny, pale-
haired, pale-eyed Klahd with a goofy grin and a kind, open
expression. Skeeve.

"Hey, Aahz, don't you like the idea of me being the
most powerful magician in the world? I'm going to make
it possible for Rattila to achieve his dream. Isn't that
great?"

My hands twitched. At the sight of my ex-partner's face
I admit a lot of emotions went though me, but on top was
outrage, followed by fury.

"You dare," I began in a low voice that made everyone
else in the store back away slowly, "to sully the good name
of my friend?"

"More than that!" the Skeeve-face gloated. "At the same

time he gives up the rest of the energy I need to become a full magician, I take full possession of him, too. He will cease to have any separate existence from my Master Card."

"Well, then, we need to cancel your account," I informed him smoothly.

I darted toward the pouch on his belt. A hand like a steel trap caught mine. He bent my wrist backward until the bones ground together.

He grinned in my face. "Want to hear me sing?"

"Not a chance!" I snarled.

I swept my feet underneath his and sent him sprawling. He had Skeeve's quick reflexes at his command, so he was up in no time. I knocked him down again with a back-handed swipe. He flicked a hand, and I floated up toward the ceiling. I windmilled, trying to get back toward the ground.

"Flying's great, Aahz! Don't you wish you could do it on your own? Oh, but I forgot," the face pouted. "You lost your magik." The pad of air under my body vanished, and I hit the floor. "You kept up a façade like you were still important. You tried to show me how wise you are, but it's all a sham. Everyone pretends they like you, that they feel sorry for you, but inside they're laughing. In this world nothing else matters but power!"

He reached out and pinched his thumb and forefinger together. Suddenly, my ears were filled with a deafening blare of music, voices, and noise. I knew what he had done: he'd destroyed Massha's cone of silence. Without its protection my sensitive ears were going to be over-whelmed by the sounds of The Mall—he hoped.

"You are so wrong, long-nose," I gritted out. "And this is going to end now!"

The ground dropped away from me again, but I had a hand on a display rack. I used my weightlessness to swing my legs around in a circle. I cringed a little at attacking one of my closest friends, but I reminded myself that this was *not* my friend but someone who wanted to drain the life out of him. At the last moment I tensed so my whole weight hit him in the head. Rattila staggered back a couple of paces, then came roaring in at me. As I swung around I smacked him in the face. He stopped, goggling. I came around the pole again and slapped him so hard he staggered and fell.

My feet settled toward earth.

"Go get him, tiger!" Massha shouted, waving a charm shaped like a scale at me.

I leaped onto the impostor. The Djinnellis and other onlookers crowded in.

"Back off!" I roared. "This one's mine!"

I hauled Rattila up by the scruff. His mouth and hands twitched. I felt something hot and gluey pour over my head, covering my eyes, nostrils and mouth. I sucked in a deep breath. The stuff solidified, but I didn't let go. I shoved Rattila into the wall and head-butted him. The shell over my face cracked away. I lifted a fist. The blue eyes opened wide.

"Aahz, don't hit me," Skeeve's voice begged me. It caught me off guard. "I didn't mean those things I said. I respect you. Really."

I cocked my head. "Sorry, partner," I replied.

It was a wish for the absent Skeeve, not for this loser. With all the strength in my body, I connected my fist with his jaw. I threw another punch. The head snapped back against the wall, and the long body collapsed in a heap on the floor. I could have stopped then, but I had a lot of resentment to get out of my system, too. I kept pounding on Rattila until the Skeeve-form disappeared, and he became a rat again.

I straightened up and kicked at him. "And your rhyme stinks, too!"

Eskina raced in and bound up the limp rodent's limbs with her cuffs. "Magnificent, Aahz!" she congratulated me. My friends and new acquaintances crowded in to shake my hand and pound me on the back. "Now, where is the device?"

I searched through the greasy black fur until I came up with the gleaming gold card.

"Here it is."

"Excellent! Give it to me! I must take it back!"

"No way," I retorted. "This thing is too dangerous to exist. Besides, it's got an imprint in it of everyone that Rattila ever ripped off."

"In spite of my firewall I can still feel a pull from its spell," Massha added.

"I, too," Chumley agreed.

"Unless you can empty it of its charge, you're not getting it back," I concluded.

"But I must bring it back with me!" Eskina shrieked. "Five years I have sought it. The scientists are waiting!"

"And what happens the next time an alchemy lab janitor can't resist the temptation?" I asked.

Eskina looked crestfallen.

"You are right," she acknowledged.

"You have the villain," Parvattani reminded her, coming up to put a consoling arm around her.

She looked up at him gratefully. "That is true," she smiled.

"You two make a good team," I told them. "Think about it."

They both looked shy.

"What about the card, Hot Stuff?" Massha asked.

"History," I snapped out.

I bent the device between my fingers. Unlike the slave cards it could make, the Master Card wouldn't break, no matter how much I twisted it.

"Let me try," Chumley offered.

But he couldn't make a dent in it either. Nor could the magik of any of the Djinnellis, Cire, Sibone, or Chloridia, nor Woofle, who had finally come out from wherever he had been hiding.

"I'm stumped," I admitted.

"Perhaps you had better let me take it back," Eskina offered, sympathetically. "It was made to withstand elemental forces."

"Elemental!" I snapped my fingers. "Jack, are you here?"

The climate-control engineer squeezed through the crowd. "What can I do for you, Aahz?"

I tapped a foot on the glowing red floor. "What'll it take to get through this to the lava underneath?"

"A snap," Jack grinned at me. "A *cold* snap." He pointed a finger at the floor. A white cone formed over the spot.

When he finished there was a round white patch on the floor. I brought a heel down on it. It shattered. Lava splashed up through the broken shards of flooring. I tossed the gold card into the liquid burning stone until the letters on it ran. A chorus of howling voices rose from it as it melted away. The remains flowed off under the floor. Jack spread his hands, and the hole sealed up as if it had never been there. I dusted my hands together.

"It's a time-honored tradition, after all," I remarked, "throwing all-powerful magik items into volcanos to get rid of them."

"I feel so much better!" Massha announced.

"So do I," Chumley agreed.

"Me, too," added Marco.

"And I," a female Deveel put in.

The chorus of voices went on and on, until everyone was looking at one another.

"And the moral of that story is," I concluded, "always look out for those hidden charges."

On the floor at my feet, Rattila groaned.

TWENTY-EIGHT

"You must take this, too, darling madama," Rimbaldi insisted, draping another pair of djeanns on Massha's outstretched arms, this one in acid green. "And accessories! Belts, bracelets, scarves, anything you like! We must make up for the things that villain took from you. My cousin Paolo does his best to repair your lovely belt and bracelets. You shall have more, more, more!"

"I'm overwhelmed, you beautiful man," Massha batted her eyes at him. "That's plenty, honest! Stop!"

All morning the denizens of The Mall had been showing their gratitude for our capture of Rattila and his mob. Massha admired herself in the big three-way mirror, attended by a troop of willing Djinnies and a couple of Rattila's ex-henchrats.

"By the way," I asked, sitting in the midst of a mountain of boxes with my name on them, "what was the deal you made with those creatures?" I gestured toward a rat who went out in search of an orange belt in Massha's size to go with the green pants.

"Well, you know, the mall-rats were scared to death!"

Massha declared, holding a scarf up to her ample chin and adding it to her heap of swag. "They're really harmless little creatures, if you overlook their penchant for picking up anything that isn't nailed down. What with all those Djinns pouring into the store, and the guards chasing them everywhere, they thought they were about to die. Once we got them all surrounded I realized they were Rattila's pawns. With Chumley's help I kept the storekeepers from killing them while I negotiated a settlement. Negotiation," she repeated with a wink at me, "is something I learned from *both* my teachers."

"Save the flattery," I growled. "Let's hear the rest."

Massha winked at me. "Well, I got the Djinnellis to agree that if the mall-rats surrendered their cards, they would hire them to help shore up security all over The Mall. As lifelong shoplifters, they know where all the holes are, so to speak, and they exploit them. Now they can point them out to the owners. Their leader, the one they call Strewth, persuaded the other mall-rats to agree, as long as they didn't have to be official, er, rats. They had a reputation to protect."

"Parvattani agreed," Chumley put in. "He told them they can work undercover. He even offered them their special undercover uniforms."

I laughed, remembering the gaudy getups we had turned down. "Inspired!"

"Indeed!" Chumley cheered. "I was very proud of Massha. I wish you could have seen how well she handled it all."

"It was nothing," Massha bridled, shoving Chumley backward into his collection of goodies.

The Troll, too, was surrounded by boxes of books, candy, grooming products, and anything in which he had ever expressed even the most passing interest. The patch of acid-singed fur on his chest had been expertly barbered and doctored by the local alchemist, all free of charge.

All the frozen clerks and guards in the loading dock had been restored to life once Rattila's power was broken. The shopkeepers of The Mall were overwhelmed with gratitude, now that the ring of thieves had been broken and Rattila hauled away by a triumphant Eskina.

The little investigator had left early that morning for Ratislava. She had persuaded Parvattani to go with her, not that he needed a lot of persuading. He was in love.

"For a tour of the most beautiful dimension of them all," she had told me, giving me a kiss good-bye. "I have succeeded in my mission, thanks to you. I shall most likely get a promotion. And possibly, a lifelong friend." She was in love, too. It was kinda sweet.

"Aahz, there you are!"

Chloridia swept into The Volcano with a hand through Cire's elbow. She stretched out two free arms to embrace me.

"I wanted to say farewell. I need to get back to Kallia. I have a documentary lined up to warn people about the trauma I have just gone through! The dangers of unbridled shopping!"

"I'm going with her," Cire added, blowing out his mustache. "Now that The Mall has cleaned up my credit, I've got some free time, and the publicity wouldn't hurt. Thanks for everything, Aahz. Friends?"

"Of course we're still friends," I tossed off, casually, shaking his outstretched flipper. "You're not half so bad as you used to be. You did good."

Chloridia gave her tinkling laugh. "You should come, too. You are the great hero of the day! Let me interview you on the network. It'd be a tremendous boost for you."

"No, thanks, sweetheart," I demurred. "All I want to do is go back to the thinking I was doing when all this started." A commotion near the front of the shop attracted my attention. "And there's the chair I'm going to do it in."

Delivery Flibberites in pale brown uniforms guided a floating platform containing a huge form under a tarpaulin through the crowds of shoppers and lowered it at my feet.

"Your new chair, sir," the lead deliveryman announced.

I threw off the covering and circled it, cackling with delight. "Look at that! Mahogany wood, dark red leather upholstery, drink-holders, magikal entertainment system, full horizontal recline—every bell and whistle!" I threw myself into it. The cushions conformed to my body as if they had been made for it, which they had. "Aaaaah."

"Stylish," Chumley commented.

"Beautiful," Massha agreed.

"Very lovely," Chloridia acknowledged, leaning over to kiss me. "Ta-ta, darling."

"Later, Aahz," Cire added. He waved a hand, and the two of them vanished.

"Mr. Aahz!" Woofle bustled over to me, a receipt in his hand. "You can't expect me to pay this amount! It's outrageous!"

Moa sauntered in after his fellow administrator. "Pay it, Woofle." It sounded like that wasn't the first time he had said it.

"But, Moa!" Woofle looked like he was about to explode in outrage.

"Pay it. He earned it. Even more than that."

I tilted my head to look up at him. "You're not going to bring up that crap about a reward again," I moaned.

I had rejected their offer last night and again this morning. Every time I did it, it was more painful, but I had made myself a promise, and I was trying to stay serene about it. Besides, Chumley and Massha were watching me.

"Why not?" Moa pressed.

"Because I did what I came here to do: restore my partner's good name and make sure it couldn't happen to him again," I stated. "I did it. Now I'm going home."

"But you saved all the other shoppers, too," Moa pointed out. "You're not going to stand on principle about that?"

I vacillated. I had earned the reward according to the deal I myself had made, but it *was* the principle of the thing. Skeeve would have made me stick to it. After all, I had done this for him. It hurt, but I said it.

"No. No reward."

Massha and Chumley let out the breaths they had been holding.

Moa's mouth quirked in a little smile.

"I'll tell you what," he suggested, "I'll make you good with Marco Djinnelli, and we'll also pick up any other expenses you incurred on our behalf, including everything from Massha's Secret. You'll at least be even."

"Even!" Woofle snorted, with a scornful gesture. "There must be ten thousand gold pieces' worth of goods here!"

"All gifts," I pointed out.

"And your service was worth every copper." Moa addressed me directly. "By the way, speaking of Massha's Secret, I just want you to know that several Deveels have all applied to open garter shops here, starting just exactly a week from when you opened yours. We were happy to oblige, since your merchandise was so popular."

"Uh-huh." I had my own ideas of who had called in the tax bureau the first time, and I suspected Moa did, too, but we would never be able to prove it. "Any of 'em read their leases all the way through?" I asked innocently.

"No," Moa replied, with a conspiratorial wink. "You'd think they would, knowledgeable businessdemons like that."

"Good," I stated, with an answering grin. "I hope they all have all the luck they deserve."

Moa waved a hand. "We'll deliver all of this to your residence, of course. Again, Aahz, thank you. Your M.Y.T.H., Inc. certainly does merit its reputation."

He withdrew, taking the protesting Woofle with him.

"I'm impressed, sugar," Massha remarked, propping her hip on the arm of my recliner. "And Skeeve would be proud of you. Are you going to tell him about it?"

"Nah," I replied. "I don't want to interrupt his education. I'll drop Bunny a line and tell her the whole thing was a mistake."

"One of these days"—Massha smiled—"someone's going to find out what a softy you are inside."

"When that day comes I'll have to rip out his guts," I asserted. "That includes the two of you if you ever tell anyone I gave anyone a major freebie. I don't want time-wasters coming out of the woodwork like that."

Chumley and Massha exchanged knowing glances.

"Our lips are sealed," Chumley assured me.

"Good," I responded, settling deeper into the uphol-stery. "After all, I've got a reputation to protect. That's the one thing you can't buy in any mall."

ROBERT ASPRIN

Robert L. Asprin was born in 1946. While he has written some stand alone novels such as *Cold Cash War*, *Tambu*, *The Bug Wars*, and also the Duncan and Mallory Illustrated stories, Bob is best known for his series: The Myth Adventures of Aahz and Skeeve, the Phule's Company novels; and, more recently, the Time Scout novels written with Linda Evans. He also edited the groundbreaking Thieves' World anthologies with Lynn Abbey. His most recent collaboration is *License Invoked*, written with Jody Lynn Nye. It is set in the French Quarter, New Orleans, where he currently lives.

JODY LYNN NYE

Jody Lynn Nye lists her main career activity as "spoiling cats." She has published thirty-two books, such as *Advanced Mythology*, the fourth and most recent in her Mythology fantasy series (no relation); three SF novels; four novels in collaboration with Anne McCaffrey, including *The Ship Who Won*; edited *The Dragonlover's Guide to Pern*, *The Visual Guide to Xanth*, and a humorous anthology about mothers, *Don't Forget Your Spacesuit, Dear!*; and written more than seventy short stories. She lives northwest of Chicago with two cats and her husband, author and packager Bill Fawcett.

The few. The proud. The stupid. The inept.
They do more damage before 9 a.m.
than most people do all day...
And they're mankind's last hope.

ROBERT ASPRIN
PHULE'S COMPANY
SERIES

Phule's Company   0-441-66251-X

Phule's Paradise   0-441-66253-6

by Robert Asprin and Peter J. Heck
A Phule and His Money   0-441-00658-2

Phule Me Twice   0-441-00791-0

No Phule Like an Old Phule   0-441-01152-7

Available wherever books are sold or at
penguin.com